TRESSA'S TRERASURES

THE KING'S JEWEL SERIES

BELINDA M GORDON

SHAGGY DOG PRODUCTIONS, LLC

Cover Design by Wesley Goulart

Cover Illustration Oleg Gekman © 123RF.com

Publisher:
Shaggy Dog Productions
221 Skyline Dr., ste 208-228
East Stroudsburg, PA 18301

❀ Created with Vellum

Sign up to be on the author's VIP List to be the first to hear about new releases, specials and contests!
Go to:

www.belinda-gordon.com/newsletter/

For my *Anam Cara,*
Paul

For all the hillside was haunted
By the faery folk come again;
And down in the heart-light enchanted
Were opal-coloured men.

—George William Russel,
The Dream of the Children

CHAPTER ONE

In my youth, we celebrated the first day of spring with fire. A custom that marked the beginning of transformation as the warmth of the new season melted away the winter frost. That year a Nor'easter swept up the coast, foreshadowing the turmoil that the coming months would bring.

I worked on an intricate filigree bracelet in my quiet shop as the storm raged. I twisted delicate silver wire into a lacey pattern, adding bits of amethyst here and there. The amethyst would bring a peaceful energy to whoever eventually wore it.

Business had been slow all day; the relentless rain and turbulent wind discouraged people from going outside. I enjoyed the sounds of the storm: the howling wind, the rustling tree branches, the rain pinging against the windows and dinging against the metal on the cars outside combined to create music that entertained me as I worked.

Holly, the young woman who runs the store for me, wasn't as happy with the lack of customers or the rain. Yet she spent the day cleaning and organizing shelves without complaint. When you sell crystal and china, the dusting never seems to end.

The storm had eased up by late afternoon, though it

continued to rain lightly. The streets became busy with people leaving work or school and those deciding to finally venture outdoors.

Most of the people walking past the store window were heading to JR's, a popular pub in the building next to us. I didn't pay much attention to the activity outside until the chimes hanging over our door jingled.

Three teenage girls wearing matching red and black varsity jackets from the local high school shuffled into the store. They chatted happily as they closed their umbrellas and wiped their feet on the mat.

Linda Singer, a cute brunette whose mother owned the hair salon down the street, led the way. The two girls who followed were her constant companions. They came into the store often to see the new pieces in the jewelry display.

I interrupted my work to greet them. "Good afternoon, girls. How nice to see you again."

They waved and continued their chatter as they scurried over to the long display case that held our jewelry.

Holly met them there. She pulled out the newest pieces, pointing out the finer details of each with the white tip of her French-manicured fingernail. Linda tried on a delicate silver bracelet accented with amazonite.

I smiled when she twisted her wrist around, showing the bracelet off to her friends. Then, as they were in Holly's capable hands, I settled back into working on the amethyst bracelet.

I had just picked up my pliers when door chimes jingled again. Sensing the relaxed atmosphere of the afternoon ending, I placed the tool back onto the workstation. I lay a protective cloth over the unfinished piece and went to greet the newcomers.

A girl of four or five skipped in on pink, sneaker-clad feet, moving with energy only a child could muster. She looked at me with a sweet, angelic smile. Then she shook her wet head, sending tiny droplets of rainwater through the air. They sprayed onto the carpet and splashed gently against the glass of a display case.

She wiped a tiny hand across her face, brushing away her disarrayed hair, revealing just the type of exotic beauty the ancients would have collected.

"Sophia."

At the sound of a deep, stern male voice, I looked up, and the child spun around. A tall dark-haired man had come through the door a few steps behind the girl. With just a quick glance at his handsome face, I could see the family resemblance.

He gave the girl a meaningful look before fumbling to close the large umbrella in his hand. The umbrella had kept him relatively dry, but judging by the girl's wet hair and jacket, he hadn't been able to keep her under its protection.

She spun back around; her grin remained in place despite his implied reprimand. "Sorry... Sorry!" she said. She spoke in a singsong manner.

I pressed my lips together to suppress a smile, not wanting to undermine her father's discipline.

"I'm Sophia. What's your name?" the child asked.

"Hello, Pretty Sophia. My name is Tressa. Can I help you find something today?"

"Thanks, but we're just looking," her father answered in his deep throaty voice.

I nodded and extended my arm to invite them to look around.

While they browsed, I went into our small bathroom to grab a wad of paper towels. I feared the child would catch a cold with her hair so wet. It may have been the first day of spring, but outside was only forty degrees.

When I came out of the bathroom, I found them in the far corner of the store by the mill goods. I walked over and crouched down to the child's level, sliding a hand along the back of my skirt to tuck it behind my knees.

"Pretty Sophia, may I dry your hair a wee bit?"

I addressed the question to her, but I looked up at her father for permission. I noticed several small scars—shaped like exclamation points—marred the otherwise smooth olive skin on his right cheek.

They both nodded, so I reached behind her with the paper towels and gently squeezed the moisture from her chin length dark brown hair. I smiled to make her comfortable with having me so close to her.

"I like this store. It's got lots of sparkly stuff," she said.

I glanced at the freshly cleaned crystal stemware. "I guess it does, at that."

"Your eyes are sparkly too."

Startled, my expression froze as I grasped the gemstone brooch on my sweater. I relaxed when I touched the cold silver and smooth stones. I stood and then turned away from them briefly, throwing away the wet paper towels and fiddling with the brooch to move it closer to my face. I hoped the action seemed natural.

"You talk funny too."

Sophia had noticed my accent, just as everyone does.

Grateful she had changed the subject, I gave her my standard explanation. "You're right, I do. That's because I'm from a place called Ireland. All of these lovely things come from Ireland too." I gestured at the merchandise in the store. "Except the jewelry. I make that myself."

"Leprechauns come from there," she said matter-of-factly. "We had a St. Patrick's Day party at my school last week." The rest came out in a rush, as though she couldn't wait to show off how much she knew. "And we saw a movie about a family of

Leprechauns. If you catch them, they have lots of gold to give you. And the Irish are lucky."

I smiled, but inwardly I cringed as I always did when reminded of the trend to glorify those nasty Leprechauns.

"Sure and that's what they say," I said, keeping my tone light.

I was about to excuse myself when the child reached out to touch one of the sweaters displayed on the shelves lining the wall. I flinched, thinking about how dirty those little hands just might be.

Whether from my reaction or of his own accord, her father pulled her hand back before she touched it. She pouted at him.

"But Daddy, I just wanted to see what it felt like!"

I crouched down again and offered her the sleeve of my sweater.

"You can feel it here," I said. "I'm wearing the same one."

That sweet grin returned to her face. Instead of reaching out for the sweater as I had expected, she put her arms around my neck and hugged me.

"I like you," she said.

This one is an enchanter for sure. I gave her a squeeze and stood.

"And I like you," I said. I left them alone to browse.

At the register, Holly rang up a sale for the teenagers. She had sold Linda a pair of tanzanite earrings, placed on discount the previous week.

"What a lovely choice, Lin, dear. They'll bring out the color of your eyes," I said.

"Thanks, Tressa. If Mike comes in, steer him toward the matching bracelet, okay?"

"Sure I will."

We grinned at our shared joke. She always made suggestions in case her boyfriend came in to buy her a gift. He had yet to set foot in the store as far as I knew.

As Linda and her friends turned to leave, the shop door flew open and crashed against the wall, making all of us at the register jump. Fred Moyer, Holly's estranged husband, staggered in, the stench of sweat and alcohol radiating from him.

Holly took what looked like an involuntary step back from the register. That single step had put her in the corner with no possibility of escape. She cringed, pulling her body inward. Already a petite woman, this made her appear even smaller, more vulnerable.

Holly's fear was justified. She had often suffered abuse at his hand before she had mustered the courage to leave him, just three weeks earlier.

Fred stumbled over the threshold with a murderous look in his blue eyes, his thin lips pressed together. He stared at Holly intently, as though he had to concentrate to stay standing.

"Away with you now, girls," I said, hastily guiding the teenagers behind him and out the door.

In my peripheral vision, I saw Sophia's face flush and her eyes grow wide before her father pushed her behind him, shielding her from danger. I felt the tension rising in him as he considered what action to take. I bit my lip in frustration. Their presence made it difficult to intercede.

"It's time for you to get your ass home," Fred growled. "Time to stop this whoring around."

"What?" Confusion filled Holly's doe eyes; she shook her head, shaking off the insult. "Stay away from me, Fred." Her quivering voice negated any impact her words may have had. "I'm staying with Eileen. You know that."

"The hell you are," he roared. "You're coming home with me where you belong. You live with me."

"Not any more I don't." She lifted her chin.

Cursing, he lunged toward her, stumbled, and lost his balance. As he pitched forward, he threw out a beefy hand to catch himself. His palm hit the glass door of a large antique curio that served as a display case. The thin glass fractured, slicing his hand.

In a rush of anger, he grabbed the frame of the cabinet with both hands and threw it down, shattering the remaining glass. The china inside flew in every direction, crashing to the floor and smashing into pieces.

Holly screamed. The sound cut into my eardrums. I covered my ears with my hands and reflexively turned away. At once, the foolishness of having my back to him hit me.

I turned back to see Fred lumbering toward Holly. He stumbled again and plowed his shoulder into her. She fell back and hit her head on a low hanging shelf on the wall behind her. Blood poured from a gash in her head, matting her carefully styled, wispy brown hair. Holly whimpered, holding her hands up in a feeble attempt to protect her face.

The sight of the blood overrode my concern over exposing my identity. I ran to help her, disregarding the audience. Sophia's father did the same, but I got there first. I jumped between them as Fred drew his cut and bloody fist back, preparing to hit Holly again.

I drew up to my full five feet seven inches. Although he was still several inches taller than I was, I locked eyes with him.

"Fredrick Moyer, husband of Holly Moyer, you will leave this building immediately and never cross its threshold again," I said with all the authority I could command. "You lousy bastard," I muttered under my breath.

Fred blinked several times, the fury in his eyes fading with each flutter of his eyelids. He ran his injured hand through his short blond hair, streaking it with blood. Then he turned and calmly left the shop.

I held my breath until he was gone.

Behind me, Holly sank to the floor sobbing. I knelt and took her into my arms, rocking her gently as she cried on my shoulder. While I murmured to her, telling her he was gone and she was safe, I heard both our hearts thumping.

Sophia's father had followed Fred, watching his retreat. He stayed in front of the door, standing guard against his return. Fred would not come back, but I couldn't tell him that.

Then I heard light footsteps. Sophia threw her body against her father, hugging his leg. He reached down and pulled the weeping child into his arms. She clung to his neck, her face buried in his shoulder.

He turned and stared at me. I cringed at his incredulous expression.

CHAPTER TWO

I led Holly to sit on the tall stool we kept near the checkout counter. Although the height of the stool made her taller than her usual five foot one, I could still look down at the gash on the back of her head. It wasn't deep, but it was long and bleeding profusely.

I searched the immediate area for something to use as a bandage and found a linen dinner napkin waiting to be re-shelved. I folded it into a square, placing it over the gash and applying a gentle pressure. I hoped it would be enough to stop the bleeding. My thoughts raced as I tried to decide my next move.

Sophia's father, still standing by the door, whispered reassurances into his daughter's ear. I wished he would take her away; surely that would help ease her fears. However, he seemed determined to secure the entrance. Slowly, her crying dwindled to hiccups. She lifted her head and looked over her father's shoulder at us.

There was something oddly knowing in her expression that cautioned me against using my essence to mend Holly's wound. The risk of exposure was too great, and not just for me.

Exposing my presence would put Holly at risk too. I needed to let the humans take care of it in their way.

I brought my attention back to Holly. Streaks of mascara stained her cheeks and her large doe eyes were filled with surprise and pain.

"I'm so sorry, Tressa. I never thought he would do this."

I crinkled my brow, confused. Fred had hit her many times before this.

"Come here, I mean. To the store, to my work place," she clarified. "This is terrible, just terrible. I'm so sorry."

A police cruiser pulled up to the curb with its flashers on just as Sophia's father opened the front door. I had hoped he was leaving, but instead, he held the door open for the two officers who had gotten out of the car. To my dismay, they left their car with the lights flashing.

I recognized the dark-haired younger officer as Tom Lynch, a friend of Fred's. He stopped to speak to my unfortunate customer, Sophia's father, who was now officially a witness.

"You saw what happened here?" he asked.

"Yes."

"Stick around; we need to ask you a few questions."

"I'm going to step outside to make a quick call."

Tom nodded.

"Don't leave until we take your statement."

Sophia's father put her down and pulled out his phone, dialing as he led her outside. The store door snapped closed behind them.

The older officer, a middle-aged black man with a rather large stomach, walked over to us.

"Holly," he nodded at her cordially. "Tressa Danann, isn't it? We haven't met, but I know your grandmother. I'm Will Clark."

I acknowledged his introduction with a grim smile.

Behind him, Tom walked the perimeter of the showroom,

looking at the broken display case and its shattered contents. He knelt and picked up one of the larger pieces of china. It had been the base of a bowl, perhaps, or a vase. He paused to examine the *Belleek* trademark stamped on its bottom.

"Now Holly, it looks like you're bleeding pretty badly from that cut on your head. I think it would be best if we go ahead and get EMS over here to take a look. Maybe take you to the emergency room," said Will in a kind voice.

"Yes, that's a good idea," I agreed. Not taking care of the wound myself turned out to be more stressful than I had imagined. I chafed with an urgency to help my friend.

"No, I'm okay," Holly said.

The door chimes clanged; Holly's sister exploded through the door and ran to her side.

Eileen, though she looked very much like her sister, was in many ways her opposite. She was taller and bigger boned. While Holly worked with feminine things like jewelry, crystal and china, Eileen drove an eighteen-wheeler.

"What's he done this time?" she asked venomously.

Eileen thrust her chin in the direction of the cloth in my hand, indicating that she wanted to see underneath it. I lifted the linen napkin from Holly's wound.

"Damn him, he split your head open." She took the cloth from my hand, taking over as nursemaid for her little sister. I suspected she had become accustomed to the role.

"He was drunk," Holly said in a monotone.

"Of course he was. Isn't he always when he starts throwing punches?" Holly started to speak, but Eileen talked over her. "And don't give me any of that 'He didn't know what he was doing' crap."

Holly crossed her arms over her stomach and looked away with pursed lips.

Tom had finished his inspection of the damage. After a moment of hesitation, he joined the rest of us.

He stood with his feet shoulder width apart, his thumbs tucked into his gun belt. Everything about his body language said he was all business. I suspected that he wanted to offset our awareness of his friendship with the offender.

Eileen turned to glare at him, flinging her ponytail over her shoulder.

"Don't you be making excuses for him either, Tom Lynch. How you can be friends with that bully I'll never understand."

Tom returned her glare but didn't respond. Instead, he effectively excluded her from the conversation by angling his body away from her and toward me.

"You want to tell us what exactly happened here this afternoon?"

"There wasn't much to it. Fred came in drunk. He threw over the display case, hit Holly and left," I said.

"How did you get him out of here?" Tom asked.

"He just left."

The scrutiny in his gaze made me uncomfortable. He glanced away from me, exchanging a look with his partner.

"Did he try to force Holly to leave with him?" Tom asked.

A bit of life came back into Holly's eyes. "He wouldn't do that," she said.

The officers nodded, their expressions remaining carefully neutral.

"Maybe he wasn't drunk this time," Tom suggested to Will.

"Come on, Tommy. He was drunk," Eileen said. "Just like he has been a thousand times. And you know as well as anyone that he's a mean drunk."

"No one's asking you, Eileen. You weren't even here," he snapped back at her. Regret instantly crossed his face.

"He was drunk, Tommy," Holly confirmed, flashing a warning glance at her sister.

"Was anyone else in the store?" asked Will.

"Linda Singer and her friends were leaving when he arrived. And a man—a customer—I don't know his name. He was here with his little girl."

"Yeah, he's waiting outside," Tom said.

"Ha. I didn't need to be here to know he was drunk," Eileen muttered, refusing to let it go.

Tom pressed his lips together as if determined not to let her get to him again. He turned back to his partner.

"Are we good here?"

"Yeah, let's go talk to the others and get this wrapped up."

The officers nodded to us and left the store.

Eileen turned her full attention to Holly's cut. The cloth in her hand was crimson red and soaked with blood. I handed her a clean one to take its place.

"Come on, Holly, let me take you to the emergency room. I really think you need stitches," Eileen said with a quiet urgency.

Holly finally agreed, though she insisted on splashing water on her face and attempting to put her hair in order first. She turned back to me before they went through the door.

"I'm so sorry, Tressa. I'll clean everything up tomorrow."

"Don't be worrying about it, Pix. I'll get it done before tomorrow's opening." I waved my hand to show how unconcerned I felt.

"But—"

Eileen cut off her protest by pulling her out the door.

Alone in the store, I debated what to do next. Surely people would expect me to stay, at least until the police leave.

I sat on an upholstered chair by the sweaters. I needed a moment of peace so I could think. Instead, my senses were assaulted from every angle.

The harsh flashing lights that flooded in through the windows made the jagged edges of the broken glass and china appear sharper, piercing to my eyes. Here and there, blood drops dulled the sharpness, but created their own affront.

I looked away from this eyesore, turning to stare out the window instead. The rain had stopped and the police lights had drawn a crowd of a couple dozen people. Their voices, filled with emotions ranging from tension to excitement to curiosity, created a turbulent, disagreeable sound. Concerned about the words being released into the wind, I made an effort to sort through the noise and pick out individual conversations.

"I saw that Mr. Moyer was real drunk and real mad. So when I left here I ran up to get my mom," Linda Singer was telling Tom. Her mother stood beside her.

"And that's when you called 911?"

"I called," said Rachel Singer. "It seemed like a good idea after what Linda told me. Tommy, you know how Fred gets when he's toasted."

The officer nodded wordlessly.

"Then I went ahead and called Eileen. She's Holly's sister, you know."

"Yeah, I know." If Tom had been trying to keep the agitation out of his voice, he failed.

I scanned the crowd and found Will Clark questioning Sophia's dark-haired father. Sophia wasn't with him.

"Did you recognize this man?" Will asked.

"No. I'm not from around here."

"And you say he tackled her, she hit her head, and he left?"

"That's what I saw."

I took a deep breath, relieved that he didn't elaborate. I couldn't afford for him to talk to people about what he saw me do today. It had been bad enough that there had been a witness at all. If word got out that I somehow forced my will onto Fred, it would be much worse.

Between his comments and Linda's, I heard nothing that would incriminate me if plucked from the wind.

I put my head down and closed my eyes to block the visual assault. I stayed like that for a while, listening as the din outside gradually faded. Someone quietly entered the store but I didn't move.

"Are you okay?" asked a low throaty voice next to me.

I opened my eyes and braved a glance at the rubble on the floor in front of me. Blessedly, the flashing lights were gone. "Sure and I will be, once this place is cleaned up."

"Yeah, it's a mess. But I was more worried about the blood on your leg."

I hadn't even noticed the cut on the back of my leg. A trail of blood ran down my calf. Now that I was aware of it, the wound throbbed painfully.

"It's nothing."

An appreciable silence hung between us. A tension radiated from him that felt like anger: Yes, definitely anger. The intensity of his aggravation seemed out of proportion with the circumstances. Perhaps it was in response to his daughter's exposure to such violence?

"I am very sorry about this—so sorry your little girl was frightened," I said, thinking that must be it.

"Me too."

He walked over to the powder room where I had gotten the towels to dry Sophia's hair. When he returned, he handed me a fresh wad of paper towels. I pressed it firmly to the wound.

I felt the weight of his gaze on my face, but I still hadn't looked directly at him, fearful of what I might read in his eyes. Did he suspect that I wasn't who I seemed to be?

He crouched down until we were level. His eyes, now so

close to mine, drew me to him like a magnet. Unable to resist, I braced myself and turned to meet his stare.

He searched my face while I searched his, looking for any hint of his thoughts. He was heart-stoppingly handsome. His dark chocolate eyes were deep, still wells that kept his emotions far from the surface, yet somehow I felt the anger draining out of him. Almost simultaneously, my own apprehension faded. A deep connection caused a peacefulness to fall over us both.

As we continued to gaze at each other, a different type of tension arose. The magnetic pull I'd felt was growing stronger. We leaned in towards each other, eyes locked, until at last he smiled and looked away, breaking the connection. He shook his head, bemused.

"Wow. I did not see you coming," he said under his breath.

And with that, the strange moment disappeared.

He peered out over the mangled showroom. "How did you do that?" he asked.

Now we had come to where I'd expected to be when he first approached me: covering up my strange behavior. I knew he was referring to Fred's abrupt departure, but I pretended to misunderstand him. I relaxed my face and widened my eyes to appear innocent and youthful.

"The flying glass cut me."

"Not that," he said impatiently. "How did you make that guy leave?"

"Me? How could I make a big man like that do anything?"

He looked at the destruction around us, replaying the scene in his mind, concentrating as if to remember all the details.

Not wanting to give him the chance to ask any more questions, I decided to run. Least said soonest mended, as my grandmother would say.

"I'd better go tend to my leg," I said, escaping to the powder room.

I closed and locked the door, leaning back against it. A wave of relief washed over me as I stood in the darkness. After several seconds of nothing to see or listen to, only the pain in my leg remained to trouble me.

I flipped on the light switch to examine the cut. It was longer than I had imagined, but not particularly deep. I wet a clean paper towel and blotted the blood away, scrubbing a couple of spots where it had dried on my skin.

Once the area was clean, I broke off a leaf tip from an aloe plant that sat on the windowsill. I squeezed the healing liquid from inside the leaf onto my fingertips. I gently spread it over the cut, infusing it with my essence—a bit of my soul, really—as I rubbed it into my skin. As the liquid expanded and grew warm, the bleeding stopped, the throbbing pain subsided, and the edges of the cut knit together until it disappeared entirely.

For the finishing touch, I took a large Band-Aid out of the cabinet below the sink and placed it over the area so that no one outside would see that it had healed.

When I came out of the bathroom, Tom Lynch was coming in the front door. Otherwise, the store was empty again.

"I wanted to let you know we're all done here," he said.

I looked past him to the street. Will Clark sat in the driver's seat of the cruiser. Fred Moyer's dazed face looked toward me from the back window.

"He was next door at *JR's*," Tom offered before I could ask. "We'll hold him at least overnight."

He turned to go, then hesitated and turned back.

"I've known Fred all my life. Truth be told, I've been drinking with him since we were fifteen. When he gets into a drunken rage, nothing stops him until he passes out."

I did my best to seem polite but indifferent to his words.

"But tonight he gets himself into a full rage, suddenly stops in the middle of it, walks away, and sits at a bar calmly having another drink?"

I shrugged.

"Something doesn't add up here. What am I missing?"

"Tommy, truly, there's nothing more I can tell you."

I traversed the stone walkway through my grandmother's terraced garden in an odd zigzag trajectory, avoiding the puddles left by the rain. Dusk was falling as I climbed the stone stairway to the back entrance of her house, queuing the garden's lanterns to sputter on.

The heavy oak door was unlocked, as always. I turned the doorknob and pushed it open to let myself in. The grand foyer ran from the front entrance back to the rear door where I had entered. I crossed to the far left, toward the half-flight of stairs that led to the small library where my grandmother would be waiting.

I was halfway across the enormous room when her butler, Shamus, bustled in. My grandmother kept several servants to run the estate. Besides Shamus there was a cook and a grounds-keeper: a small staff, compared with the one she had employed when her husband was alive.

Shamus, though one of many Brounies that lived on the estate, was the only one who came out during the day. My grandmother brought him with her to the estate when she retired. Her servant for centuries, I was sure she couldn't imagine her home without him.

Shamus had wiry, red-brown hair, the ends of which stuck out even though he used grease to slick it back. He had a terribly old-fashioned and formal disposition. I'm afraid I annoyed him a great deal with my habit of making myself at home in his mistress's house.

He tagged along behind me as I continued on my way to the library. I moved briskly, impatient to see my grandmother. He worked his short legs hard to keep up with me while maintaining his starched demeanor.

"Miss Tressa, if you can't wait for me to open the door for you, won't you please allow me to announce your arrival to Mistress Órlaith?"

"No need, Shamus my friend. She knows I'm coming," I said over my shoulder as I approached the library door. I had to raise my voice a notch to be heard over the American country music blaring from behind the door; oddly, my grandmother had acquired a taste for it since moving to the states.

When I entered she was shuffling towards the bookshelves by the cold fireplace. She dragged her left leg slightly more than usual as she walked, leaning on her mahogany cane for support. When she saw me looking, she tried to hide her limp with her next step. Her pride would not allow her to admit weakness. I rushed to greet her with a kiss on her smooth cheek.

"Welcome home, *a leanbh*," she said with a warm smile.

She pointed at the book she wanted. I lowered the volume on the music before taking it down and walking with her to her favorite chair by the bay window.

My grandmother's appearance had changed little since I was a child. Her long, thick hair still shimmered in the light. Now, however, the color was gray instead of golden blonde. Her face, though lined, was as regal as ever. No one would have guessed her true age, despite her labored gait.

The way I felt in her presence hadn't changed either. The sight of her calmed my nerves and made my heart swell.

"How was your day?" I asked.

"I had a fine day, as a matter of fact. I sat watching the effect of the storm on the gardens. Isn't it wonderful how it makes everything shine?"

"Sure it is."

I kissed her cheek again before sitting on the floor at her feet and leaning against her, just as I'd done since childhood.

"Oh Mamó, I had some trouble today."

She stroked my hair gently. "Tell me about it."

"Holly's husband—you've met him, haven't you? Fred Moyer?"

"Yes, I believe so. He has dark coloring, does he not?"

"No, actually he's blonde with blue eyes."

"Aye, that's the one."

Such nonsensical remarks were characteristic of my grandmother. Years of experience had taught me that trying to make sense of it was useless; I let the incongruent remark pass.

"He came into the store this afternoon drunk and looking for a fight. He threw Holly against the wall and she bashed her head. I fear he would have done worse, but I was able to stop him."

The hand that had been stroking my hair slipped under my chin and lifted it until she could see my face.

"You called *Dominion* over him?"

"Mamó, what choice did I have?" I searched her face for a reaction. My own expression pleaded for approval.

She sighed.

"No other choice at all," she said.

"He destroyed most of the *Belleek* china and one of the old curios," I lamented, remembering the shattered pieces that had littered the shop floor.

"You're hurt." Her voice took on an edge when she noticed the bandage on my leg. "Why haven't you tended to it?"

"Oh, I did. I put this over it so no one would notice." I pulled off the Band-Aid as I explained. No trace of the cut remained.

"And Holly was injured? Did you tend to her as well?" she asked.

The question surprised me. She knew the consequences of using my essence to heal Holly as well as I did. Certainly she wouldn't have approved of my being so reckless. "I thought it best to let her sister take her to the emergency room. Would you have wanted me to do differently?"

"No. The timing isn't right."

I puzzled over her comment, but again I let it pass, continuing with my story.

"Eileen called to tell me Holly needed several stitches, but there was no concussion. The police picked up Fred next door at *JR*'s. They assumed he was in a drunken stupor."

She smiled sadly and patted my cheek. I laid my head back in her lap and she went back to stroking my hair as she spoke.

"You did it to prevent an act of violence. The *Decree of the Ancients* is clear that this is one of the situations where you can call *Dominion* without it being reported to anyone at home."

"Hmmm. Unfortunately, that isn't the real problem. Holly was too traumatized to realize what was happening, and Fred won't remember any of it, of course. However there was another man in the shop at the time. He saw everything."

"*A leanbh*, that is unfortunate."

"I've never seen him before. He's not from around here. Surely he was a tourist who will go home and forget all about it. At least, that's what I'm hoping." I bit my lip, silencing the small part of me that hoped he would stay.

Determined to shake that thought, I reminded myself what was at stake. I had dangerous enemies. Several of my friends had lost their lives just by being close to me. The memory made my stomach churn.

I had found a haven here at my grandmother's Pine Ridge Estate. Here, people liked me for myself, rather than for what I was. Here, disappointment didn't attack me at every turn. Deaglan Mór didn't know I was here. To keep everyone safe, I had to keep it that way.

"The episode has made me think about my life, and how I would feel if I had to leave," I said to my grandmother. "I'm fond of this place. I've never fit in anywhere the way I do here. It's my home, now."

"Ah well, that's not a surprise to me. That's why I brought you here," she said.

We sat in companionable silence for a few more minutes.

"You need to get dressed for dinner. We have guests coming," she said, patting my shoulder.

"Guests?"

She loved to entertain, so the fact that people were coming wasn't unusual; however, I was hardly in the proper mood.

"A geologist from Marywood University will be staying at the guest house for a while. He and his assistant will be joining us."

"Are you taking in renters?" I asked, surprised, as I got to my feet.

She chuckled.

"Hardly that. He's a guest lecturer and only planning to be there for a semester. Evidently it was quite a coup for them to get him, even for such a small amount of time. I met him this morning and I must say, I have a good feeling about him."

Mamó was notorious as a sound judge of character, so her good opinion was high praise.

"Then I look forward to meeting him. Do you need any help before I go?"

"No, child. I've only to go dress as well."

I WALKED HOME, retracing my steps on the stone walkway that led from her back door to mine.

My home was humble compared to my grandmother's grand manor. It was the 18th century farmhouse originally built on the property. Whereas when you entered the main house you had a grand foyer, my little house had no foyer at all. The front door opened directly into the main living area.

I went upstairs and took a quick shower before picking out a dress from my closet. Its deep turquoise color would set off my coloring well. It was a flattering choice that would make Mamó happy.

I sat at my dressing table, deft fingers pulling apart the long braid I had worn all day. I picked up my brush and ran it through my hair.

My people were the Sidhe of the *Tuatha Dé Danann*. Others thought of us as vain and superficial beings. Though my brethren often deserved the stereotype, I pride myself on being different.

Having said that, I admit that my hair is my one vanity. I admired it as I brushed. The color was a brilliant coppery blonde with golden highlights that shimmered in the light. I had big, wild curls. No matter how often I ran my brush through it, I never managed to tame them.

My final step before leaving the dressing table was to put on some jewels. I chose a necklace and a matching bracelet: simple strands of chrysocolla with its soothing, tranquil properties. Unfortunately, my ears have no real lobes, making wearing earrings virtually impossible: a sad thing for a jewelry designer.

I went nowhere without wearing some kind of jewel or

gemstone. This was an important part of what allowed me to live among these people without having them discover whom, or rather what, I was.

My glamour—the magic that kept all humans except the rare Sidhe Seer from seeing my faceted eyes, the sheen of my hair, my pearly skin, and the points on the end of my ears—was rooted in these luxurious blossoms of the earth.

Our code of laws, the *Decree of the Ancients*, required that we live anonymously among humans. This was more important for me than for most but with my love of jewelry and stones, living this way had never been an issue for me.

The big grandfather clock downstairs struck the hour; I was running late. I took one last look in the mirror and, satisfied, I slipped into my heels and rushed back to Mamó's house.

I WENT to the front entrance of the manor house this time, as befitting the more formal occasion. I rang the bell and waited patiently for Shamus.

I suppressed a smile when he opened the door. It took effort to avoid commenting on his appearance. His butler's suit was newly cleaned and starched. His coarse, reddish-brown hair was slicked back with an abundance of hair gel that succeeded in keeping all but the very ends flat to his head.

"Good Evening, Miss Tressa."

"Shamus," I nodded as I stepped inside.

I had started toward the formal living room to the left of the entrance when I heard Shamus clear his throat. I slowed, turning back to look at him.

"They are in the study, My Lady."

I gave him a chiding look. He knew not to address me formally as long as we were in the human world. However, that annoyance faded as I digested the rest of his words.

"In Móraí's study? And she has guests with her?"

My grandmother generally avoided going into my grandfather's study since he had passed away. I followed Shamus as he led me to the back of the house.

"Perhaps I should announce your arrival formally," he said. The twinkle in his eye told me he was goading me but the idea was appalling.

"Shamus, you wouldn't! No titles today."

"As you wish, My Lady," he said, grinning.

With a grand wave of his arm, he gestured for me to enter the room. He bowed slightly at the waist as I crossed in front of him.

The room looked dark and broody, lit only with a couple of lamps. At first, it appeared to be empty. Then I noticed a man there, standing with his back to me. He stood in front of the case that held my grandfather's large collection of gemstones and crystals.

I flipped the switch that turned on the lights inside the case to give Mamó's guest a better view of the stones. The light danced around my grandfather's collection, creating the feeling of movement and life.

The man turned toward me and our eyes met with mutual recognition. I sucked in my breath in surprise. I thought back over my conversation with my grandmother, to what she had said about her dinner guests. Surely this could not be the man to whom she had rented the guesthouse. This man was supposed to be on his way out of town.

To his credit, Sophia's father looked taken aback as well.

"You again! Surprised twice in one day," he said.

"You say that, and yet you're the one showing up at my place," I retorted.

He laughed aloud: a good, hearty sound.

"Fair enough," he said.

His breezy attitude calmed the nervous tizzy going on inside me. I remembered my role as host, joining him by the display case.

"This collection is a rock hound's dream," he said.

"Aye, my grandfather was quite the collector."

"Do you see that Pineapple Opal?" he said. He leaned closer to point to a stone made of a cluster of milky white opals, which did indeed resemble a pineapple. He smelled of earth and intoxicating spices.

"What a fantastic specimen," he said. "They're only found in the opal fields of the White Cliffs of New South Wales. They're very rare. Most of them have been cut up; they're made of such excellent opals."

"That's what I would do," I said.

He placed a hand over his heart as if wounded. "And destroy such a beautiful piece?"

"It does no good, trapped there in the case. Opals bring emotional stability to those who wear them." They can also normalize blood sugars over time with the right amount of fae essence, but I didn't say that.

"How very New Age of you," he said with a smile. It was my turn to laugh.

"More like old world, I would say."

We both leaned in, almost touching, as he pontificated on a large, uncut taaffeite on one of the lower shelves.

I took a reluctant step away from him when I heard voices coming toward the door of the study, realizing we were much too close to each other.

"Ah, here is my granddaughter now," my grandmother said as she entered the room. She spoke to a lanky black man who looked at me through small, round wire-rimmed glasses.

Shamus helped Mamó to a well-worn, brown leather winged chair: part of an intimate seating arrangement surrounding the cold fireplace, before quietly leaving the room. Mamó sat with such dignity, she might have been holding court at the palace.

The lanky man held out his hand. His smile broadened to reveal exceptionally white teeth.

"Hi. I'm Matt Johnson."

I shook his hand.

"I'm Tressa Danann."

"Do you guys know each other?" Matt asked. His inquisitive look suggested that he thought he had interrupted something. To my embarrassment, I blushed.

"Not really. He was in my shop today with his daughter," I said, looking at the man beside me. I didn't even know his name.

"I haven't introduced myself," I said, surprised at my lack of manners.

"Alexander Mannus," Sophia's father said.

"Tressa. Pleased to meet you." I shook his hand as well.

His grip was weaker than I anticipated. I looked down as he pulled his hand away and saw a wide, white line of a scar scrolling through his palm and up his arm, disappearing into his shirtsleeve.

Introductions finished, we joined my grandmother in the comfortable leather furniture.

"So hey, you work at that store?" Matt asked. "The one with all the excitement this afternoon?"

"You heard about our little incident?"

"I was there, though not for long. Xander asked me to pick up Sophia."

"And where is the child now?" my grandmother asked.

"She's with my folks. They live over in Tobyhanna," Matt answered. Then he turned to me and asked, "You weren't the one who got hurt, I hope?"

"No, it was the young lady who works for me."

Alexander raised an eyebrow, and belatedly I realized I had

made a critical mistake. I hadn't thought to re-bandage my leg. Why would I have, not knowing who our dinner guests would be?

My grandmother changed the subject, saving me from further questions. "Why don't you tell us how you came to know each other?" she asked the men.

Matt happily complied. Mamó and I learned that the two men had been in the military together. I knew nothing about the inner workings of the armed forces and therefore I didn't understand all of what Matt said, but from what I gathered, Alexander had been his superior officer and they had fought together some-where in the Middle East.

Matt prattled on, however I wasn't listening anymore. All my attention was on Alexander, though I tried my best to hide it.

I remembered the thick scar that coiled around his palm and up his arm. How had he gotten it? Fighting in the gulf, most likely.

My attention jerked back to the conversation as Matt's words echoed my thoughts.

"Xander came back to the states to recuperate. When he was discharged, he started prospecting, of all things."

"Not such an odd thing for a geologist," Alexander interjected.

Matt nodded his head and kept going.

"Anyway, I started working with him after he made his big find. I help him with his prospecting, but I'm also his lapidary." He turned to me and grinned. "I'm sure you'll agree, Tressa, when I say the stones are only as good as how well they are cut and polished."

Shamus interrupted Matt's story to announce that dinner was ready. Our small group got up to move into the dining room. Just as we had earlier in the day, Alexander and I acted with the same objective. We both moved to help my grandmother.

This time, Alexander arrived before me. Without hinting at any concern other than escorting her into the dining room, he offered her his arm, which she accepted with great dignity.

In that moment, I liked him very much.

I STUDIED Alexander's attitude during dinner, trying to see if the odd events of the day lingered in his mind. Yet I spent most of the evening distracted by my unanticipated attraction to him.

He spoke infrequently through dinner, which gave me little chance to learn about him through the tone and choice of his words. My senses needed a great deal to occupy them, so with my hearing next to idle, my vision went into overdrive.

I scrutinized every part of his face. He had smooth, flawless skin, except for the two small scars by his right ear and a thin, two-inch long scar that marred the edge of his strong jaw line. His dark, almost charcoal hair had a silky, gentle wave. That being said, his eyes were his standout feature. They weren't multifaceted like mine—refracting the light back to where it came—but deep, rich brown pools that pulled you in.

When I wasn't looking at him, I could feel Alexander's eyes on me. Whenever he stole a surreptitious glance a flutter ran through me that I couldn't identify. Was I worried he was becoming suspicious of me or did I hope he was attracted to me?

While Alexander and I pretended not to study each other, Matt and my grandmother got to talking about gardens. Not typical back yard gardens, but the large formal ones found on grand estates, palaces and such.

I would have thought it an odd conversation for the young man except that his round glasses gave him such a bookish look. He couldn't have landed on a subject more dear to my grandmother's heart. Her joyful expression as they discussed their favorites was a pleasure to see.

"I understand you have some fantastic gardens here on your estate, Mrs. Danann." Matt said as he fiddled with his tie.

"How nice, you must come by often to enjoy them. I designed them myself."

Something seemed to roll around in Matt's mind when she said this. As if a memory was moving from deep inside to the forefront.

"Wait a minute, Órlaith Danann," he said, not speaking to her but as if the name meant something to him. He smacked his head with the palm of his hand.

"How did I miss that? Órlaith Danann designed some of the most famous gardens in Europe during the 19th century! Are you related?"

I hid my amusement and waited to see how she would answer his question.

"Sure and I'm her namesake," she said.

Well, that was almost true. She was the Órlaith Danann who designed those gardens, but confessing that fact would show her age; or more likely, since the truth would be impossible in their minds, they would believe she was crazy or demented.

To dissuade any more probing from Matt, I drew Alexander into the conversation saying the first thing that came to mind.

"Mr. Mannus, your daughter is completely charming."

He beamed. The corners of his eyes crinkled and those dark chocolate pools drew me in deeper.

"Thank you, she likes you too. When I left her with Matt's mother this evening she still hadn't stop talking about you."

Though his response was pleasant enough, I regretted mentioning Sophia the second the words escaped. The comment had to remind him of how we met. I reprimanded myself for indirectly mentioning the very thing I wanted him to forget.

"Will Sophia be with you for your entire stay, or will she be spending time with her mother too?" my grandmother asked.

Alexander's body tensed. "Her mother's not with us anymore," he said, his voice had a gruff edge that discouraged continuing that line of conversation.

CHAPTER FOUR

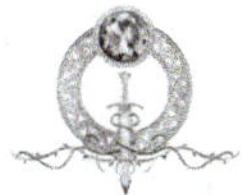

ALEXANDER

After dinner, Shamus delivered boxes with at least thirty large thick journals to the guesthouse where I was staying. Brion Danann had kept copious notes on the exploration and research he did in the area.

I did my prospecting on instinct, just going where my gut told me. I couldn't imagine what information the journals contained that would fill so many volumes, especially when the information covered a relatively small geographical area. You could cover every inch of the entire state of Pennsylvania in so many volumes.

I had been staring at the leather bound books for hours. I'd put them into chronological order, or as close as I could figure. The older volumes were written in an unfamiliar language. They also had drawings, diagrams, and calculations, and I hoped that would give me enough to go on.

The book in front of me had to be the oldest, although the pages weren't yellow or showing any sign of age. Hand drawn maps showed the area around the estate, the woods and mountains to the north. The nearby town was no bigger than a trading camp. It probably illustrated the territory as it was in the 18th century—when the area was the frontier.

Such strange research. There were sketches of the estate's first farmhouse and barn, along with detailed floor plans, livestock and planting records. Equations—no, lists of latitudes and longitudes... areas he was excavating? And this here—this is a list of names? Townspeople? Farmhands? Slaves?

I sat back into the deep cushioned sofa, pinching the bridge of my nose and squeezing my eyes closed. I was getting a headache from trying to understand the scratchy handwriting that filled the half-dozen journals I had spread out on the coffee table in front of me. It was late; time to call it a night.

I picked up the small velvet bag sitting on the table next to the journals, opened the drawstring, and dumped the small stones inside into the palm of my hand. I studied them, rolling them around with my finger, remembering the day I found these stones inside the small package from Mrs. Danann. I was flabbergasted.

After over a decade searching the world for stones that matched my ring, out of the blue, some are mailed to me from this elderly woman. I set the velvet bag back on the table. Then I put the stones and my ring on top of the bag so I could see them together.

Something else had come in the mail that day, too: an invitation to be a guest lecturer at a university only twenty miles from where this woman claimed the stones had been found. I was sure they must have seen the article about me in the Rock and Gem magazine. I had also been in the news when I discovered a new mineral, so my name was out there... Still, it all seemed too coincidental. I shook my head just thinking about it. There was something off about the whole thing.

I slid forward to the edge of the sofa, resting my forearms on my knees. I scrutinized the journals again. Could the information I need be here in this strange mix of science and domestic bliss?

A sense of reassurance fell over me, convincing me that without a doubt, my answer lay within these pages. I had learned to trust my intuition. It had never served me wrong before; why would it now?

Feeling rejuvenated, I looked again at the indecipherable handwriting. What language was this? Gaelic? I'd get what I could from the books and then hire someone to translate them.

I took a sip of coffee from the mug on the table, forgetting I had brought it from the kitchen hours ago, and grimaced. The cold coffee tasted disgusting. I wouldn't stay awake much longer without another jolt of caffeine, so I took it back to the kitchen to get a fresh cup.

I dumped the stale coffee into the sink then switched the cup to my right hand. My injured hand wasn't strong enough to lift the heavier coffee pot. Just as I tilted it to pour the hot brew, words popped unbidden into my mind: She can't sleep. She's getting up. It wasn't like hearing a voice; it was more like a thought mixed with absolute conviction.

I gazed through the kitchen window towards the old field-stone farmhouse, whose origins I had just been trying to interpret. A light popped on in one of the upper windows. I wondered if I would catch a glimpse of my pretty, redheaded neighbor, but all I saw were shadows moving across the window shade.

Speaking of something off, there was something not quite right about her. I wasn't used to surprises. I usually had a general sense of things before they happened—at least the important things. This woman had surprised me twice today.

I couldn't believe she jumped in front of that maniac at the store. The hulking man might have killed her, but instead, he meekly followed her instructions and left the store. It was all very odd.

There was something ethereal about her, and yet at the same time, down-to-earth. Gorgeous, long red hair. Her delicate face and eyes that looked somehow wounded and wary. What had caused that pain?

My coffee cup slipped from the grasp of my weaker hand, crashing off the corner of the counter and hitting the floor with a bang. It broke into pieces. I cursed quietly, mindful of my sleeping daughter.

"That's what you get for obsessing over the pretty girl," I said out loud.

Still, unable to resist, I glanced back out the window. But the farmhouse was dark now. I sighed, kneeling to pick up the pieces of the broken coffee cup.

"Daddy?" Sophia stood in the doorway in her pink cotton nightgown and bare feet, rubbing her eyes sleepily.

"What are you doing up, sweetie?" I asked as I threw the broken ceramic into the garbage bin.

"I heard a noise."

"Yeah, I'm sorry sweetie. Daddy accidentally dropped his coffee cup. Come on, let me put you back in bed."

I hiked up my baby onto my hip. It was time we were both in bed.

TRESSA

THE DAY'S events spun around inside my head, keeping me awake.

At first I refused to get out of bed, confident that eventually I would fall asleep. When I was still awake at three in the morning, I decided some fresh air might help. I threw on a pair of yoga pants and a thick wool sweater. I grabbed a woven throw blanket from a chair in my bedroom and headed outside.

A warm front had rolled in after the day's storm, and the air felt more like spring in that early morning hour than it had during the day. The slim crescent moon gave off scant light to help me see my way across the lawn. I strolled carefully to my favorite spot by the lake.

My destination was a glider nestled under a tree: part of a landscape grouping created by my grandmother years ago, designed not only to be aesthetically pleasing, but also to give a degree of privacy to anyone enjoying the sitting area.

I often came to this spot to decompress and relax. When I reached it I draped the throw around my shoulders and lay down on the glider. Resting my head on one smooth, rounded sidearm, and curling a leg over the other. I let one foot dangle to push the glider, creating a relaxing rocking motion.

As soon as I had settled there, my thoughts returned to the endless circle that had kept me awake. I suppose those thoughts should have surrounded the events in the store that afternoon.

It wasn't often that I called *Dominion* over someone. Not because it was difficult to do—it wasn't. It was easy, as natural as breathing for a Sidhe. None-the-less, I believed it was wrong to trifle with people by overriding their free will with your own. In many cases it was prohibited. Consequently, I spent a great deal of effort suppressing what was, in fact, a natural behavior.

However, I confess my thoughts weren't on that incident at all. I agreed with my grandmother's assessment and felt guilt free in doing what I had done.

What my mind wouldn't stop running through was the evening's small dinner party. The real danger to my freedom wasn't the unusual thing I had done that day, but the thing I do every day: hiding my true self. I was certain that Alexander Mannus had the potential to become too curious about things he had seen and cause trouble for me.

The night sky began to lighten as the sun came closer to breaking the horizon. When a fluttering sound came from the trunk of the old maple tree next to the glider, I sat up expectantly, pulling my feet up to rest on the edge on my seat. I wrapped my arms around my legs and hugged them to my chest.

The Pixies tumbled out of a hole at the base of the tree. I heard their sweet, high-pitched giggles as the three of them rolled, tumbled and danced around each other. Their blatant display of abundant energy made me acutely aware of just how exhausted I was. I yawned.

The sound of my yawn caught the attention of the tiny creatures, and their heads looked up at me almost simultaneously. They pushed off the ground in a jump-like fashion and fluttered their thin wispy wings to fly up to me, their voices jingling together calling, "Tressie, Tressie, Tressie!" in youthful exuberance.

They hovered in front of my face, their wings flickering lightly.

"Good morning, wee ones," I said, smiling.

It was a rare soul who could be in the presence of a Pixie and not smile. They resemble human toddlers, and so invoke a similar affection on sight. However, they are only three or four inches tall and have wings attached at their shoulder blades, shaped not like butterfly wings, as often depicted, but like dragonfly wings.

If their adorable looks weren't entertaining enough, they spent their time romping around the garden, dancing and playing. Two of the Pixies, Megan and Kerry, flew one to each side of my face and kissed my cheeks affectionately before returning to the ground to resume their play.

Brenna, my particular favorite, twirled in front of me. Her flame red hair and feathery skirt swirled around her as she turned. I laughed at her when she stopped and dizzily tried to keep herself aloft.

It was no wonder I came to this location when troubled, I mused. What a shame that people generally weren't able to see the Pixies. Although they were as solid and as real as any other creature, their appearance had a translucent quality that made them all but invisible to the human eye, their tiny voices inaudible.

Brenna became serious, as serious as a Pixie can be with their childlike demeanor, as she fluttered over to sit on my shoulder.

"Trouble, Tressie. Heard trouble in the wind."

My thoughts sluggishly turn toward Alexander. My mind was finally as exhausted as my body.

"Trouble, Precious Brenna?"

"Handsome trouble."

I chuckled at her characterization.

"Handsome indeed." After a moment's reflection, I added, "I'm drawn to him in a way that's unfamiliar to me. It worries me."

We sat for a minute in silence as I stared at the sunrise. Brenna repositioned herself to lie with her stomach along my shoulder, her head facing mine. She rested her chin in her hands, bent her knees, and crossed her legs at her ankles.

"I should avoid him, of course, but what do I do with this pull he has on me?" I hid my face against my knees, knowing before I asked the question that I wouldn't like her answer.

"Follow it, Tressie. Have some fun. Tressie, he could be...fun."

I started at her innuendo. It was easy to forget that she wasn't a child. I thought about what she suggested: an affair, a tryst... was that what I wanted? Most Sidhe would bed the man without hesitation and think of it as an afternoon's entertainment, but most Sidhe didn't have the enemies I did.

"He could destroy everything."

"Silly. It was a little thing. He'll forget."

"Maybe."

I thought of his perceptive eyes and wasn't convinced, but I let the conversation end there. I had made up my mind to suppress my strange attraction and avoid him, because that was what needed to happen. There wasn't any reason to discuss it further.

"Sleep now, Tressie," Brenna whispered into my ear.

A Pixie, calling my name and nudging my arm, roused me from a deep sleep. As I awakened, I realized that it couldn't be a Pixie. The hand on my arm, although small, was too big to be one of theirs.

I fluttered my eyelids but wasn't quite ready to open them. Instead, I adjusted the blanket crumpled under my head and curled deeper into the glider.

"Wake up! Come on, Tressa, wake up!" the small voice pleaded.

I opened my eyes and found myself face to face with little Sophia Mannus. She shook my arm once more, her mouth set in a pout.

"Good morning, Pretty Sophia," I said, biding my time until I could get my bearings.

"Ha. Not morning—afternoon," said a masculine, familiar, and disapproving voice.

I sat up slowly, twisting to place my feet on the ground. I pushed my arms up over my head and arched my back, stretching my muscles awake.

It was indeed full daylight, though I didn't believe it was really past noon. More like ten o'clock, maybe ten-thirty. Brenna must have thrown some Pixie dust over me to help me sleep.

I patted my lap and Sophia climbed up, sitting with her back to me as if it were an old habit. I hugged her around her waist.

"What's wrong, Shamus? Don't you approve of my slovenly ways?"

While I teased him, Brenna flew up and kissed him on the tip of his nose. Shamus crossed his eyes to look at her, and Sophia giggled.

Brenna flew higher and sat on the top of his head.

Shamus sucked his teeth in disapproval. I didn't know if he meant the derogatory noise for Brenna or me—perhaps it was for both of us.

"I do not approve," he answered me. He shook his head with a quick jerk, causing Brenna to tumble from her perch. An inelegant noise escaped from my throat when I tried to suppress a burst of laughter.

"Ms. Órlaith said we should go find you," Sophia told me as she swung her legs—signaling, I thought, that she was ready to get down and get moving. I released her and she slid off my lap.

"She did? I wonder why," I said.

What I really wondered was how Sophia had come to be here at all. Here with my grandmother, here with Shamus. Had she and her father moved into the guesthouse that quickly?

Shamus interrupted my thoughts. "Mistress Holly called the house. She is distraught that you haven't contacted her. I gather she expected you at the store early this morning."

"Damn."

My playful mood vanished. I closed my eyes in dismay; I had told her I would come in early to clean up the store. Holly was a worrier, and after yesterday, it wouldn't take much to send her into a panic.

"I better get going. Thanks, Shamus."

"Hum," he grunted.

Now that I was fully awake and he had dutifully delivered his message, Shamus turned to leave. I said goodbye to Sophia. She took hold of the grumpy butler's hand and walked with him toward the main house. I had to smile as I watched them go.

When they were out of sight, Brenna called down to me from the tree where she was walking tightrope style across a twig.

"Come back soon, Tressie?"

"Sure I will." I gathered up my blanket. "Thanks for the sleep, Precious Brenna."

She nodded absently as she concentrated on walking the edge of the twig. She held her arms out to keep her balance and carefully placed her left foot down directly in front of her right.

When her foot was securely place, she looked up.

"Bring your fiddle?"

"I will."

I threw her a kiss goodbye and rushed away.

A QUICK LOOK at my cell phone told me I had missed four calls from Holly. I sent her a text message telling her all was well and I would be there soon, though I knew she would worry until she actually saw me.

After a quick shower, I dressed. Although I rarely wore pants into the store, I decided I would on that day. They were a better choice for cleaning, and I wouldn't need to worry about covering the nonexistent wound on my leg.

In the midst of wrapping a string of amethyst around my neck, a thought struck me. I hadn't been wearing any gemstones when I went to the lake last night. So I hadn't been wearing any when Sophia and Shamus found me.

Insignificant to Shamus, but with people now living at Pine Ridge, I had best start wearing some jewels at night. Oddly,

Sophia hadn't seemed to notice the difference. I mulled the thought over as I rushed out of the house.

The estate was several miles outside town. My store was in the town's small business district. I could ride the wind to get back and forth to the shop, but I drove my car to keep up appearances. Twenty minutes later, I parked in the public lot on Church Street, two blocks from the store.

I enjoyed the feel of the spring air on my skin as I crossed the road, hurrying down Church Street. As I passed Saint Francis Church I bowed my head to the holy presence there, as was my custom. When I rounded the corner to walk up Fifth Avenue a breeze brushed past me, flicking strands of my hair back away from my face.

Tressa's Treasures was on the other side of the street, nestled between The *Apple Dumpling Café* and *JR's Bar and Grille*.

The storefront looked charming with its colonial door surround freshly painted a rich mahogany and the rich green, and a gold-lettered sign above. The sunlight touched the crystal displays in the window. It actually did make the store sparkle.

I stepped onto the macadam and moved across the road even as I looked to my right to check for approaching cars. I was already halfway to the other side when I turned to look to the left. Suddenly, the sun blinded me. I couldn't see if any cars were coming, though I heard no engine approaching.

Foolishly, I squinted and kept moving as I strained to see. Abruptly, the sound of screeching tires rapidly accelerating exploded from that direction. With a rush of adrenaline, I jumped the last two feet to the sidewalk to get out of the way. I whipped my head around to catch a glimpse of the vehicle as it sped past. For a mere second, Fred Moyer and I locked eyes. He smirked.

Had he really been trying to hit me? It would take more than a bit of aloe to recover from that. I took several deep breaths to calm myself, watching his red Ford pickup round the corner at the end of the block. I felt profoundly grateful that sweet little Holly had finally gotten away from him.

Dismissing him from my thoughts, I continued on my way to the store. When I reached the door, I heard an unexpected sound: laughter. Holly was laughing.

Curious, I hurried in and stood in the doorway for a moment, appraising the scene before me.

Things appeared much changed from last evening. Most of the broken china and glass had been cleared away. A large cardboard box lined with a green plastic garbage bag sat on the floor serving as a garbage pail for the debris.

Holly, broom in hand, swept together the smaller pieces that lingered on the floor. Standing near her and getting ready to move what remained of the curio was Matt Johnson.

Holly dropped the broom handle against the checkout counter and hurried over to hug me. I held her at arm's length so I could take a good look at her.

She looked her usual self. Her hair, perfectly styled, covered the stitches on her head. She wore a beautifully sculpted blue blouse over sleek black twill pants, no doubt purchased from one of the designer outlets nearby. Her makeup was flawless.

No one would imagine, just by looking at her, that she had suffered an attack less than twenty-four hours ago. My surprise melted into understanding: this is how her relationship with Fred had gone on so long without those of us closest to her suspecting abuse.

She spoke in a rush as I looked around.

"I'm so sorry I bothered your grandmother, but when you didn't show up and you didn't answer your phone, I was sure something awful had happened."

"Pix, you shouldn't worry so much. But I do apologize for oversleeping."

I looked at Matt, who appeared much more comfortable in the plaid shirt and jeans he was wearing than he had in a suit and tie.

"Mattie, what a nice surprise."

"Wow, no one's called me Mattie for years," he said, chuckling.

"That's our Tressa—a nickname for everyone," Holly laughed. "I suggest you let it go. She's been calling me Pix for two years now. There's no stopping her."

"Pix?" Matt looked at me quizzically.

I shrugged. "She reminds me of a Pixie."

"Like Tinkerbell, with the wings and the tiny dress? Yeah, I can see that."

Holly slapped his arm in mock outrage while he pretended to cower, a wide grin on his face.

I smiled but didn't respond. Actually, Holly's reddish- brown eyes reminded me of Brenna's, although Holly's were constantly on guard while Brenna's were full of mischief. Holly's petite and frail frame made her appear delicate and childlike—just like the Pixies.

"So, what brings you here today?" I asked Matt.

"Xander sent me. He had a class, so he told me my job this morning was to get this place back in shape."

"How nice of him." *Surprising of him.*

"Can you believe Matt and I went to the same high school?" Holly interrupted. "We were just talking about the old days."

Her face lit up as she spoke. It had been a long time since I had seen Holly that animated.

The chimes over the door jingled. Ida Krauss, a tall woman in her sixties with a rather square and hefty figure, came in carrying a bakery box. Ida was the owner of the Café next door and a legendary baker.

"Good morning, Tressa. I saw you go by and thought I would bring you a treat."

She gave Matt a curious once over and looked at me expectantly. I introduced the two as she placed the box on the checkout counter. Holly eagerly opened the lid.

"Oh good! Shoofly pie," she said.

I met her eyes and smiled. This was Holly's personal favorite. I was very fond of sweets, especially chocolate, but I'd never really liked this particular pie. It wouldn't do to let Ida know that, since she was so proud of her baking. Long ago, Ida had come to the idea that the Shoofly pie was my favorite too, and we chose not to correct her.

"Come on, Ida, let's take this in the back and slice it up," Holly said. "Matt, you want a piece?"

"Thanks, but I better not. I've got a lunch in a few minutes."

He watched her leave the room with Ida by her side.

"You know, she doesn't remember me from high school," Matt said, "but I sure remember her. She was a year ahead of me and she was something else."

"Really? What was she like?"

"She was an angel. Everyone's dream girl. She was a cheerleader, homecoming queen, always the center of attention. But she wasn't just popular—she was really sweet to everyone. Even a science geek like me." He smiled ruefully.

He hesitated then, as if not sure he should continue.

"She seems different now."

"She's still very sweet." Even as I defended her, I knew she wasn't the vibrant girl he had just described.

"She is, but subdued somehow. Her eyes are so sad." This was an unusual observation for a man, and completely true. "And she never used to wear so much makeup."

I chuckled. Now that sounded more typical, especially from a man who appreciates nature.

The other women returned, each holding a paper plate with a slice of pie. Holly perched on the stool behind the counter to eat hers. Ida handed me the other. I ate a forkful to be polite before setting the plate down on the counter.

The older woman made a show of looking over the broken display cabinet, which still lay on the floor. It wasn't much more than a wooden frame, now that the glass doors and sides had broken out.

Her investigation seemed to remind Matt of his purpose.

"Tressa, where should I put this?" he asked, righting the broken cabinet.

"Would you put it in the back of the storage room? Anywhere that's out of the way is fine." I would decide later if it was worth repairing.

He gripped it carefully so as not to cut his hands and slid it out of the room.

"Tressa, I hear you were the hero yesterday," Ida said.

"Oh? What did you hear?" I asked, stiffening with worry. This must be why she had come—to create drama. She would probably talk about this incident for days.

"I heard you stood up to Fred. It was about time someone did. And, oh dear, so much damage to your pretty little store," Ida said with undue sadness.

"It was nothing," I said, careful not to give her anything to add to her gossip.

Holly had flushed at Ida's words. She dropped her plate of half-eaten pie onto the counter, grabbed the broom, and went back to brushing the glass and china fragments into the dustpan.

"We have it nearly all cleaned up," she said as she dumped the last bit of broken glass into the box.

"You've done a good job," Ida said, nodding her head. "But all that beautiful china! And it isn't just that it was imported.

People collect that stuff. It must be expensive! And the cabinet needs to be fixed... It's really going to add up." She shook her head, dismayed.

Holly's face paled with each word she spoke. I pursed my lips to hold back the anger building in me. Ida didn't seem to see what she was doing to Holly.

"Pix, don't worry. It wasn't your fault and it's not that much money," I told her.

The damage would be costly by Holly's estimations, but I wasn't worried about the money.

"Of course it's not your fault, Holly!" Ida said indignantly. "It's that oafish husband of yours."

I knew Ida had meant to make her feel better, but instead, tears welled up in Holly's eyes.

"It's almost noon," Matt said. None of us had noticed him come back into the room. "They must be busy next door with the lunch crowd."

"I suppose I should go," Ida said reluctantly. A moment later, the door chimes rang out, distracting her from this thought.

Matt looked at me with lifted eyebrows as if to say, "I tried." He grabbed the box with the broken glass and headed back toward the storage room. I followed him with the broom and dustpan, leaving Holly to deal with the newly arrived customers.

Matt carried the box through the back door to the dumpster. He came back in and glanced at his watch.

"Tressa, I'm sorry, but I have to go. I'm supposed to meet Xander for lunch in ten minutes."

Please don't apologize. I'm grateful for your help."

He nodded to acknowledge my thanks.

"Like I said, it was Xander's idea. I'm on the clock, and I'd rather be with you lovely ladies than looking at his ugly mug."

"Why do you call him Xander? Isn't Alex the common nickname for Alexander?" I was just too curious to restrain myself from asking.

Matt chuckled before answering my question.

Xander is what his men called him. We thought it sounded like the name of a comic book superhero. He has deadly reflexes and unbelievable instincts, and a real 'might for right' attitude that sometimes makes him seem larger than life."

I smiled, amused. "Well if that's so, I surely do *not* want to be on his bad side. Let's get you out of here."

We returned to the showroom together. Ida was gone and Holly was busy waiting on customers. Matt hesitated, clearly wanting to say goodbye to her. When it became obvious she would be some time, he waved to her and hurried out of the store.

CHAPTER SIX

I went into the small room where I create my jewelry. My worktable is against a wall with a cutout into the showroom. The back of the table protrudes six inches into the other room.

This setup allows me to see the showroom, the door, and part of one window while I work. Visitors to the store can also watch me work if they so choose.

I uncovered the filigree and amethyst bracelet I had been working on the previous day. I held it up to examine my work under the light before deciding how to proceed.

A few minutes later, after her last customer had gone, Holly came over to the worktable. She leaned against it with her elbows. I looked up at her expectantly, however, she wasn't looking back at me. She fidgeted with the sleeve of her blouse, her gaze turned down. Her clouded expression took me off guard. I put the unfinished bracelet, now forgotten, back on the table.

"Tressa, I've got something to tell you. Some news. Good news," she clarified, but her voice held only worry.

"You don't sound very happy."

"No, I'm happy, but—" She shook her head. Before she could continue, the door chimed.

Tom Lynch entered the store. He wore his navy police uniform and a serious expression. As with the night before, he entered cautiously, as if he didn't want to be there.

Holly cursed under her breath, and I couldn't help but agree with her. I wanted this whole ugly incident behind me.

"Hey Tommy, what's up?" Holly asked, trying a bit too hard to be nonchalant.

"Actually, I need to speak to Tressa."

He walked halfway to me then stopped. I saw the reluctance in his hazel eyes. Whatever he had come to say, he didn't look forward to it. I tensed. It must be something unpleasant.

"Of course," I said. I went back out to the showroom. "Good to see you again." I smiled at him politely.

He dropped his head and shoved his thumbs into his gun belt.

"Well, I doubt that."

The three of us stood in awkward silence. While I waited for him to continue, he shifted his weight uncomfortably.

"Well, you probably know that Holly decided not to press charges against Fred over last night's... blowup."

I looked at Holly pointedly. However, I didn't correct him.

"You had a considerable amount of damage to the store. So what do you want to do about making charges yourself?"

I sighed. I truly wanted this incident behind me, and I didn't want further involvement. However, I didn't understand what Holly was thinking. She had taken the hardest step toward getting rid of this man when she left him. Why let him get away with this now?

"Tressa, please, I really need to speak to you for a second before you say anything." Holly tugged my forearm and led me a few feet away.

"What's this about, Pix?"

"Tressa, I'm sorry. I wanted to tell you before he got here."

I made a waving gesture with my hand, encouraging her to move the story along.

"Last night I called Tommy back to the emergency room and told him it had been an accident—that Fred had been so drunk he fell and hit me."

"Why did you do that?" I asked. "Even if that were true, he meant to hit you again, and he's hurt you so many times before this."

"That's just it. He was going to hit me again, and he didn't. He got ahold of himself and walked away. Don't you see?" she pled. "He's never been able to do that before. He's never stopped before passing out, to be honest. I think my leaving has affected him, made him at least begin to understand that he needs to change."

A two-pronged disgust ran over me: disgust at her description of Fred's past behavior and disgust that my own behavior had resulted in her thinking better of him.

I had already decided, although I didn't want to, that I would need to go along with her new story, but she wasn't finished.

"There's a more important reason I need you to let it go." She looked down shyly, her expression unreadable. "They told me something last night in the emergency room. I'm—I'm pregnant. I'm having a baby." Once she broke the news, her words came out in a rush. "I didn't know before. It's early on—just the second month—so it's really too soon to tell people, but... I'm due in October."

A baby. I felt as though she had punched me in the stomach. Instinctively, I placed a comforting hand on my abdomen. A shocked numbness spread across me. A baby for her—with this despicable man, and in this terrible situation?

I felt another blow at my jealous and ungracious thoughts. A baby was always a blessing, no matter the circumstances. I took a second to pull together an appropriate outward reaction.

"Pix, that is some news. A baby..." It was the absolute best I could do at that moment. "But what does this have to do with our guest?" I pointed the top of my head toward Tom, who continued to shift his weight from one foot to the other while he waited.

"If Fred is arrested for this, he'll lose his job. No matter what he's done, I need his financial help to raise this baby."

The fight just flew out of me. She was rationalizing this to fit some happy ending scenario, but I didn't have it in me to try bringing her to her senses.

I nodded. I would do as she asked. She smiled, and her face glowed with happiness as I went back over to Tom.

"Well, I suppose since Mr. Moyer was drunk and not in control of his actions, I'm okay with dropping the whole thing... this time."

His expression remained grim.

"He won't come in here and bother you ever again. I swear." He spoke with an intensity that made me wonder what had taken place between the two men.

"I know he won't," I said truthfully.

We shook hands and Tom left the store. I suppose I remained still after he left, staring at nothing, for too long.

"Tressa, are you all right?" Holly asked from behind me.

I didn't turn around. I couldn't be with her right then; I needed some breathing room.

"Holly, I have a bit of a headache. If you're okay here, I think I'll go home."

"Sure, yeah, I'm good. You go ahead."

. . .

I AWOKE from a nap feeling slightly better for having caught up on my sleep and decided a walk to the lake would help lift my spirits. I grabbed my violin before leaving the house, remembering Brenna's request from earlier that morning.

The air outside, laced with the smell of nature reawakening, was surprisingly warm for March. The forsythia bushes along the side of the farmhouse had begun to bloom, and daffodils were sprouting throughout the landscape.

There was a blue truck parked in the driveway I shared with the guesthouse. I assumed it was Alexander's. I looked around to see if he was within eyesight. When I didn't see him, a strange tinge of disappointment ran over me.

I did, however, notice Sophia in the distance with my grandmother in the rock garden that surrounded the main house. Mamó leaned heavily on the cane she relied on since her stroke.

It pleased me to see Shamus hovering, as usual. He wouldn't let her do anything she shouldn't, like pull weeds or rearrange the stones.

I couldn't hear their conversation, but I knew from the way Mamó leaned in toward Sophia and ran her finger over the leaf she held that she was teaching the child about the plants. She had done the same with me when I was young, as well as several generations of Sidhe children.

I didn't linger to watch them for fear that my grandmother would wave me over to join them. Instead, I strolled lazily down to the lake, taking my time and enjoying the transformation happening around me. The woods behind the lake had a red tinge from the buds that covered the tree branches. The grass was turning from brown to a vibrant, yellowish green.

Yellow flowers covered the forsythia bushes in the landscaping around the glider. The leaf buds on the taller trees would burst open over the next week or two.

I settled comfortably onto the glider and scanned the area as

I tuned the violin strings, but I didn't see any of the Pixies. Without an audience to please, I made a selection to please myself and played a slow, melancholy ballad perfectly aligned with my mood.

I closed my eyes as I played to fully experience the tautness of the strings beneath my fingers and the emotions evoked by the music. My hands lingered in position after the final note, letting the sound linger in the air.

"Not too late," someone whispered, and I opened my eyes. Brenna hovered next to my ear. She flew to my shoulder and sat, knees bent to her chest.

"It is too late, Precious Brenna." I caught the sadness in my voice and cleared my throat.

Brenna pouted, crossing her arms and shaking her head stubbornly. I let the subject go and started playing another melancholy tune. When the song ended, I told her what I had been thinking.

"These humans become pregnant with such recklessness. It doesn't matter if their relationship is stable, if they are in a good situation to raise a child, or even if they are fit to be a parent.

"Meanwhile we Sidhe folk, with all our abundant resources and who raise children as a community, only become pregnant under perfect circumstances. It hardly seems fair." I swallowed hard, pushing down the injustice.

"Not fair. Not too late," Brenna said sagely. "Play jig please." The tone of her voice made it more a demand than a request.

She flew down to join her sisters, who were now sitting on stones near my feet. While I played, the three of them danced in a circle, holding hands. I continued at once into another song in the same mode, finishing this one with a bit of flourish.

The Pixies dropped London Bridge style to the ground in a fit of giggles. I surprised myself by laughing with them.

"Now what, ladies?" I asked, eager to continue the effects of their frivolity on my mood.

The three of them scrambled to their feet, Kerry doing a somersault before standing. Once on her feet, Megan cartwheeled into Brenna, knocking them both to the ground again. I laughed for a second time at their silliness.

ALEXANDER

I DID A FEW GOOD STRETCHES, grabbing each foot one at a time and pulling it up toward my rear. When I felt nice and loose, I took my therapy ball from my pocket. I was used to squeezing it as I ran to strengthen my weak hand. After shaking each leg out in turn, I started a slow jog, heading toward the woods in the distance.

I increased my speed until I reached a comfortable pace. When I came to the end of the clearing, I found a faint trail that ran in front of the tree line and looked as if it would wind around the lake. I took up the path.

I quickly got into the zone-that place where you know nothing but the sensation of using your muscles and the rhythm of putting one foot in front of the other.

The scenery was peaceful. The forest, on one side of me, was just beginning to show signs of spring. On the other side, the trees were reflected in the water. The late afternoon sun shone in my eyes.

I was just beginning to tire when I rounded the far end of the lake, putting the sun to my back. As I ran towards home, music broke the silence, slow and moody at first but then abruptly bright and cheerful. As I came closer to the source, it stopped with a fanfare. In the silence, I heard someone speaking.

I came around a row of trees and stopped short. Tressa sat in front of me, violin in hand. It struck me each time I saw her: She was gorgeous.

"Oh, hey," I said.

I gasped once or twice for air, more winded than I should have been. I looked around to see who she was talking to, but no one was there.

"Looking for something?" she asked.

"I thought you were talking to someone."

She looked up and smiled at me. Well, not really at me. It seemed like she was looking around my head, not actually at my face, but her smile seemed genuine even if her eyes looked wary.

"No, just speaking to myself. 'Tis a bad habit, I know." She set the violin into the case next to her on the glider.

That answer didn't feel right to me. In fact, it felt like someone was watching us. I looked around again, but I still didn't see anyone. I decided to let it go; just another item in a long line of odd behavior.

"You play the violin," I said, stating the obvious. "I heard you while I was running. It sounded good."

"Thank you. I'm glad you enjoyed it. And thank you for sending Matt to help me earlier. It was so kind of you."

I shrugged, a little embarrassed by the compliment. "The damage to the store seemed to make you sad, and I wanted to help. I would have come myself, but I had a thing I couldn't get out of."

I turned to look across the lake, feeling awkward and not sure what to say to her. I continued squeezing and relaxing my grip on the stress ball—a nervous habit. The muscle in my scarred forearm flexed each time I gripped the ball.

"Would you like to sit?"

"No, thanks. I've got to get cleaned up and get Sophia. She's with your grandmother; they're expecting me soon."

I turned back to her and noticed her staring at my hand. I froze in mid-squeeze, suddenly self-conscious.

"What a lovely ring. May I see it?" she asked.

I relaxed. She was staring at my ring, not my damaged hand. I slipped off the ring I wore on my pinky finger and handed it to her. The agitation caused by having it out of my possession started the hand tick up again.

"This stone is lovely, and quite unique. Where did you get it?"

"You could say that ring is the reason I'm here. I thought you knew the story?"

She shook her head and continued to examine the ring. It reminded me that she was a jeweler; naturally she would be interested in such a unique piece.

"My mother gave me that stone when I was a boy. She wore it on a chain—she never took it off. Then one day she put it around my neck and told me I should always wear it. I had the stone reset into the ring some years ago."

The old sense of loss returned like it always did when I told this story. I cleared my throat. She watched me, now showing more interest in my story than the ring.

"Did she tell you where it came from or how she got it?"

I laughed derisively. If she had told me that, I wouldn't have spent my life looking for the source.

"She only said that it was special and that I should always wear it. She disappeared a week later. I never saw her again."

"Oh. I'm so sorry," she said hastily. Her sad eyes looked alarmed at the direction the story had turned. I regretted being so blunt.

"It was a long time ago."

"How old were you?"

"Seven."

Her brow wrinkled, obviously concerned for the seven-year-old me. But she also nodded, as if it made sense somehow. As if the age seven may have had some significance.

I wanted to see her reaction to the most recent part of my story, so I continued. "After my mother's disappearance I became obsessed with learning what the stone was and what made it so special—not easy, as it turned out. I got a degree in mineralogy and geology and searched every book I could get my hands on without luck. I've traveled the world looking for another stone like it. I guess I always thought figuring out the mystery of the stone would lead me to answers about my mother."

"And has it?"

"No. I've spent over twenty years looking without luck."

"And how did this bring you to Pine Ridge?"

I watched her closely as I continued. "Two months ago, a story about my research ran in a trade journal. Your grandmother saw it and sent me a letter containing fragments of the same stone. She said she's a friend of my maternal grandmother's, and that her husband found these fragments while exploring this region. Then she invited me to come look for myself."

"How lucky that she read the article." She handed back the ring and I slipped it onto my finger. There was nothing unusual in her reaction.

"Yeah, extraordinary, isn't it?" I kept my voice neutral, not wanting to show her how uncomfortable I was with the coincidence. Any doubtful thoughts I had got pushed to the back of my head. I had never been so close to my goal, and I didn't want anything to get in my way.

Her lyrical voice brought me back to the present.

"So you're on a treasure hunt." Her smile, again, didn't reach her eyes. "You must tell me if you find some."

TRESSA

I WENT LOOKING for my grandmother where I had last seen her, in the rock garden near the Manor House. She was still there, sitting on a bench with her hand resting lightly on the hooked handle of her cane.

She smiled as I approached her and greeted me warmly. A basket made of woven vines lay on the bench next to her. I picked it up, sat in its place, and put it on my lap. Inside the basket was an assortment of pine needles, seeds, leaves and stones. I recognized them as the ingredients to a potion I concocted for her that helped relieve the damage done by her stroke.

"I ran into Alexander down by the lake," I said.

"That's nice, dear."

"I was able to get a good look at that ring he wears. He told me that it's the reason he's here."

"Did he now?"

I marveled at the complete lack of pretense in her voice as I contemplated what to say next. It was notoriously diffi-cult to get information out of my grandmother. Plus, I had to be careful: we were outside, after all, and anything I said could be carried on the wind. Only a select few knew I was here.

Then I heard light footsteps running toward us. Seconds later, Sophia came around the bend with a handful of bright yellow flowers with needle-like pedals around a bumpy round center.

"I found some! I found some!" she sang and lay the mess of flowers, stems broken and bent, into Mamó's lap. "Hi Tressa, do you see what I found?"

"Aye, where did you find them?" The plant was coughwort, also sometimes called coltsfoot, though many people confused it for dandelions, which were more common locally. I used these flowers in a tea to help with respiratory problems. I knew Mamó had a planting of them on the west side of the rock garden, but I feigned ignorance.

"Just over there." The child pointed to where she had come from.

"So what have we collected today?" Órlaith asked.

"White pine needles, sage pepper seeds, St. John's wort—" she ticked off each ingredient on her fingers while simultaneously jumping and landing with her right foot forward, the next time with the left foot forward and back again. "—amber, and..." here she stopped jumping, seeming to think hard, "the yellow flower. Ummmm, ponyfoot."

"Coltsfoot," I corrected her.

"Coltsfoot!" She held both her arms high overhead in triumph.

"You did good, child. That's enough for today. You have this old lady all tired out. Take the clippings and go find Shamus, will you? It's time that your Da must be expecting you."

Órlaith put the flowers into the basket and I handed it over to Sophia. There was no need for the girl to go find Shamus; he came out through the side door just as Mamó spoke. He exchanged greetings with us before reaching down to take Sophia's dirty little hand.

Mamó and I sat in silence as we watched the unlikely duo go.

"You're teaching her the Sidhe ways," I said. It was a statement, not a question. She nodded her head.

"Do you think that's wise?"

"What could be the harm in it?"

"She'll learn who we are."

"Yes, she may."

"You know you will grow attached to her, and she to you, as it has been with every child you have nurtured. She won't be here that long; just long enough for both your hearts to break when she goes."

"It's true; I've loved all the children I have nurtured. However, that's the Sidhe way. We nurture all the children around us for as long as our lives intersect. I could ignore a child in my home as easily as I could change the color of my eyes."

I had known she felt this way. Children were precious to any Sidhe community since the birth rate was so low. It was for this reason that Sidhe children were raised by all the adults in the community, not just their parents.

I too was in danger of growing attached to the charming little girl, and of getting my own heart broken when she left.

Mamó's voice interrupted my thoughts. "Perhaps they won't be leaving," she said.

Her use of the word 'they' brought Sophia's father back to mind, reminding me of my purpose in seeking her out.

"Mamó, the stone in his ring is River Rock. He said his mother gave it to him. What was his mother doing with a stone that can only be found in Faery?"

"She came upon it honestly."

"So that means what? From his grandmother, whom you say you knew? I guess she was fae."

"Aye, she was fae. She was my best friend from childhood. She was killed in the last big battle of the last Unseelie war. Her daughter, her only child, fell into such a grief that she left the Otherworld and resolved never to return. I helped her cross a threshold. It was she who brought his stone here, her only memento of her mother and now Alexander's only memento of his." She sighed.

"He says he came here expecting to find more. You wouldn't deliberately mislead him on something that is obviously so important to him. Mamó, what haven't you told me?"

"All will be revealed in due time."

I left my breath out in a huff, the only sign I dared give of my impatience. We sat in silence as I thought over everything she had told me. As my thoughts fell into place, my agitation grew.

"He said his mother told him to never take the stone off. She must have left the stone with him to protect him, to hide him." I dropped my voice to a mere whisper to keep my next words as contained as possible. "She had some reason to fear that the Unseelie would be listening for news of him on the wind. If this is true, being near me can only be dangerous for him."

Here was another sign, if I needed it, that I should stay away from this man. Every new revelation reinforced the realization that getting too close to him would be bad for both of us.

"What was once true doesn't always remain true." Mamó leaned toward me and kissed my temple. "He is here, as he is meant to be. They may go; they may stay. Either way, all will be as it should be."

I smiled at her, knowing she would tell me nothing more. She was giving me another of many lessons in patience, as she had since I was younger than Sophia.

Shamus was beside her then, holding her elbow to steady her as she rose.

"I have guests coming for dinner, *a leanbh*. You are welcome if you would like to join us."

CHAPTER SEVEN

It didn't take Alexander long, considering the overall length of his search, to find more of the River Rock. Three weeks later he followed Matt into the store.

It was the first time he had come back to the shop since the fateful afternoon of his arrival. This time, he had obviously come directly from work. Both men wore their dirty work clothes and mud covered boots.

"Howdy, Pilgrims," Matt said in his best John Wayne imitation.

Holly, who had been moping around, brightened. It made me wish he would come around more often. Her mood seemed to get lower every day, and it was a joy to see her smile again.

"Matt, where have you been?" Holly greeted him at the door with a kiss on his grimy cheek. "I thought you'd visit once in a while when you told me you would be working nearby."

I hid my amusement when he blushed.

"I would have been here sooner if my boss weren't such a slave driver. He never gives me a minute's rest."

She made a sympathetic noise. "Bad, huh?"

"He sure is, ask him yourself," Matt said, his voice teasing as he turned to indicate Alexander behind him.

This time, it was Holly's turn to blush.

"Geez, are you trying to embarrass me in front of your boss?" she chided him.

"Who, me?" He grinned widely.

"Well, the least you could do is introduce me."

She stretched out her hand toward Alexander as Matt began the introductions, but then dropped it before he could take it.

"Do I know you? You look familiar."

"Alexander was here a while back with his daughter," I told her, wishing she hadn't recognized him. I could see the change in her the moment she realized who he was. The frown was back in place and her neck flamed with embarrassment.

"So what brings you gentlemen in this evening?" I asked brightly.

"My treasure hunt," Alexander said in his low throaty voice— deeper than I remembered.

"Indeed?" I said, intrigued. "Come. Sit and tell me about it."

I led him to the stools by my workstation, leaving Matt and Holly engaged in their own conversation.

Alexander pulled a small cloth bag out of his pocket before sitting. He opened the drawstrings and dumped the contents onto the counter.

Three ragged-edged nuggets clicked onto the countertop. I pulled the arm of my magnifier over and held one of the stones beneath the glass.

The silver specks were striking in contrast to the navy when magnified. Unlike the stone in his ring, this one was unpolished and rough-edged, but it was definitely River Rock. I stared at it in disbelief.

I felt the warmth of his gaze on my skin as he scrutinized my face. Finally, when I could no longer take the heat, I looked over at him.

"You found some," I said, surprised. Only then did I realize that I hadn't thought that he would.

Happiness glowed from his dark chocolate eyes. "Well, if I'm being honest, Matt found it."

"Where? How?" I stumbled on my words. How had these pebbles from the Otherworld come to be on a mountain in Pennsylvania?

"He found them in a stream created by the spring runoff coming down the mountain." He shook his head as if he didn't believe it himself. "I come here after over fifteen years of searching, and in a couple of weeks: success. It's incredible."

Yes, I said to myself, it certainly is. Somebody must have placed them there, but who? Mamó couldn't have, at least not recently. Shamus? She could have asked him to do it for her. My grandfather might have done so many years ago, but that seemed improbable.

I didn't understand what my grandmother was trying to do by bringing Alexander to Pine Ridge. Would she have gone to such lengths just to get her friend's grandson close? That didn't seem like her, though.

"Does this mean you're done? That your treasure hunt is over now that you found the stones?"

"Hell no. There's still a lot to do. These stones were lying on the surface. I need to find the source, and finding the source is just the beginning. Then the real science begins."

I smiled genuinely at his enthusiasm, though his words filled me with dread.

"So now what?"

"Well, first I need to go back and read more of your grandfather's journals."

A frightened gasp from the other side of the store interrupted our conversation. Something outside the window had startled Holly, who stumbled backwards. Matt grabbed her elbow to steady her.

Alexander and I couldn't see what was outside from our vantage point. Alexander rushed out the door while I went to the window to get a look. I made a cursory glance and saw nothing.

"Holly, what's wrong?" I asked.

"Nothing. I'm fine. I'm just being silly. I thought something was out there," she said sheepishly. "I'm sorry. I didn't mean to startle everyone."

"Was that the ex?" Matt asked angrily. "Has he been harassing you?"

Alexander came back in as Matt asked his question. He nodded his head, answering him when Holly hesitated.

"He's just checking up on me," Holly said, falling back into old habits. "He wants to be sure I'm okay. I was just startled to see a face in the window, that's all. Let's drop it, can we?"

Alexander gathered up his bits of stone. I encouraged him to let me know if he found any more, and the two men said their goodbyes.

When they left, I turned on Holly.

"Tell me what's going on with Fred," I demanded.

"It's nothing. Really."

I didn't respond; arms crossed, I stood and waited for more. Eventually she sighed and continued.

"He's called a couple of times to tell me I should come home. Uses every reason in the book. He says I owe it to the baby, that I should try again for the baby's sake."

"Does Eileen know about this?"

"He calls me on my cell, but she knows."

I relaxed a bit, knowing Eileen would keep things under control. She wouldn't let Fred manipulate Holly.

Holly's voice interrupted my thoughts.

"I keep seeing him checking me out through the window. It spooks me every time. He told me he wants to be sure I'm okay. I don't know why he doesn't act like an adult and just come in and ask..."

I bit my tongue to keep from answering. Fred would never come into the store again.

ALEXANDER

I FOUGHT the urge to push Shamus aside and rush past him as I followed him through the foyer to the porch at the back of the house.

Shamus stopped when we reached the porch. He turned and faced me, blocking the doorway and giving me a measured look.

"I'm not leaving until I speak to her, so you might as well let me in."

"Not if I think you mean her harm," Shamus said, squaring his shoulders and standing as tall as his five-foot frame allowed.

I had to give him credit for standing up to a man so much bigger than he was. It made me realize how angry I was, and how that came across to him: as a threat. I relaxed my free hand, which was in a fist, and took a deep breath.

"Listen, Shamus. I'm not going to hurt anyone. I just want to talk to Mrs. Danann."

Shamus stood his ground for a few more seconds weighing the truth of my words. Then, with a stout nod, the little man opened the door and stepped out onto the porch.

"Madam, Mr. Mannus to see you."

I stomped into the room without waiting for her reply. Mrs. Danann stood by an arrangement of plants, pruning the dead ends with her fingers. She smiled when she saw me.

"What a pleasant surprise."

I went to the table close to her and slammed down the book I was carrying. It was one of Brion's journals, the last one in fact.

"Mrs. Danann—"

"Órlaith, please."

I bit my lip to keep from cursing.

"Órlaith. Please explain to me what my mother was doing at Pine Ridge the day after she disappeared?" my voice came out strangled as I worked to control my temper. "I want to know exactly what's going on. What kind of game are you playing?"

Undisturbed, Órlaith made her way from the plants she was pruning to a seat at the table where I had dropped the book.

"Why don't you have a seat, Alexander?"

"I don't want to sit. I want you to tell me what's going on."

"As I told you, your grandmother and I were close. In fact, she was my best friend. Unfortunately, she died too young. I looked after your mother after she was orphaned, doing my best to ensure that she was okay, which wasn't easy. She had a terrible stubborn streak."

"Okay, but that all happened years before. I'm talking about when I was a kid. She came here to you. Why? Was she in some kind of trouble?" I walked away from her, hoping that putting distance between us would diffuse my anger.

"Were you aware that your mother had the gift of Second Sight?"

"Excuse me?" My voice went up a few notches, and I chuckled in disdain. Could this conversation get any weirder? "Second Sight? Are you trying to say she was a mind reader or something?" I barely kept the scorn from my voice.

"No, I'm saying she had visions of the future. She was extremely talented; I never met her match when it came to the accuracy of her visions."

"You really expect me to believe this?"

"Young man, there is much more to this world than you realize. Now, if you want to hear any more, come here and sit down. You're wearing me out just watching you."

I grudgingly pulled out a chair and dropped myself into it. "So she had a vision that made her leave?" I asked.

Órlaith shrugged. "She came here speaking of a vision."

"The journal says something about this area fitting the descriptions in folklore, and that whatever Brion was looking for was close to the estate. But it doesn't say what he was looking for."

"He was looking for the same thing you are looking for. That is why I brought you here."

"Brion was looking for some rocks? Sorry, but that doesn't ring true. His writings make it sound like he was looking for something—I don't know—bigger than that."

"You are looking for something bigger than that."

I shook my head, frustrated. Did this woman ever give a straight answer?

"So she comes here, tells Brion what he's looking for is close by, and then vanishes? There has to be more to it than that. What aren't you telling me?"

"She told me to bring you here. She said I would know when the time was right. I did as she asked. Let it be enough to know you are here by her request. The vision will reveal itself in time."

"That's not good enough. All due respect, but I don't like being played a fool by anyone."

I picked up the journal and stood to go. She grabbed my arm before I could leave.

"Stay the course, Alexander. Your mission here is more important than I dare tell you. Continue your search and you will get all of your answers."

I gave her a sharp nod. I wasn't happy, but I wouldn't give up my search now.

As I walked away, again I felt that deep conviction that I

would get the answers I wanted if I continued looking for more of the strange gemstone.

"You don't need me to convince you. It's not about trusting me," Órlaith called as I left. "You need to admit to yourself that you already know what I'm saying is true."

I turned back to her, meeting her eyes. "I'll stay for now. If I change my mind, I'll give you two weeks notice. If nothing else, I accepted a position with you and I'll see it through."

"One last thing." The urgency in her voice kept me rooted in place. "Whatever you find in the place where the stones take you —no one is to learn of it but me."

"I have Matt working with me. He may find something before I do, or he may be with me when I find it."

"He won't," she said evenly. "I need you to swear that you will tell me—or Tressa—and no one else exactly what you find on my mountain. Do you so swear?"

"Yes." Suddenly the conversation had the odd sense of an oath-taking, and I answered her with solemn conviction.

I nodded to her again and then turned to go.

"You will know when the time is right to reveal your find to others..."

TRESSA

SOMEONE POUNDED on the front door as if it was their enemy, which they certainly didn't need to do to get my attention. I heard them approaching before their foot hit my front porch.

I left the tomato I had been slicing, ran water over my fingers to clean off the juice, and dried my hands quickly on a dishtowel.

I peeked out the window to see who was responsible for abusing my door. Alexander stood with his hands on his hips. A vein along the side of his neck pulsed madly. I released the latch and pulled the door open.

We stood looking at each other in silence. I waited for him to open the conversation; anyone pounding on a door so aggressively must have something pressing to say. Why he remained silent, I did not know, but as he stood looking at me, his stance and his heart rate relaxed. Eventually, he spoke.

"Did you know that trying to get information from your grandmother is impossibly frustrating? She just makes cryptic comments and refuses to tell you what you want to know."

I laughed.

"Aye, I know. And I can tell you from experience, it does no good to push. She will tell just so much and no more."

I stood to the side to allow him to enter.

"I'm making a salad for dinner. Would you like one?"

"A salad? For dinner? Thanks, but a salad isn't dinner. It's a side dish."

I smiled to show I appreciated his humor.

"Sure and a salad is my dinner when I'm not dining at the Manor House."

"Excuse me for interrupting your meal, but I wanted to talk to you for a minute if you don't mind."

I ushered him into my small living room.

I sat in the corner of my overstuffed settee and motioned for him to take a seat as I pulled my feet up under me and settled in. He ignored the invitation. Instead, he walked over to the fireplace and leaned on the old timber mantle with both hands, arms outstretched, hanging his head down between them. He seemed to gaze at the vase of hydrangeas I had nestled into the hearth. When he spoke, his back was to me.

"You seemed genuinely surprised when I showed up for dinner that first night, but I need to ask. Did you have anything to do with helping Órlaith get me here?"

"I'm not sure of your meaning, but rest assured, you were a surprise."

"So you don't know the real reason she hired me?"

What *were* Mamó's intentions? It was a good question. Clearly she had a purpose in this. She wanted Alexander to stay and search for River Rock, which should be impossible to find here. Yet he had found some, and quite easily at that.

I hesitated as I searched for something to say that might help. However, my hesitation only served to bristle his already jagged nerves. He pushed forcefully off the mantle and spun around to face me.

"You do know what she's up to."

I sighed. Nothing clever had come to me, so I simply answered honestly.

"Truly, I don't understand what she's doing. She wouldn't tell me either."

"But you know something."

I knew that I wanted him to stay... but I also wanted him to go. I took a rare few seconds to glance directly into his dark eyes. In the space of those seconds, I had the overwhelming urge to tell him everything. I took several quick swallows to bring my emotions under control.

He sat and turned his body toward me, resting his knees against mine. He covered my hands with his.

"Tressa." He spoke gently now. "There is something odd about this place. About the people on this estate. Something odd, yet oddly familiar. I don't understand what it means. Won't you please tell me?"

His deep, throaty voice and the touch of his skin on mine was a seduction stronger than any Sidhe song, compelling me to open myself to him. I leapt from the settee to break the spell, stumbling a step or two before I steadied myself.

"Alexander, I wish I could answer your questions, but you

need to trust me when I say that knowing too much about us will put you in the path of a danger you can't possibly understand. You don't want to get tangled up with us."

He stood, growling his frustration as he grabbed my upper arms and pressed them tight against my body. I felt myself melting under his touch.

"I'm already tangled up in this—whatever it is. My mother wanted me here for a reason, and I'm not leaving until I understand why." He lowered his face close to mine, forcing me to look him in the eye.

"Tell me who you are. For me? For Sophia? Tressa, tell me what's going on here," he whispered.

For one tantalizing moment I thought he would kiss me. I wanted him to kiss me. If he did, I would be defenseless against his pleas. I held my breath, but in his moment of hesitation I gained enough control to pull gently away from him.

"Find whatever my grandmother has you hunting for and then take you and your daughter as far from here as possible. It's far too dangerous for you to get too close to me."

I WENT BACK to the kitchen after he left, intent on finishing my salad. First, I heated a cup of water to make tea, hoping it might help the dull headache developing behind my eyes. My heart throbbed in my ears, but nothing would help that.

I finished slicing the tomato and thought about Pine Ridge. My little piece of the world, which had seemed so safe just a few short weeks ago, now seemed absurdly dangerous when I considered becoming involved with Alexander.

It was no exaggeration to say it could mean his life. Deaglan Mór and his Unseelie rebels hunted for me and they didn't care who they had to go through to get to me: in fact they enjoyed hurting those closest to their enemies. Three of my dearest friends had already been murdered because of me.

I tossed the tomato slices onto of a bed of lettuce. I peeled and sliced half of a cucumber and added it as well.

Alexander was part fae. I hadn't previously allowed myself to think of him in that way. However, to my kin, half human was human. They didn't consider anyone part fae. You were either fae, or you weren't.

His mother came to live here among the humans, apparently seeking solace in much the same way as I had two years ago. Alexander's existence was proof she had found her *Anam Cara*, her Soul Mate, in his father. A Sidhe with her Soul Mate and a child of her own. What could have compelled her to leave them? It didn't seem possible that she would just run out on her family the way some humans did.

I added two slices of onion and some cold chicken to the salad and retrieved the salad dressing from the refrigerator as I continued trying to piece the story together.

River Rock muffles the sound of humans on the wind. It makes it nearly impossible for any fae to track a human by listening for noise of them. However, a fae diminishes the protection if they stay close to the person. So she gave him the stone, but she had to leave to protect him.

Why would the Unseelie come after him? Did they have a grudge against her—enough to want to punish her through her child? Maybe it was the grandmother. Had she played a critical part in the Unseelie defeat in the war?

When I finished preparing my salad, I had no answers. Only more questions, and my head still pounded. I decided to eat, and if my head still ached afterward, I'd make myself a tonic.

CHAPTER EIGHT

Over the next several weeks, my life fell into a new routine. I spent an absurd amount of time keeping track of Alexander's whereabouts in order to maintain a safe distance from him. Or so I told myself.

He never returned to the store, and even though on one level it rankled me—as though not making another appearance was somehow an insult to my cozy little shop—it enabled me to relax when I was there.

My worktable became my sanctuary. I bathed in the energy that radiated from the stones and metals I worked with, absorbing the healing powers they offered.

At home, I looked for him constantly. If I heard or saw him in one direction, I went the other way. This made for some interesting routes from my house up to Mamó's house.

One evening I saw him from my living room window, kicking around a soccer ball with Sophia in the yard behind the guesthouse. His back was turned to me, so I allowed myself to watch him.

He looked good in a faded pair of jeans and a t-shirt

stretched tightly across his broad shoulders and hung loose over his narrow hips.

I wondered if soccer had been his game before he injured his arm. He had talent with manipulating the ball's movements. I would have imagined he played baseball, not soccer—probably because I thought all American boys played baseball.

Several other times, I watched him and Sophia on their porch. She often sat on his lap as he read to her. The rocking of the chair lulled her to sleep every time. It created a sweet and tender picture.

Occasionally I would catch a glimpse of him preparing food through the kitchen window as I pulled up to park in our shared driveway.

I began to check through my window before stepping outside the house to be sure he wasn't around. I even pestered Brenna to listen to the wind for him. She often heard him jogging while I was at the lake with her, but he never stopped by the glider again. I thought I was the one avoiding him, but perhaps he was avoiding me too.

Being around Sophia was much easier; she was an absolute joy. I saw her almost daily when she spent time with my grandmother and Shamus.

I even saw Matt more often. The Bed and Breakfast that served as his temporary home was located a couple of blocks from the store. He stopped in to visit Holly and me several times a week on his way home from work. His lanky figure and bright smile were always a welcome sight.

ONE MORNING IN MID-MAY, I arrived at the store to find Holly busy with a young couple looking at the *Waterford* Crystal. My earlier bout of jealousy and self-pity had been short lived, and I now enjoyed seeing her with a pregnancy glow.

She looked radiant. Every wisp of her short brown hair was perfectly placed. She had applied her makeup with an expert, if somewhat heavy, hand.

She hadn't started wearing maternity clothes yet, but she was in her fourth month. Her normal clothes would soon be too tight to wear.

Over at my worktable, a man stood with his back to me. I couldn't see his head. He leaned over to look at something, his body blocking it from view. I could tell by the plaid shirt, worn jeans and work boots, not to mention his lanky build, that it was Matt.

When I got closer, I noticed he was reading a newspaper he had sprawled out on the store side of my worktable. He looked up at me and smiled as I rounded the corner.

"Morning," he said.

A small bag of green grapes sat next to the newspaper; Holly had gotten into the habit of bringing fruit into work to snack on. Matt picked one out of the bag and popped it into his mouth.

"You're here early," I said.

"Yeah, Xander is across the street at the outdoor sporting goods store. I decided I'd wait for him here instead of in the car."

"Oh?" To my embarrassment, my heart thumped. "He's coming in, then?"

He grabbed a handful of grapes and ate them, tossing one at a time into his mouth. "What? Oh, in here? No, I told him I'd meet him at the car."

I turned away from him and stowed my purse to cover my disappointment. We both sat down then—me on my workroom chair, him on the stool on the other side of the table.

"What's the temperature like today?" I asked.

He understood me at once and snorted. Holly's moods had been wildly unpredictable recently. He looked at her with such affection that I understood for the first time how much he cared for her.

"Well, Miss Pix is in quite a tizzy this morning. Something about something-or-other in the paper, but I haven't found anything to get all that excited about yet."

The bells above the door chimed when the couple Holly was waiting on left the store. She finished up at the register and joined us.

"Tressa, have you read about this strange illness in the area?" she asked, her soft voice filled with anxiety.

"Which story are you talking about?" Matt asked her. "I couldn't find it."

She paged through the newspaper and pointed to a headline on the third page. "See this?"

"Holly, this says some people in Niagara Falls are sick... so what?" Matt asked after taking a second to read a bit of the article.

"It's contagious. They've found six people with strange, flu-like symptoms since the beginning of the month."

"Yeah, so?"

Holly blew out her breath in a huff. "Matt, I'm pregnant. I can't be around some strange disease. If I get sick, something might happen to the baby."

Matt worked to suppress a smile. "Niagara Falls isn't really that close."

"Don't laugh at me." Holly slapped him on the arm. "These flus usually begin in places like China or Mexico. Compared to that, New York is right around the corner."

I flipped the paper around to read the article, losing myself in thought and barely hearing their conversation. Suddenly, I real-ized they were both looking at me and waiting for a reaction.

"I'm sure it will end up being something easily explained," I said, all too afraid that I already knew the cause. "It's not even flu season." I must have sounded reasonable, because they both nodded.

"Hey, are you eating my grapes? You can't eat my food, that's not right! I'm eating for two now."

"Not right? What about me? I'm still a growing boy. I need my sustenance too..."

I tuned out their banter as suspicion and fear welled up inside me. *The story had a strange set of coincidences in it, but they could be just that—coincidences, right?* My leg, bouncing under my worktable, told me I hadn't convinced myself.

"Well, I better get going. I'll see you guys later," Matt said. I wasn't listening and didn't respond.

"Tressa, Matt's leaving," Holly said, pulling me back to the present.

"Sorry. Off in my own world, I guess. Top of the morning to ya, Mattie me boy." I gave him a facetious grin and he hooted with laughter.

With a quick wave goodbye, he left.

I looked at Holly as she watched him go, hoping for any hint of deeper feelings for him. Although I hadn't expected to find anything but friendship, I was disappointed when there was nothing more in her expression.

She turned back to me, the movement of her head was accompanied by a soft glittering at her ears.

"New earrings?" I asked.

She wore diamond studs—large, expensive and meant to be impressive.

I, however, was not impressed. Diamonds are, in effect, selfish stones. They're too hard. They share nothing of their essence with the wearer. Almost any other stone would have given her something of itself.

An unmistakable flash of guilt crossed her face, making me

all the more curious about her new baubles. She reached up and fiddled with one.

"Um... yes. Fred gave them to me." Her doe eyes darted around, looking anywhere but my face.

"Oh Pix, don't tell me you're back with him again?" My heart sank at the idea of her taking such a huge step backwards.

"Well, not exactly. I'm still staying with Eileen, but we're trying to work things out." Her eyes settled on her hand as she twisted her wedding band around her finger.

"Do you think that's a good idea? What does Eileen say?" I wondered how it was possible that Holly's pit-bull of a sister hadn't been able to stop this backslide.

Holly's eyes flew up to meet mine, her neck flushed.

"It's not up to her," she said harshly. She sighed and took a deep breath. "She's been working a lot recently, taking longer trips to make extra cash."

From that remark, I gathered that Eileen didn't know that Fred was worming his way back into Holly's life.

"I just think that with a baby coming, and because he tried to stop himself at the end of that last... well, incident... he deserves another chance to get it right."

Her expression was so sincere and hopeful that guilt ran through me. If only I could have explained that I forced Fred to leave the shop that day against his will.

"I don't think people change that easily," I said.

I wished that I could solve the whole situation by just holding *Dominion* over her and instructing her to stay away from him. However, she was entitled to make her own decisions. Suddenly I remembered one bit of protection I *had* been able to create for her.

"Listen, Pix. I won't bring it up again if you promise me one thing."

She shrugged.

"Sure, Tressa, I'd do anything for you. You know that."

"If he has reformed—great. But if you are ever afraid, or if you ever need to get away from him, you come here to the store. You come directly here, and you call me after you get inside. Will you promise me that?"

"I don't understand. Why here?"

"Please just trust me on this. If you ever even think it's a possibility he might lay a hand on you, or if he gets started on another drinking binge, come here as quickly as you can and think about your next step after you're here."

She looked puzzled, but she nodded and smiled tentatively.

"Sure, Tressa. No problem. I'll come to the store and call you if I need help... but I won't. I'm more worried about this new flu than Fred. So don't worry about me, okay?"

I pretended to be reassured, made all the harder because her comment brought back a different concern. I needed to speak to my grandmother.

It was late afternoon before I could leave the store without raising Holly's curiosity. Twenty minutes later, I turned off the road onto the long driveway that led to Pine Ridge Estate.

When I let myself into the back door of the Manor House, as usual, the house was oddly quiet: no music blaring, no Shamus running up to bother me.

I was standing in the foyer wondering where everyone was when I caught the aroma of melted chocolate and burnt sugar wafting through the air. I turned right and headed toward the kitchen.

The long, marble-top island in the middle of the room held the source of the chocolate aroma: a platter of large round chocolate cookies with chocolate icing smeared clumsily on top.

Two baking sheets of cookies sprinkled with colored sugar

lay next to them. Jenny Jamison, Mamó's cook, stood at the far end of the island.

Sophia stood on a chair at the foot of the island, covered in flour and holding a rolling pin. A ball of dough lay in front of her.

"Tressa!" Sophia exclaimed with such joy I couldn't help but smile.

"Hello, Pretty Sophia. You look like you're having fun."

I caught a movement out of the corner of my eye. Shamus sat over by the window, smoking his pipe. His chair leaned back on its two hind legs and he propped his feet on the windowsill.

"Shamus?" I said, shocked at seeing him relaxing in the middle of the day.

"Nothing wrong with your eyesight, 'tis me all right. Mistress Órlaith is napping, so I'm tending the child for her." He made a 'humph' noise intended to show he wasn't obligated to explain anything to me.

"Seems like JJ's tending the child."

"Oh, I don't mind," Jenny said with a grin. "We're having fun."

"Shamus, I need to speak to Mamó." I moved closer to him, dropping my voice. "It's important."

"She'll want her tea before long. I can put an extra serving on the tray and you can join her then," Jenny suggested.

"Sure, that's a good idea," I agreed. Shamus wouldn't wake my grandmother unless the world was ending.

Jenny sprinkled flour over the ball of dough in front of Sophia. She took the rolling pin, placing it into position on top and holding it there as the little girl took hold of each of the handles.

Sophia leaned over the rolling pin, using her weight to help flatten the dough. Jenny's expert hands guided the girl's clumsy ones. They cut the dough with a cookie cutter and placed the butterflies onto cookie sheets. Jenny praised her work, though the dough was far thinner in the middle than on the edges, making the cookies a little lopsided.

Sophia and Jenny were covering the newly cut cookies with colored sugar when Shamus put his pipe down and stood.

"Mistress Órlaith is ready for her tea now," he said.

"Oh sure, let me get the tray together."

Jenny washed the flour and sugar off her hands. She pulled a silver tray out of its slot along the line of bottom cupboards.

Shamus loaded it with the necessary dishes and silverware while Jenny retrieved a three-tier curate stand from a cupboard in the island. She placed raisin and currant scones on the top tier, crustless sandwiches cut in delicate triangles in the middle, and three of the large chocolate cookies on the bottom. She took a plate of lemon slices out of the stainless steel refrigerator.

In a matter of minutes, they had the tray ready to go. Shamus lifted it and balanced it on his left hand.

Jenny shook her head as she watched him bustle out the door. "How does he know the minute she wakes, or the second she needs him?"

"They have a bond," Sophia said matter-of-factly.

Jenny and I both laughed. The grownup sentiment sounded funny coming from the four-year-old.

"I guess that happens when people are together so long," I said. "Ladies, it's been fun, but I've got to go. Oh, and Pretty Sophia, you make wonderful cookies." I winked at Jenny to show her I knew where the real talent lay, then waved goodbye to both and followed after Shamus.

I mulled over Sophia's last comment as I walked up the stairs toward the master bedroom. Could she possibly understand that Shamus and my grandmother have been bonded for over two hundred years? Did she know that Mamó could summon Shamus telepathically? I had dismissed this line of thought as ridiculous by the time I reached Mamó's bedroom suite.

My grandmother's suite was a study of rose and cream fabrics. Its Imperial style suited her old-world, aristocratic mannerisms.

When I entered the room, Shamus was assisting her to the cream silk sofa in the sitting area. The tray with the tea service already lay on a small table close to the sofa.

The sitting area overlooked the labyrinth she had planted on the lower lawn, about an acre behind the house. From this second story view, the garden had the estate's namesake woods as its backdrop.

I stood holding the back of a chair as I waited for her to get comfortable. Shamus held her elbow as she eased down onto the sofa. He walked to the table to serve the tea.

"*A leanbh*, what a pleasant surprise."

I went to her and kissed her cheek, inhaling deeply. She smelled natural and soothing, like pine needles, jasmine, and vanilla.

If she had been sleeping, there were no signs of it. Her hair was neatly in order. She wore her usual clothes, and her eyes were clear and alert.

"Mamó, I need to show you something."

I pulled the newspaper article from my pocket, unfolding it and handing it to her. I stood in front of her, watching her face intently as she read. Her expression remained impassive. My anxiety rose, and I grew impatient for her to respond.

"People started getting sick around Beltaine just when the walls between the Otherworld and here were thinnest. Anyone could have gotten through if they tried hard enough."

"I see that," she said, her tone entirely too calm for my liking.

"And at Niagara Falls, of all places. It's the closest threshold to where we are right now." Agitated, I paced to the window and back.

"And a flu outbreak, in May. It's peculiar don't you think?"

Mamó finished reading, setting the paper down and staring trance-like into the space in front of her. She came out of it only when Shamus reached out with her tea. She smiled at him as she took the delicate china, placing a palm under the saucer and holding the handle with her other hand. She took a sip, nodded her approval and smiled again at Shamus before speaking.

"It is quite an unusual set of circumstances. And you're suggesting that this is the work of a band of Unseelie Rebels?"

It sounded absurd when I heard it said aloud, and that made me feel better. I needed to be wrong about this. I had just gotten my life back in order, however tenuous my hold on it may be. Unseelie Rebels would mean chaos and danger all over again.

I took a deep breath and blew the air out sharply, letting a measure of stress escape with it. I dropped into the chair.

"So I'm just imagining things. There's nothing to worry about."

"Well, I don't know. Shamus, come look at this." She handed the article to him.

I watched his face as he read it and was not encouraged. Although I wouldn't have thought it possible, his usual stern expression grew more so.

When he finished reading, his eyes locked with Mamó. They conversed without speaking and I quickly grew impatient with being left out of their thoughts.

"Well, what do you think?"

"It's probably just what it says: humans getting sick." He shrugged. "Their resistance to this kind of thing is so low."

This was exactly what I wanted to hear: that it was unrelated to us. However, something about his contemplative tone made my anxiety return.

"The Unseelie haven't moved against the House of Finna in decades, and it's been longer still since any have gotten past the threshold guards," Shamus said.

"That we know of," Mamó said. "We never unearthed the truth of who or what was behind the so called Bird and Swine flus."

"Why don't we check with the Pixies to see if they've heard anything?" I asked.

Mamó nodded. "Better yet, Shamus, send a dispatch with Kelly. Find out if anything unusual is happening in Faery.

"It's unlikely that this will amount to anything. But we lack the level of protection here we would have at home—that calls for extra diligence on our part."

Shamus made for the door, but my next question stopped him short.

"What could they be after? Just hurting humans seems unlikely." I hesitated, taking a steadying breath before I spoke my deepest fear. "Mamó is the likely target, isn't she? If it's Unseelie Rebels, they must be planning to assassinate her."

Shamus glanced at my grandmother before answering. He startled me by addressing me by my formal title, which he rarely did.

"Princess Tressa, since your grandfather died and your grandmother retired, she is no longer the Queen. She is the Queen Mother. Though she is well loved by all her people, she holds no political power. She could be a target, but not the most likely one."

I had a moment of blissful relief. No one was hunting my beloved grandmother.

"Your grandfather may be gone, but you are still the King's Jewel. You may still be the one of whom the prophecy speaks," Shamus continued. "You, Princess Tressa, are the most likely target."

CHAPTER NINE

I watched, dumbfounded, as Shamus scurried out of the room. Why would he suggest there was still hope for me to be the Jewel foretold in the prophecy?

When he was gone, I turned back to my grandmother.

"Surely time has shown that I am not the King's Jewel of the prophecy. That must be as clear to everyone in the Otherworld as it is to me." I shook my head to emphasize how wrong he had to be.

"Tressa, I believe that is exactly who you are," Mamó said in a hushed voice.

My eyes widened with shock and dismay. I groped for the arm of my chair to support the turmoil growing inside me.

Speculation regarding the likelihood of me fulfilling the King's Jewel Prophecy had dominated my entire youth. My people had adored and blessed me at first, but as time passed, they began to disparage me. It began to seem like the moment would never come when I would conceive and take the next step in becoming everyone's savior. Yet not once had I heard my grandmother remark on it, let alone make such a proclamation.

Mamó would never speak blithely about such a serious

matter. She held my gaze with her own stoic stare, still managing to show empathy for my anxiety. She broke our connection and gazed out the window.

"Do you see the labyrinth out there?" She waved a graceful hand toward the garden. "Life is like that labyrinth, full of pathways that seem like the right way, but end up being detours. We go one way and then another until we find our true path."

"Aye, there certainly have been detours," I remarked sardonically.

"A few affairs with men who your grandfather and uncle thought of as politically advantageous was hardly the way to find your *Anam Cara*. You will find your way when the time is right."

I said nothing. I didn't know what to say. Arguing with Mamó was foolhardy—she was never wrong.

The weight of my race's deliverance pressed down on me, suffocating me. I gathered my strength, closed my eyes and pushed away the burden of their expectations.

My grandmother's attention wandered while I struggled with my thoughts, giving me some mental space. She appraised the food on the curate stand. After a moment of silence, Mamó patted the seat next to her on the sofa.

"Come sit next to me and have tea," she said gently.

I refilled her empty teacup and poured a cup for myself. When she waved off a fresh slice of lemon, I put it in my own cup instead. I dropped two lumps of sugar in each of our cups. Then I fixed a plate for each of us with two sandwich triangles. I cut a scone in half, spread cream on both sides and put one half on each plate.

I settled down in to the space next to her on the sofa. She sipped her tea and smiled approvingly.

"Did you see the child when you came in?" she asked.

This lighter topic was an unexpected and welcomed turn in the conversation.

"She's in the kitchen making cookies with JJ. They made the chocolate ones there." We both took a bite of chicken salad sandwich.

"Do you remember when I said that I had a feeling about her father—about Alexander?"

"Of course, Mamó."

She was quiet again, as if deciding how to continue. Her hesitation proved my first impression wrong; we weren't going to have a casual chat. Instead, she was weighing the consequences of telling me something important.

"Having 'a feeling' about someone isn't unusual for you, is it?" I said, encouraging her to continue.

"True enough. Actually, I get a feeling about everyone." She smiled ruefully. "Since I rarely ever explain what I mean by that, most fae conclude I have a vision, or some kind of second sight —a *Darna Shealladh*."

"Well, don't you?"

"Not at all."

"Oh?" I picked up a second piece of sandwich, making sure my movement was smooth and natural, feigning a sense of calm. She was about to reveal something that, until now, she had kept deeply hidden.

"You are aware, of course, that I can see auras?"

I nodded.

"Everyone's aura is different. They can tell you a great deal about a person."

"Is it true that your aura shows the quality of your character?"

"Auras come in many colors. The shade of that color is what you are referring to."

"White for good and black for evil, like in storybooks?"

"Yes, essentially, but in reality they are normally shades of gray. Angels have the purest auras, so much so that they are difficult to look at. I saw one once. Her aura was so pure, so flawless that it burned my eyes to look upon her.

"Fallen angels are the opposite; only Lucifer himself could be more devoid of light. I've never seen one myself, and I've never been sorry about that. I always believed seeing one would have a negative consequence.

"We Seelie Sidhe come closest on the spectrum to the angels, and the Unseelie to the fallen. Though we have variations, our auras are discernibly lighter or darker than humans.

"The colors and textures are harder to explain. They're subtler, and they take a while to understand when you first receive the gift. They can tell you many things—for instance, how artistic, healthy or intelligent the individual is.

"When you know these things about a person's makeup, it isn't hard to predict that a person with a dark aura may end up in jail one day, or that the marriage of a person with poor health to a person with little fortitude will fail."

It was a lot to take in.

"I see what you're saying. However, if you excuse me for saying so, you encourage people to misunderstand your ability when you make half statements or refuse to answer questions."

She smiled and nodded. "Aye. I find it's best not to reveal all you know about a person, otherwise they behave differently around you. The aura is an even more useful tool when you compare someone's behavior to their true nature. If they know about what I can see, they become cautious." She held my gaze with a look in her eyes that I didn't quite understand. It looked almost like a warning.

I tried to imagine what it would be like to be born with such a gift, and then I remembered something.

"Wait—earlier you said 'when you first receive the gift'. 'Receive' seems like an odd word to use for something you're born with."

"Aura Sight isn't something you are born with. We pass it down through our family, but not by genetics. It can only be bestowed upon you by the one who last possessed it. My great-aunt Tressa, for whom you were named, bestowed it on me when she passed on. I was a great favorite of hers, and I loved her dearly."

Her gaze became distant, reliving her past in her mind's eye. Sadness cloaked her face when she spoke again.

"She died when I was a child, suddenly and violently. I was quite young and had no warning. I did not understand what had happened. It was terrifying at first. The auras were so strong— overpowering, really. They blocked the physical person from my sight. However, I quickly learned to control the ability. Now when I meet someone for the first time, their aura is bold and obvious, but I'm able to tone it down." She sipped her tea before continuing.

"It's like when you meet someone with big ears. The ears are all you notice at first; you can hardly keep your eyes off them. But when you get used to the person, you stop noticing their ears, except every once in a while when it hits you: Joe really has big ears."

I nodded. "Do auras change?"

"Sometimes, but it's rare. As I see them, anyway. It may have been different for the others before me, but I've only seen it happen once in my considerable lifetime."

She patted my knee.

"I suppose we better place wards around the estate in case any Unseelie fae have entered this realm. Will you go to the herb garden and get some cuttings for me?" she said, effectively ending the conversation.

"Of course, Mamó." As I put our dishes on the tray I asked, "Would you like me to take Sophia with me?"

"Let her be. Her father will return soon. And you can leave the tray there; Shamus will take it downstairs."

I leaned over and kissed her cheek. I was halfway to the door when she spoke again.

"Oh, and speaking of her father, I meant to tell you something about him." I turned back to her.

"What was that?" I had forgotten that she had mentioned him.

"His aura is different. Certainly not like any other human's I've ever seen. You're fighting your attraction to him, but you shouldn't."

"You know that just from seeing his aura?"

"You think running from him will keep him safe. However life isn't that simple. There are never any guarantees, no matter what you do. Don't miss out on love because of the things that might go wrong. There will always be bad in the world; grab onto the good while you can. Trust me. Better yet: trust your instincts."

I GRABBED a pair of garden clippers and a long flat basket from a cupboard in the kitchen. With the handle of the basket hanging from the crook of my elbow, I headed outside and walked north. I strolled, surveying the changes to the foliage as the season made ready to turn into summer.

All hints of brown had left the grass. It was now in its young yellow-green stage, and it would soon be the blue-green of summer. The forsythia bushes had lost their yellow flowers and were covered in small green leaves instead. In fact, leaves covered all the trees, and the estate looked lush and healthy.

The garden my grandmother sent me to was not the herb garden used by Jenny, planted near the kitchen door of the main estate, but the one in the far northern edge where the clearing met the forest, almost a mile from the buildings. It didn't look like a garden at all, but it appeared to be the forest's natural attempt to extend into the clearing. This was intentional to avoid the curiosity of the non-fae.

The first clipping I collected was the three-leaf sprig of a poison ivy plant. I had no concerns about touching it, despite the rash it would give a human. Next, I grabbed the base of a horseradish plant. The textured leaves were course beneath my fingers. I gave it a firm tug and pulled it out by its fleshy root. I shook it to dislodge any loose dirt before placing it on top of the poison ivy leaves.

Lastly, I moved to the feverfew plant. I picked out a stem with several open flowers, held it between my fingertips, and used the clipper to cut it at the base. After placing it in the basket I reached for another stem. My hands froze in midair when I heard someone approaching from behind me.

It was Alexander. He was still some distance away, so I quickly finished taking the clippings I needed and walked toward him to greet him away from the plants.

I smiled cordially as I got closer to him, more relaxed than when I had encountered him in the past—Mamó's influence no doubt—and my smile became genuine.

His gait was smooth and agile. He had the small rubber ball in his hand that he squeezed and released rhythmically with his stride. I wondered what his aura looked like to my grandmother.

He returned my smile, seeming genuinely happy to see me. Perhaps he hadn't been avoiding me.

"Good afternoon, Alexander." I looked away from him awkwardly when I said his name. I could never come up with a nickname for him. Without an alternative name to use, I avoided eye contact when I said his name—though I'm sure it looked rude.

Nicknaming people was something I did regularly. Since I couldn't hold *Dominion* over someone unless I used their full and proper name using nicknames was a habit I had gotten into long ago to avoid any accidents. We fae folk didn't use our true names, for if a fae knew your name, they could control your every action.

"Can I help you find something?"

He chuckled. "Actually, I was looking for you."

The space between us closed, and he turned and walked with me as I continued back toward the house.

"First you're avoiding me, and now you're looking for me?" The question popped out before I could censor it.

This time he laughed that good hearty sound I liked so well. "No, I've just been helping you avoid me," he said. I blushed, embarrassed that he knew what I had been doing. Then I told myself that it only showed that he paid as much attention to me as I had to him.

"I rarely come to this end of the estate; it must have taken you a while to find me. Did you go to the lake first?" I worried that he may have found Shamus there while he was talking to Kelly. What would he have made of that?

"No, I figured you would be here."

"Why would you assume I was somewhere that I rarely go?"

He shrugged but didn't seem inclined to answer.

"Well here I am. What can I be doing for you?"

"Matt and Holly ambushed me after work. It seems it's Eileen's birthday, and they want us to come to *JR's* tonight to celebrate."

"Us?"

"Yes. It seems they have it all arranged. Matt's mother is taking Sophia for the weekend. Her granddaughter is visiting and the girls like to play together."

"You're not wanting to go?" I asked.

"It's not that. I just didn't think you would want to go with me."

"Sure, and how could I not, with such an enthusiastic invitation?"

His neck flushed red. Perhaps I should have felt remorse for my sarcasm, but his reluctant invitation had hurt my pride.

When we had come up to the yards behind our houses I could see Shamus returning to the Manor House. He must have just finished his conversation with the Pixies. I called his name and waved him over.

"Shamus, my friend, will you take these clippings in to Mamó?" I put the clippers into the basket and handed it to him. My cell phone vibrated, and I absentmindedly reached into my pocket and pulled it out while I continued talking. "How are things at the lake?"

"Very calm; nothing new there." Shamus's answer told me both that he understood my question and that the Pixies hadn't heard of any trouble in the air.

He nodded once to me, once to Alexander, and then bustled off with my basket of clippings in tow.

"He is a strange little man," Alexander said when he was out of earshot.

"Indeed, he is." I laughed harder than the comment warranted, giddy with the added assurance from the Pixies that my worries about the story in the paper were unfounded.

I swiped my phone open to read a waiting text message as I started to say goodbye to Alexander. He startled me by taking my free hand before I could speak. His hand felt warm, strong, and inviting.

"Tressa, would you please go out with me this evening?" His voice was as smooth as a caress.

"Well, that was better."

With my grandmother's words still ringing in my ears, the thought of lowering the barriers I had been framing between us was enticing. I looked down at the open phone in my hand to give myself an extra second or two to think and laughed again.

Looking up into his dark eyes, I grinned.

"Yes." I held the phone out for him to read the message.

JR's 7pm say YES! Pix

CHAPTER TEN

$\mathcal{A}$lexander leaned against his truck, his arms crossed over his chest as he waited for me. An evening out with Holly meant you had to look good; she was always at her best. But this evening I took special care with my preparations for that one moment, when I met him outside: to see his face light up.

It surely did light up. I may not have been your typical Sidhe, but I was vain enough to enjoy his admiration. He took in every detail as I walked toward him.

"Wow. You look fabulous," he said.

His dark eyes were so penetrating that even his briefest glance went soulfully deep. I allowed myself to be open to his scrutiny. It was freeing to relax my guard after spending so much time hiding.

The wide collar of my blouse slipped over the curve of my shoulder, exposing my collarbone. He reached out and ran his fingers over it. His caress was warm and gentle. I took a deep, faltering breath.

"Why did I wait so long to do this?" he asked.

"To touch me?" I'm not sure if I meant to be flirtatious, but the words came out that way.

He smiled, crinkling the corners of his eyes. "To ask you out."

We held hands as we walked around the front of the truck. Alexander reached to open my door, but then pulled his hand back. He turned his body toward mine and studied my face. His expression went from thoughtful to resolute. He slid an arm around my waist, pulling me close against him.

Then he kissed me. It was a gentle kiss. Then he pulled back just enough to see into my eyes, gauging my reaction. Finding no sign of resistance, he ran his fingers softly up from the nape of my neck until my curls tangled around them. He lowered his lips to mine and kissed me again: a deep, lingering kiss.

"Is this how you start all your dates?" I asked, breathless.

"I didn't want to risk missing the opportunity again." He wore a rakish grin.

Alexander helped me into the truck before getting into the driver's seat. He fumbled the key as he tried to slide it into the ignition. After several attempts, he gave up using his right hand and twisted his left arm awkwardly to insert the key. The engine came to life and he drove down the driveway.

The truck was surprisingly clean, considering that its owner worked outdoors. However, there were telltale signs that a child was a frequent passenger: a booster seat and a variety of stuffed animals and baby dolls littered the backseat.

There was a packet of wet wipes in the storage area between the front seats. Next to it were two therapy balls. I picked up a black one and squeezed my hand around it. The ball was harder than I anticipated. It didn't react to my grasp. I rolled it around my palm with my thumb and fingers.

"Does this help?" I asked tentatively, not sure how sensitive he was about his hand.

He glanced over to see what I had and then took a minute to answer.

"The doctors say dexterity will always be a problem, and I

won't recover any more strength in my hand or arm. I figure there's no harm in working on it. If everyone stops their therapy when told to, how do they really know that doing more won't help?" He shrugged as if it wasn't important, but the muscle working in his cheek told me otherwise.

The conversation turned to his work at the university, though my thoughts remained on his injured hand.

Alexander pulled the truck into a parking spot that had just been vacated directly in front of *JR's*. We met at the front of the truck, Alexander taking my hand. Holding hands felt natural, as if we had been doing it for years.

The sign on the sidewalk by the pub's entrance announced that *Steamtown*—a popular band out of Scranton—was the live entertainment for the evening. They played here often and were popular. The pub would be crowded.

Inside, *JR's* was exploding with noise. Alexander tightened his hold on my hand and guided me through the crowd standing around the bar. Several of the patrons called out to me as we passed; I waved and smiled but didn't stop.

When we entered the dining room, Holly stood and gestured in our direction. She looked great, as I had expected, and ours wasn't the only attention her waving attracted.

She caught the eye of several of the young men in the pub, including the band members on the little stage preparing to begin their set. They saw me walking toward her and acknowledged me with a nod and a smile.

Holly was at our regular spot: a large table along the far side of the room that was actually two tables pulled together.

I introduced Alexander to everyone. Eileen sat in the middle of the group as the guest of honor. Holly and Matt sat on one side of her; Rachel Singer, from the salon down the street, and her husband sat on the other.

Matt introduced a woman I didn't recognize as his sister,

Kendra. Kendra shared Matt's big smile and generated a warmth that made me like her instantly.

The two open seats were across from Holly and Eileen. Alexander pulled out my chair for me, but I hesitated to sit. Holly grinned and shook her head.

"Sorry, Tressa. I forgot." She leaned over a candle on the table in front of her and blew it out. A small black line of smoke curled up from it and disappeared. "Kendra, would you get that one?"

Kendra looked puzzled, but did as she requested.

"Thanks, Pix." I winked at her as Alexander and I sat.

"What was that about?" Alexander asked.

"Pyrophobic," I said, pointing to myself.

"Sorry?"

"Fire phobic."

"Okay, good to know. So, no candles?"

"No flames of any kind," Holly told him.

"No gas stoves, no campfires or barbecues." Eileen ticked off with her fingers.

"No kerosene lamps," Holly added.

"No romantic fires in the fireplace?" Kendra asked.

I shook my head.

Alexander held up his hands. "Okay, enough! I get it."

Steamtown's first song drowned out everyone's laughter. I smiled as I looked around the table. My friends had easily welcomed and accepted Alexander and me as a couple.

The waiter arrived with frosted mugs of beer for everyone except Holly, who got a glass of orange juice.

"Alexander, I hope you don't mind, but we ordered a beer for you. If you don't want it you can order something else. It won't go to waste with this crowd," Holly said.

"This is fine," Alexander assured her.

I lifted my glass and held it out toward Eileen. "A toast for the birthday girl."

Everyone followed my lead and lifted their drinks. They looked at me, faces alight with anticipation. I stood to give a grand effect as I toasted the guest of honor.

"I wish you health, wealth, and happiness, for as long as you shall live. And may all the love be showered on you that the world has to give. Happy birthday to Pix's big sis!"

"Happy birthday!" The group shouted and clinked their glasses.

"So are we going to order? I'm hungry," Holly said as soon as she swallowed a sip of juice.

Matt, Kendra and Alexander picked up menus from the pile that lay on the table. The rest of us knew the selections so well we no longer needed it.

Alexander opened his menu on the table between us. He placed his arm across the back of my chair and brought his mouth close to my ear. I warmed, imagining romantic intentions behind his move.

"What are you thinking of ordering?" he asked. I realized he thought I would have trouble hearing him over the music if he didn't speak into my ear. I liked having him so close, so I didn't tell him any different.

"I'm afraid it's nothing fancy. Bar food really," I said.

"I don't mind that," he said and then hesitated. "I guess I'm not very hungry."

"Too many cookies?" I said with a sideways glance.

He looked surprised and laughed. "How did you know?"

"The chocolate ones were delicious."

Our eyes met in shared amusement.

"Tressa, Alex, you're up." Matt's voice drew us back to our surroundings. The waiter stood next to Alexander, pen and pad at the ready and looking at us expectantly.

"A bowl of soup?" I suggested to Alexander.

He nodded his agreement. "A minestrone soup for both of us," he told the server and handed her his menu.

While we waited for the food, Matt told stories from their high school days. Holly and Eileen laughingly corrected him when they thought he told it wrong.

Alexander took my hand underneath the table, interlacing his fingers with mine. Our paired hands lay comfortably on my thigh. My breath quickened as he caressed the side of my hand with his thumb.

The arrival of our meal interrupted the conversation around the table, but the raucous stories continued once everyone had their food and the servers were gone.

Holly placed her hand on Eileen's arm, as if to add something to what she was saying, but stopped mid-sentence. Eileen stiffened in response to something behind me.

Before I could turn around, Eileen said, "Tressa, sing for us. Please." She glanced up to the stage. "It looks like George is taking his break, anyway."

She gave me a pointed look that warned me not to ask questions.

"Yes! Please, Tressa." The rest of the group latched onto the idea.

Eileen waved to George, the leader of the band, to get his attention, pointing at me in a type of crude sign language. He grinned and nodded, not surprised by the request.

I squeezed Alexander's hand before releasing it. Although I enjoyed singing to this crowd, I was reluctant to lose the intimacy of his touch.

Once on the stage, I greeted George with a kiss on his cheek.

"May I use your guitar?" I asked.

"Sure," he agreed before turning to speak into the microphone.

"Okay folks, we're going to take a break, but we have a real treat for you. Tressa's going to sing."

The crowd murmured with pleasure. I pulled a stool out to the microphone and took the guitar George handed me. He and the rest of the band left me alone on the stage.

I settled onto the stool and checked the tuning of the guitar. Once satisfied with its sound, I scanned the crowd. It didn't take long to understand what had upset Holly. Fred was there with several friends, including Tom Lynch. They sat at a booth along the wall, across the room from our table. I thought I recognized another of the men as Fred's brother. Fred was glaring in the direction of our table. Holly kept her eyes downcast as Eileen glowered back at Fred.

I pushed the unfolding drama to the back of my thoughts and smiled at my audience. "Good evening, everyone. You may have heard that it's my friend Eileen's birthday today..."

ALEXANDER

TRESSA HAD CHANGED. I noticed it earlier in the day. She had lost the wariness she had assumed whenever I was around her. Instead of averting her eyes, she looked directly at me. She appeared relaxed and comfortable.

I didn't want to scare her by being too aggressive, but the impulse to touch her was intense. The sense of connection I felt when holding her hand was deeper than anything I had felt during the entirety of many of my past relationships.

Eileen asked her to sing, which annoyed me because it meant she had to let go of my hand and leave my side. Evidently she often performed for the bar patrons. Their anticipation was palpable as she took the stage.

She took the guitar from one of the band members and sat on the tall stool he offered her. She looked at the instrument, plucking the strings individually and then in various combinations. The room held their collective breath, exhaling when she looked at the crowd and smiled.

"Good evening, everyone. You may have heard that it's my friend Eileen's birthday today. If it's okay with you, I'd like to play one of her favorites for you tonight. What do you say?"

The audience whooped their approval; then became quiet when she strummed the first note.

As she played the song's introduction, she looked down at her fingers again. Her reddish gold curls fell across her shoulder. Then she lifted her face and sang, pleasure shining in her eyes.

Her voice was mesmerizing—an effect, I realized, the entire audience experienced.

"My god, she's fabulous," Matt said.

"Outstanding," Kendra agreed.

When the song ended, the audience let the last note fade before breaking into thunderous applause. Several people in the crowd called out requests. Tressa let them talk her in to a second and then a third song before begging off.

"Sure, and it's the band we all came to hear tonight," she said. "I'll not be taking any more of their time."

The audience thanked her with applause and cheers as she made her way back to the table. There was an ethereal quality to the way she moved. She nearly floated across the floor.

The band started their next set with a slow song. I asked Tressa to dance before she could retake her seat.

I wrapped one arm around her waist and hugged her close. Her body was warm and soft against mine. I took her hand and curled my arm until I held her hand next to my heart.

We didn't speak. She laid her head on my shoulder as we moved our bodies with the rhythm of the music. We fit together as if designed for each other. When the song ended, I waited until the couples around us fell away before I reluctantly released her.

She smiled up at me. "You're full of surprises. What a wonderful dancer you are."

"That's right; you never know what I might come up with next," I agreed with a wink.

A new song began as I followed her toward our table. I stopped short of colliding with her when she stood still and cocked her head to one side.

"Tressa, are you okay?" I asked.

"It's not me. Fred's bothering Holly over by the restrooms."

I looked in the direction she gestured, but I couldn't see through the crowded dance floor.

"How can you tell?"

"I can hear them."

It seemed impossible that anyone could hear anything over the music, let alone a conversation on the other side of the room, but I turned and led Tressa in the direction she had indicated.

The restrooms were in an alcove at the far corner of the dining room. I maneuvered around the packed dance floor, clearing the way as Tressa followed behind me. As we got closer, I heard raised voices.

"Holly, come on. You know I didn't mean to hurt you. We're going to be a family now. It's time to come home."

"Fred, please just go away." Holly pleaded.

"Not until—"

We stepped into the alcove just as Eileen bolted between Fred and Holly, who had streaks of black mascara smeared across her face.

"Holly, go ahead to the ladies room," Eileen said. Holly didn't move, though she seemed to shrink into her sister's protective shadow.

Tressa hurried past me, hugging Holly and shepherding her towards the restroom. "Come lass, let's get you cleaned up." They disappeared into the ladies room.

I stayed in the doorway, monitoring the situation. I didn't want to intervene in a family squabble, but I would not let him hurt any of the women.

Eileen held her ground, blocking Fred's path. Though she was much smaller than he was, the look of determination on her face made it clear that he wasn't getting past her.

"Fred, I'm telling you for the last time: leave Holly alone. Find someone else to abuse," Eileen hissed.

"She's my wife, she's having my baby, and we're going to be a family."

"Not if I have anything to say about it."

Fred's voice dropped. "You don't have a say."

He grabbed Eileen's wrist and twisted it, trying to wrench her out of the way, but she held fast to her footing.

"Let me go," she yelled.

"Hey, don't touch the lady," I warned, taking a step toward him.

"Fred, what are you doing, man?" Tom Lynch yelled as he came onto the scene.

"Oh good, the cops have arrived." Eileen's tone was mocking.

"Give it a rest, Eileen. Come on, Fred. Let's go back to our table."

He put a hand on Fred's arm and attempted to usher him away. Fred jerked away from Tom but finally released his grip on Eileen.

"Don't you get it? This bitch has turned Holly against me," he said.

He balled his fist and stepped toward Eileen. She stood her ground, unflinching. Tom and I both moved toward Fred. He dropped his fist when he saw us, looking at us with contempt.

"Man, I'm out of here," he said.

Tom trailed after him. "Fred, you're drunk. Let me take you home."

"Screw you."

As they faded out of sight, Eileen took in a deep breath and let it out in an audible whoosh, slumping as the tension rushed out. After a second deep breath she looked at me.

Thank you," she said.

I shrugged.

"No worries."

The restroom door opened slowly; Tressa and Holly stepped out. Holly had washed her face free of makeup. Her fresh face and petite size made her look more like a child than a grown woman.

"I'm sorry," she said. "This is so embarrassing."

"Please stop apologizing for that jerk, Holly," Eileen said. "You're not responsible for what he does."

"Yeah, well, that's not the way it feels."

She looked ready to cry again. Her sister hugged her.

"Come on, forget him. Isn't this supposed be my birthday celebration?"

Holly looked at her fondly. "That's right. Let's go have a party."

When we returned to the table, the rest of the group did a great job of joking around and teasing the funk out of Holly's mood.

The ladies got up to dance when the next song started. I begged off, as did the other men, when they asked us to join them. Conversation was impossible with the loud music, so we sat in a comfortable silence and watched the people on the dance floor.

While Tressa danced, I appreciated how her hips moved to the beat. The soft drape of her blouse emphasized her curvy chest.

After a couple of songs, Rachel came over and insisted that her husband join her on the dance floor. Eileen soon followed, grabbing Matt and playing the birthday card to get him up and dancing.

I suspected I would be next. I quickly reconciled myself to the idea, though I would've preferred to continue to watch Tressa from where I sat.

She came over just as the band started a new, slower song. My reluctance vanishing, I grabbed her hand when she held it out to me.

I pulled her into my arms again, happy for the excuse to hold her. I placed her hand on my chest and then reached up to run my fingers down the cascade of curls on her head—an experiment to see if they felt as soft as they looked, which they did.

Curiosity satisfied, I placed my hand back on top of hers. I closed my eyes and took a deep breath, enjoying the scent of her shampoo.

When I opened my eyes again, I saw Matt and Holly sitting alone at the table. Matt had moved around to sit next to her. He leaned towards her, intent on their conversation.

I looked around the dance floor for the rest of our crew. The Singers were laughing at something while they held each other close. One of the local boys had claimed Kendra for a dance.

Where was Eileen?

The minute her name passed through my thoughts, I knew she was in danger. My body stiffened, and I stopped moving. Tressa stepped away from me.

"What's wrong?" she asked.

"Where's Eileen?" My tone had a sharper edge than I had intended.

Tressa looked confused, but she dutifully scanned the restaurant. "I don't hear her anymore. Maybe she left."

I raced over to Matt and Holly without letting go of Tressa's hand. "Holly," I barked. "Where's Eileen?"

She squinted and appeared to think about my question. Matt, accustomed to my outbursts, was quick to answer. "You just missed her; she said something about going to a friend's place for the weekend."

"We've got to stop her," I said. Anxiety weighed on my chest as I spun toward the door.

"Xander, wait. I'll go." Matt was jogging through the crowd toward the door to the parking lot before I could argue.

"Alexander, you're scaring Holly," Tressa whispered. "What's happening?"

Torn between answering her question and going after Matt, I settled for keeping my eye on the door as I explained.

"I don't know—a bad feeling. Something about her truck," I thought for a minute then nodded. "Yeah, something is wrong with her truck."

Nothing more came except that I had to stop her from driving a truck. I cursed myself for being so useless.

"Well she wouldn't be driving her truck now, would she, Holly? I mean, she wouldn't have the truck if she isn't working, right?"

"No, she didn't bring her rig here," Holly agreed.

I took a deep breath. Perhaps we had time to get to her.

Matt reappeared at the door. He shook his head, telling me he hadn't been able to catch her.

"Okay, so she didn't leave in her truck." I said as I concentrated, trying to get a better sense of what was happening.

Holly's brow wrinkled in confusion. "Well, she didn't leave in her rig, but she drives a pickup truck."

Pure panic rose inside me. "Call her cell. Quick, call her cell. Tell her she needs to pull over."

Flustered, Holly pulled out her phone but her hands shook so badly that she fumbled as she tried to make the call. Matt took the phone from her and pressed the screen several times.

The band ended their song at that moment, so we all heard the buzz of a cell phone vibrating. Holly dug around until she found Eileen's cell phone, forgotten in the mess on the table.

"I'm going after her." I looked at Tressa. What an awful way to end such a beautiful night. She looked sympathetic; maybe she wouldn't hold it against me. "Matt, will you take Tressa home?"

"Don't worry about me," Tressa said. "I can get myself home."

"What do you want me to do, boss?" Matt asked.

"Wait," Holly said. "Somebody explain what's going on here."

Matt sat next to her again and tried to sooth her. "It's probably nothing. Xander gets these gut feelings sometimes, but it could be anything. This could be nothing more than indigestion."

"Okay, so no need to be worried?"

"None at all," Matt said, but over her head, his eyes told me a different story.

"You had better take her home," I said. Matt gave an almost unperceivable nod.

I couldn't rush out without saying goodbye to Tressa. I pulled her away from the table. There was so much I wanted to say, but I didn't have time. I curled her hand to my lips to kiss it.

"How will you get home?"

"Not to worry. Go."

"I'm sorry to end our evening like this."

She nodded, met my eyes, and smiled tenderly.

"Go."

CHAPTER ELEVEN

TRESSA

*E*ileen's brakes failed while traveling down US380 on the way to her friend's home near Tannersville. The state police reported that, when she came down the last big descent, her speed climbed past one hundred and twenty miles per hour before she lost control—or so the paper said.

Eileen was the first friend I had lost since coming to live in the Human World. A tragedy for her family, but it broke my heart as well to see someone so young leave this world. She was a mere twenty-eight years old—a child by Sidhe standards.

A human's life span was woefully short. However, this girl had hardly any chance to live. My own parents' lives had ended too early, but they had lived more than a century longer than this young woman.

I didn't hear from Alexander in the days after her death. How many times had he had such a premonition without being able to remedy it? Not often, I hoped. How devastating, to know something awful was going to happen and to not be able to change things.

I tried to reach out to Holly. My healing abilities are mainly in the physical arena, but I hoped my presence would bring at least some comfort to her grief.

I bought one of Ida's shoofly pies and brought it with me to Eileen's apartment. However, Holly's father refused to let me in. When I asked after Holly, he nearly slammed the door. His rudeness shocked me; humans were usually enthralled by the fae.

I stayed for a moment outside the door, listening, hoping to use the timbre of Holly's voice to gauge how she fared. My breath caught in alarm when I heard Fred's disdainful voice instead. My only comfort was that Holly wasn't alone with him. Surely her parents wouldn't let him hurt her? At least she hadn't moved back to his house.

I DECIDED NOT to reopen the store until after the funeral; I didn't have the heart to put on a cheerful face for customers.

To pass the time, I worked on a project I had been rolling over in my head for the last couple of weeks. Ever since meeting Alexander, I had been thinking about how to heal his damaged hand. It wasn't going to be easy.

First, the injury was old. I hadn't been able to heal Mamó entirely after her stroke. In that case, not only had the injury been old when I got to her, but Mamó was old as well. I wasn't sure how much each of those factors influenced her healing process.

Second, healing a wound required including my essence, my life spark. Once exposed to enough of a fae's essence, a human would be able to see through the glamour of all the fae. While not strictly forbidden, it was dangerous.

For my part, it increased the chances of my enemies finding my sanctuary here at Pine Ridge. For the human? Well, I was not the only fae living incognito here. Many fae felt threatened by humans who could see through their glamour. The danger lies in how they chose to deal with the threat. Not all fae had the same moral standard.

It had taken me a while to work out the details. After doing extensive research in my grandfather's library, I believed I had found a way to make it effective and safe by using a talisman to hold onto my essence and release small doses of healing power over time.

I took advantage of the seclusion of the closed and quiet store to create the talisman and make it beautiful. I disliked grieving in idle silence. At home, the family's Banshee would help carry the weight of everyone's sorrow with her keening.

I sang instead of chanting the required invocation as I worked. Breaking the silence with a song, though it wasn't the same as a keening, helped sooth my grief.

THE FOLLOWING MONDAY, Matt stopped by the store at the time of his usual morning visit. This surprised me; his visits were usually an excuse to spend time with Holly.

I opened the door and hugged him. He gave me an extra squeeze before letting go. He hadn't known Eileen well, yet pain lined his face. It helped to have a companion to mourn with me.

I insisted he sit while I brewed a special tea for him. My yearning to heal someone needed to be satisfied. If I couldn't work on mending Holly's heart, I would try to help Matt.

I can't say if the tea was actually effective. We were a broody pair.

"Holly told me her parents think she should go back to Fred and try to work things out, now that she's pregnant," he said. "They think she's exaggerating about the beatings."

I nodded. I had guessed this when I heard Fred in the apartment with them.

"They won't let me in to see her." His voice cracked when he spoke.

"They wouldn't let me in either," I said, tears welling up in my eyes.

"I think they're keeping her isolated so they can convince her to return to that ass. After everything she's done to get away..." Matt said.

It was true. Without Eileen, Holly wasn't strong enough to stand up to both Fred and her parents.

"Well, he won't hurt her again if I can help it." Matt drank the last of his tea and stood to go. I walked him to the door, where he hugged me again.

"Thanks for listening, Tressa. You managed to make me feel better," he said.

Perhaps the tea had helped after all. I patted his cheek before he left.

I DIDN'T SEE Alexander again until late Tuesday evening. He knocked on my door just as I was slipping into bed. I padded downstairs in my nightgown, barefoot. As I opened the door, a gust of wind swirled the flimsy fabric of my nightgown so that it wrapped close around my body.

Neither of us moved nor spoke. We consumed each other with our eyes. He opened his mouth as if to speak, but closed it again without a word. I ached, seeing his pain.

He tried again, this time choking out some words.

"Sorry to come by so late. I took Sophia to spend time with my dad. I just got back."

His eyes carried on the real conversation. They spoke of sorrow, pleading with me not to blame him for being absent and out of touch. Mostly, they begged me to forgive him for not getting to Eileen in time.

When I had regained my ability to move, I pulled him into my embrace. At last—I'd found someone to whom my presence alone was a tonic. A sense of peace coursed through me as his body relaxed against mine; he was my tonic as well.

Relief turned into burning tension as I felt his desire. I flamed with hunger for him, but the time wasn't right. With great effort I stepped away, holding onto his hand in the hope that it would make my movement less offensive.

I wanted him, but not like this. He didn't know who or what I was, and I still held lingering doubts—not about him, but about the consequences if he were to enter into a relationship with me.

He coughed to cover his discomfort.

"I came by to ask if you wanted to go to the funeral with me tomorrow."

"Yes, I would like that," I said, smiling sadly.

"It starts at ten. I'll come get you at 9:30?"

"Okay."

He hesitated before he leaned forward and kissed my cheek. He gave my hand a soft squeeze before letting it go.

"Goodnight."

"Goodnight." My strangled voice was just above a whisper.

I DECIDED on a simple black dress for the funeral. Not wanting to look over embellished, I wore a single strand of pearls around my neck and another around my wrist. Pearls weren't the best stone to hide behind, so I smoothed my hair over my ears to cover their points and wound it into a knot at the nape of my neck to minimize its metallic sheen.

I also wore a black pillbox hat with black netting that fell over my eyes. It was perhaps a bit too circa 1950's, but better to look eccentric than to have my faceted eyes shine for everyone to see.

I held the bracelet I had worked on over the weekend wrapped in tissue paper. I fidgeted with it, wondering how Alexander would react to the gift. His mother's ring was the only piece of jewelry I had ever seen him wear. I would have to get him to wear this piece without telling him why. I hoped he wouldn't resist the idea.

I stepped outside when I heard his footsteps on the path between our homes. His lips turned up into a small smile when he saw me.

"Stunning," he said before kissing me lightly.

He walked me to his truck. Before I got in, I pushed the tissue paper package at him. He looked puzzled, but he took it willingly enough.

"What's this?" he asked.

"A gift."

He crinkled his brow. "What's the occasion?"

"No occasion. You inspired this new design, and I wanted you to have it." I smiled and motioned with my hand for him to open the package.

He tore the paper away to reveal a cuff bracelet carved from an agate crystal I had taken from my grandfather's collection. It was a luscious stone with blue marbling. On its surface I had etched an intricate geographic design.

He held it gingerly, examining the artistry.

"Tressa, you made this? It's magnificent."

"Will you wear it?" I asked.

Alexander slipped it on, using his good left hand to slide it over his right wrist, just as I had imagined.

EILEEN HAD BEEN A POPULAR GIRL, and she had lived her entire life within a thirty-mile radius of Saint Francis Church. Naturally, a large crowd attended her funeral. People packed the pews and lined the walls of the church. Alexander and I found a spot to stand along the back wall.

Looking out over the congregation, I was able to pick out everyone who had attended that fateful birthday celebration. Rachel and Ricky were on the far left, their daughter sitting between them. Kendra and Matt sat near the front, just three rows behind Holly and her parents.

In fact, the whole town seemed to be there.

An unmistakable sadness permeated the congregation. Quiet sobs and sniffles punctuated the sound of the mourners' hushed conversations.

I trembled with anger when I saw that Fred was one of the pallbearers. Eileen would have hated just having him in attendance, and her parents had given him this honor?

A red-eyed Tom Lynch took the spot behind him. His relationship with Eileen had been more complicated; they had been sweethearts before Tom's loyalty to Fred ripped them apart. I believed his grief was genuine.

The service was a conventional funeral mass. While in the church, Alexander and I took part in the service but didn't speak to each other. We went wordlessly to the car when it was over to join the funeral procession to the cemetery. It was a companionable, if sad, silence.

The cemetery was on a steep and rocky hill. Eileen's freshly dug grave, canopied with a tent, was near the peak. Alexander looked with concern at my high-heeled sandals.

"Are you going to be alright?" he asked.

"Sure and I'll be fine," I assured him.

He took my hand and steadied me as we climbed the ten yards to the gravesite. We stood on the fringe of the crowd, which seemed appropriate, as we weren't her closest friends or family.

A warm breeze kicked up as the priest finished his service,

carrying the final words of his prayers to heaven. Goosebumps covered my arms as I felt the grace in his words brush past me. Alexander put his arm around me, pulling me close.

The priest had just invited everyone to come forward to say our final good-byes when Holly called out to me.

"Tressa, will you sing?" Her request came out choked with tears.

"What are you doing?" her mother mumbled under her breath, unaware that I could hear her.

"Eileen loved Tressa's singing. She would want her to sing now," Holly hissed back. It was the first bit of feistiness I had seen in her since the accident.

Alexander helped me over to the head of the casket where the priest had stood. I looked over at Holly for confirmation. Her eyes were dull and lifeless, but she met my gaze and nodded.

I began my lament as the mourners passed by the gravesite, offering their condolences to the family. Several people stopped at the casket to say a quick prayer or to pull a flower from one of the arrangements to take with them.

By the time my song was finished, most of the mourners had left or were walking to their cars. Only Holly, her parents, Fred and a few stragglers remained. Alexander, of course, still stood beside me.

I took a moment to allow my own feelings to open, mourning the young woman being laid to rest. Unconsciously, I closed my eyes and murmured a traditional Sidhe funeral invocation.

Midway through the prayer, Alexander startled me by pushing me aside. He had moved in front of me to block Fred, who advanced at me swiftly.

"Stop that. Stop it now, you witch," he shouted at me, finger raised and pointing.

"Fred, stop. What are you doing?" Holly called, dissolving

into sobs that wracked her entire body. Her anguish broke my resolve, and my own tears overflowed at last.

"Back off, man," Alexander ordered, raising his hands to thwart Fred's progression.

Fred continued his rant, addressing Alexander this time. He was still trying to come at me.

"That woman is a witch. She bewitched me, and she probably has you under her spell too."

A chill ran through me as the breeze picked up again. This time it rustled past Fred, catching his words and taking them with it as it moved. I willed them back, but it was too late.

"Damn it, I said you better back off." Alexander strengthened his stance, squaring off with the other man.

Fred appraised him as if seeing him for the first time. He snickered when his gaze rested on his damaged hand.

"Yeah? What's the cripple going to do, hit me?"

"I know you prefer to hit girls. Cripple or not, believe me, I'll teach you the difference," Alexander said, as his hands balled into fists.

Tom rushed over and stepped between them.

"Alright guys, knock it off," he ordered. He turned his back to Alexander, speaking to Fred in an undertone.

"You just convinced Holly to come home. Do you really want to spoil things now, after you've worked so hard?"

His words filled me with dismay. I looked over the cemetery and saw her parents putting the still sobbing Holly into the limousine.

Fred started down the hill after his wife, but turned to make a parting shot.

"She's with me now. You'd better stay out of my way or I'll see you burn in hell, witch."

Alexander took a menacing step toward him, but Tom put out a hand to stop him.

"Enough."

Tom looked more composed than he had during the service. His body language proclaimed that he was in cop mode and was more comfortable there.

"Mannus, I've got a few questions for you. I can ask you now, or you can drop Tressa off and come to the station. Which will it be?"

Alexander looked over at me.

"Ask whatever you want. I've got nothing to hide."

"I understand you were at *JR*'s with Eileen on Friday night?"

"Yeah, I was there. I wasn't 'with' her, if that's what you're asking. I was with Tressa."

"Is that right?" He made it more of a sarcastic statement than a question.

"Yes, that's correct," I spoke up, choosing to act as though it were a question.

"Did you leave the restaurant at any point during the evening?"

"No."

"Not even to have a smoke or make a call?"

"Tom, he was with me all night."

"You were up on stage for a while," Tom pointed out.

"Yes, and I saw him at the table the entire time."

"I understand you got into an argument that night."

"Not me, that's on your boy there. I just tried to back him down. But you know that already. You were there." Alexander lost his patience. "Listen, why don't you tell me what this is about?"

"Someone tampered with Eileen's brakes while she was in the restaurant. But you already knew that, didn't you?"

"I read it in the paper like everyone else, so yeah, I knew. What exactly are you implying?"

"Witnesses at the restaurant said you were upset when you

found out Eileen had left the restaurant. They said you tried to stop her." He stepped closer to Alexander, eyes narrowed and glaring. "Why would you do that unless you knew something was wrong with her car? You were somehow involved in this."

My stomach tightened when I remembered Alexander's desperation to stop Eileen. Surely his premonitions were a form of *Darna Shealladh*, but most people didn't believe in Second Sight so he couldn't tell Tom the real reason for his panic that night.

"Don't be ridiculous. She forgot her cell phone and I was trying to get it to her is all," Alexander told the officer.

"Your wife was killed in a car accident, wasn't she?" Tom threw the words at him like a punch.

Alexander, shocked, stepped back as if the words had physically hit him.

"Yeah. So what?"

"Isn't it true that she died because someone tampered with her brakes?" And there it was: Tom's knockout blow.

"No, you son of a bitch, that's not true."

If Tom had hoped to provoke Alexander into a physical reaction, he had failed. The more enraged Alexander grew the more still he became, like an animal preparing to attack. I took his hand to calm him. He took a deep breath.

"She dropped a bottle of water while she was driving and it got lodged under the brake pedal. Nothing was wrong with the car. It was a senseless accident."

"There was an investigation."

"Isn't that routine with you law enforcement types?" Alexander shook his head. "Listen, if you're looking for a suspect, you should look at your boy Fred. If you have nothing more constructive to ask, we're leaving." We started toward the car, not bothering to wait for Tom's acknowledgment.

"Don't leave town without my okay, Mannus," he called after us.

CHAPTER TWELVE

I dreamt I was in the ballroom at Uncle Lomán's castle in Faery. The crystal chandeliers shimmered like jewelry. An orchestra played a heavenly waltz as smiling couples spun round the dance floor.

At first, I danced with my father. His eyes shone as he told me how proud he and my mother were of me. Seeing him quenched a thirst I hadn't known I had. I drank in the details of his face—the lines at the corners of his eyes, the way his cheeks dimpled when he smiled—knowing I would not see it again in this life.

Then another lost face, my grandfather, swept me across the dance floor, looking as he had the last time I saw him: tall, straight-backed and proud with his silver hair and glittering purple eyes.

"You are the Treasure, my darling girl," he said, looking at me adoringly.

"You mean *a* treasure, Mórai, not *the* Treasure." I corrected him more assertively than I ever had in life. I no longer wanted the expectations of that title hanging over me. Had I ever wanted it?

He smiled at me indulgently.

"No, my darling girl, I spoke correctly. You are the Treasure. Your Mamó says it is so."

The old king faded, replaced by the current king. My Uncle Lomán whirled me around faster than the music called for. Faster than comfortable.

"You are the Treasure," he said.

Next, my brother Gilleagán spun me so fast that my head began to spin as well.

"You know what they do to the Treasure, don't you?" He hammered the words at me in a nasty stinging tone, just as he had in our youth. "Deaglan Mór will hunt you down and burn you alive, like his grandfathers burned the King's Treasures before you."

He laughed maniacally, his face morphing until it was Deaglan Mór himself whirling me around, still laughing. His eyes were a blazing, crackling fire-red.

Suddenly, everything and everyone around me burst into an inferno of flames.

I WOKE WITH A START. My sheets were damp, and I glistened with sweat. Darkness surrounded me. Only the moonlight coming through the window disrupted the pitch black of my room.

It took a couple of panicked breaths before I realized that the electricity was out. The digital clock on my bedside table, which usually illuminated the room, was dark.

My breathing gradually returned to normal, but the hot, stuffy room kept me sweating. I slid out of bed and padded carefully down the hall to the bathroom.

Feeling my way around the windowless room, I turned on the cold tap and splashed the refreshing water onto my face. I took a few deep breaths to rein in my emotions, splashing my face once more before toweling dry.

Our electricity often failed at Pine Ridge. I kept a flashlight in the drawer of my nightstand for these occasions. However, on that night, my flashlight refused to turn on—apparently the batteries were dead. I didn't keep candles, matches, or lighters of any kind in the house, so the room remained dark.

I opened the window and found that the air outside was as hot and humid as inside: more like a midsummer's evening instead of mid-spring.

The gibbous moon and a galaxy of stars gave a silvery glow and a sense of vastness to the night sky. My room began to feel even darker and more claustrophobic when compared to the view from my window.

The lake in the distance called to me with its open air and clear, cold water. It promised to relax and refresh me.

I went as I was, holding tightly to the banister as I made my way down the steep old staircase. When I reached the outdoors and I could see properly, I ran barefoot with my nightgown flowing behind me.

I pulled the nightgown over my head, tossed it onto the glider, and ran naked into the water. With long, forceful strokes, I swam toward the middle of the lake.

My hot room had summoned the nightmare of fire and Deaglan Mór, the Unseelie prince. I let the soothing sensation of water flowing over my body and cooling my skin dispel it.

About a hundred yards into the lake, I flipped onto my back and relaxed into a float. I lazily picked out constellations from the starlit sky.

Once the water had done its work, I began to grow cold. I started back to shore at a slower pace, in no hurry to return to the darkness of the farmhouse. Halfway back, I saw him.

Alexander stood at the edge of the lake. He wore jeans and nothing else; even his feet were bare. His tousled hair and unkempt look made it clear that he had recently abandoned his bed as well.

He stood looking at me with his hands on his hips, the bracelet I made for him still wrapped around his wrist. We stared at each other across the water for a heartbeat or two.

I watched, unable to turn away, as he peeled off his jeans and joined me in the water.

My nightmare had been a blatant reminder of the danger I brought with me into this relationship. Yet I was about to be tested, and I knew I would fall short of the challenge.

There was no avoiding this. I swam closer to where he stood, now up to his waist in the water.

"How did you know I was here?"

"I woke up and just knew," he said.

I swam around him, keeping far enough away so he couldn't see me clearly with his human eyesight.

"You're a *Fáidh*?" I said, part question, part statement. He looked quizzical. "You have Second Sight. Visions of the future," I explained.

"No. I'm just a normal guy who gets a gut feeling once in a while." He stepped toward me, closing the distance between us, but I splashed away from him. "The better question is: who are *you*?"

"Wha—What do you mean?" I halfheartedly tried to keep up my ruse.

He held up the wrist that wore the bracelet.

"I've been working on this hand for years. You put a bracelet on it, and in less than twenty-four hours, it's completely healed." He shook his head. "What are you?"

His hand had healed. He could see me. Oh no, no, no. I had

done something terribly wrong with the talisman; it had healed him too quickly. I splashed backward again, this time in a real panic.

"Tressa, please don't be afraid of me." He started toward me again.

"I'm not afraid of you. I'm afraid *for* you."

His eyes, those deep, penetrating eyes, told me there could be no more pretending. He had to know everything. Afterwards, it would be safer for him if I left. Silent tears wet my cheeks when I thought of parting from him.

"I couldn't live with myself if something happened to you," I said, a vision of Deaglan Mór appearing in my mind. My pain-laden voice echoed my thoughts. "Evil hunts for me. I must leave so that it doesn't come after you."

He lunged, grasping my wrist and pulling me to him.

"You can't leave. I won't have it."

Heat radiated out from my wrist where he held me until my entire body felt flushed. I stretched my foot to test for the bottom and found the water was shallow there; I stood and the water barely came to my breasts. My senses tingled, intensely aware of my nakedness and the closeness of his body.

He reached out and gently ran his fingers through my hair pushing it back to unmask my face. He gasped and I ducked my head, feebly attempting to cover myself. He wouldn't allow me to hide. He lifted my chin, met my eyes, and smiled.

"Don't hide. You're safe with me." His eyes explored my face, fingers tracing a line from my forehead, circling around my eyes, and then following the wet tracks down my cheek.

He stroked the points of my ears before moving his hand to caress the length of my neck as he took a deep, shaking breath. When he exhaled, the outflow of air was so ragged it seemed painful.

"My god." He took another faltering breath. "You're beautiful."

"You will never again see me or anyone like me as you did before now." My tears returned. "I've made you a target. You must leave Pine Ridge as quickly as you can. Tell no one what you can see."

"Damn it, woman," he hissed, his anger mixed with lust. "I'm telling you: neither of us is going anywhere."

He was right. Perhaps it was without logic, for some would say I barely knew him, but I knew I loved him. And I trusted him—with my life, and with his. The time for doubt had passed.

He wrapped his arms around my waist, pulling me tightly against him as if overwhelmed by need. He groaned as my naked body met his. The touch of his flesh destroyed my defenses. I pressed my body along his length and lifted my face to his.

A curse escaped his lips just before he brought them down on mine. His kiss was hard, almost brutal, as though he were punishing me... or perhaps himself. Then a frenzied longing swept away the anger.

The water lapped around us as we tore at each other, frantic to explore each other's bodies. Our need for release was such that neither of us had the patience for long caresses. I reached up, locked my fingers behind his neck, and wrapped my legs around him. He lifted my bottom and let me down as he entered me. Almost instantly, unable to hold back even if we had wanted to, we both exploded.

We stayed locked together as he kissed me thoroughly. Then we started again, this time going slower, taking the time to enjoy the details of each other's bodies, prolonging the buildup until at last, we came to another explosive conclusion.

· · ·

LATER, in the small hours of the morning, we lay together in my bed. Alexander leaned against the headboard comparing his hands, which he held out before him.

He closed his right hand into a fist and then opened it again, stretching his fingers wide. He touched each finger to his thumb in turn, testing their dexterity. It looked as fragile as it had before the bracelet: the scar still wrapped around the center of his palm and ran up his forearm, and the muscles around the scar still appeared atrophied. However, I noted with pride, his arm and hand were strong, functioning as well as they had before the injury.

He rolled to his side, supporting his head in his hand and staring at me as he had been doing all night. He ran his fingers down a lock of my hair, watching the curls flatten as he stretched it out and bounce back when he released it.

"It's amazing. Your hair looks like fine-spun copper, but it's as soft as silk." He leaned forward and kissed me. "You never told me what you are," he scolded.

"As if I could have," I said with mock defensiveness. "It isn't as though you've given me the time."

"Hmmm," he wore a satisfied smile. "Yes, I guess that's true... Tell me now."

He continued to play with my hair as I tried to find the right words to explain. His expression grew concerned when I had taken too long.

"You're not afraid, are you? I promise it will be okay."

"No, it's not that. I've never tried to explain to anyone who I am, so I'm not sure where to begin. I can tell you that I am a Sidhe of the *Tuatha Dé Danann*, but I don't know if that would mean anything to you."

"No, I'm afraid it doesn't." He rolled onto his back, rearranging me until I was curled on my side with my head resting on his shoulder. Perhaps he suspected it would be easier for me to continue if we weren't looking at each other. Whether or not he'd planned it, avoiding eye contact did indeed make it easier.

"Some people call us faeries, or the 'Good People'. 'The Others'."

"You're a faery." His tone held no surprise, revulsion, or disbelief; only simple acceptance. "And what, exactly, is a faery?"

"Hmmm. Do you know anything about angels?"

He barked a startled laugh. "As much as anyone, I guess. You're an angel?" He sounded dubious.

"Not exactly. The Sidhe are descendants of the Dominions—one of the nine choirs of angels."

He sobered.

"You're serious, aren't you?"

I nodded.

"Okay... Please explain that."

"Let me back up a bit. You see, all angels are God's messengers, but it was the job of the Dominions to make God's plan for the universe known by communicating His commands to both angels and humans.

"In the beginning, the nine choirs of angels roamed all of creation at will—the heavens, the earth, and everywhere in between. However, the Dominions began to spend much of their time interacting with the people here on earth.

"The humans began to call these angels gods and goddesses. While the Dominions didn't promote this idea, they didn't discourage it either.

"The Thrones—a choir closer to the Throne of God—were in charge of doling out justice and dictating the lower angels' access to God. They disapproved of what they called the Dominions' 'sin of omission.'

"The Thrones knew their God was a jealous God and would

not stand for this behavior. They gave the Dominions an ultimatum: end their association with the people or lose all access to our Lord.

"The Dominions had seen the terrible fate of the angels who had sided with Lucifer in his battle against God, and at once, they came to their senses. Now it's a rare thing for a Dominion to make himself known to a mortal."

I took a deep breath; the heavy and burdensome nature of the story made me ill at ease. I fidgeted as I continued, anxious to have it told, to know his reaction.

"The Sidhe are the result of the Dominions' physical relations with the people of earth. Neither fully human nor fully celestial, we are of the Otherworld. Free to live with our human relations if we wish, but unable to enter heaven until our physical self has passed away."

I stopped speaking when his body went still beneath me. The silence in the room fed my anxiety; perhaps it had been too much too fast.

"Making love to someone even part-angel seems wrong," he said at last.

I laughed, relief replacing my concern. "You might think differently if you met any of my family." I patted his arm. "We're several millenniums removed from the Dominions now. We've evolved into our own race."

I felt him relax, comforted by my words.

"Why do you look different now?" he asked.

"This is the real me." I smiled wryly, insecure for a moment. "We use glamour to make ourselves blend in. I use gemstones, crystals—different elements of my jewelry—to anchor the magic. Most of us do, though there may be other ways."

"What's changed? It has something to do with the bracelet, doesn't it?"

"Aye. I have the gift of healing, but it requires at least a spark of my essence to knit the wounds back together. The glamour doesn't work on a human infused with a bit of fae essence.

"I just—I wanted so much to help you. I thought I could avoid opening your eyes by using the bracelet. Obviously, I was wrong." I looked up at him, heart full of guilt.

Shaking his head, he dismissed my regret. "You have to know—this is like a miracle to me." He opened and closed his hand, testing it again. "You said you have the gift of healing. Don't all the Sidhe?"

"No, but most of us have a special gift. A talent. My grandmother sees auras, and my cousin Rosheen can tell when someone is lying."

"Wow. That must be tiring; people tell lies all the time," Alexander said, amused. Then, his eyes narrowing, he asked, "Tressa, who are you so afraid of?"

I sighed and laid my head back on his shoulder. I took his hand in mine. As I continued my story, I traced the line of his scar, musing that the path created a simple Celtic knot.

"Long ago, the Sidhe divided into two factions: the Seelie court—my people—and the Unseelie Court. For centuries each court controlled equal shares of the Otherworld, but the Unseelie always fought to takeover.

"The last war reduced them to rebel gangs fighting guerrilla warfare. The House of Mór is all that remains of the Unseelie Court. They have had a blood feud with the current royal family since Lucifer fell; they believe they are the true rulers of all of the Otherworld."

"Are they after all of the Seelie, or you in particular?"

"Well, both. I'm part of the royal family, the House of Finna, so I'm a target twice over."

I couldn't bring myself to tell him everything. Too many years of adulation for my station made me loath to admit that I was the King's Jewel. I dreaded the possibility that the affection in his eyes—which had nothing to do with hidden agendas—could turn into the bitter disappointment I saw in so many others' eyes. The longer I kept the prophecy out of this, I reasoned, the longer it would be before I had to face that pain.

"The royal family?" Alexander asked.

"My uncle is King Lomán the Third, King of the Otherworld."

"And what exactly is the Otherworld?"

"The Faery Realm. I was born there, in a place called *Tír na nÓg,* which means land of the young."

"The land of the young," he repeated as though the translation bothered him. "Are you immortal?"

"No. We're part human, so we are susceptible to disease and mortal wounds, just as you are. We do, however, age slower and live longer. But we do grow older, as you can see with my grandmother."

"Sure. I should have thought of that," he said.

We fell silent for a while, and I thought perhaps he had fallen asleep. Eventually, he spoke up again.

"Tressa, how old are you?"

Human women, I have heard, often lie about their age as they get older. I lie about my age when I need to, if only to protect my anonymity. This didn't seem like the time to bother with human concerns. I laughed as I imagined his reaction to what I was about to say.

"Oh no," he said. "This will be bad."

I laughed even harder.

"Xander, I'm sorry to tell you, but you've just been with a seventy year old."

He flipped me over and pinned me down by rolling partially on top of me.

"Hottest damned seventy year old I've ever laid eyes on. And what's with calling me Xander all of a sudden?"

"I've decided Matt's right... you *are* a super hero." I batted my eyelashes for emphasis.

His eyebrows went up suggestively.

"Why don't we test out that theory..."

CHAPTER THIRTEEN

*L*ater that morning, I left Alexander asleep in my bed and walked down to the glider with a cup of tea. I settled in, sipping the tea as I appreciated the clear blue sky and the backdrop of lush, green trees behind the lake.

Beneath my calm façade, turmoil twisted inside me. I could not regret the decision I had made the night before, but I still worried about what would happen to Alexander if an Unseelie came after me here.

I heard a fluttering by my ear and grinned.

"Told you so! Told you so!" Brenna gloated.

"Welcome back, Precious Brenna. When did you get here?" I asked, a bit concerned that Alexander and I had not been alone last night.

"Not soon enough." Brenna flew in front of my nose, shaking a finger at me. "The wind is full of interesting noises."

I decided to take the high road and ignore her.

"Have your wee companions returned with you?"

Brenna zigzagged over to sit on my shoulder, curling up along my neck.

"Aye. Sleeping. Travelling hard."

I knew her relaxed mood was probably a good sign, but I was too afraid of what she may have learned in the Otherworld to take it at face value.

"Don't fall asleep now, Precious Brenna. You haven't told me what you learned."

She roused herself and flew over to the tree. She found a branch she liked and settled down on it. She leaned her elbows on a leaf in front of her, resting her chin on her hands. She crossed her legs at her ankles and swung them back and forth.

"Good news," she said. "Nothing at home about Unmentionables in human world. No reports of any Unmentionables trying to cross the border."

I let out a breath I didn't know I was holding.

"Anything else?"

"Top bad guy spotted in Faery just a week ago."

"Okay, that's good then." Perhaps, as long as we stayed here, I could relax about the danger to Alexander.

"Bad news."

"What bad news?" I asked, my nerves on edge again.

"Strange things on the wind."

"What kind of things?"

The Pixie struggled to keep her eyes open. She barely managed to keep them at half mast.

"Brenna, wake up," I said sharply. "Tell me what you heard."

The Pixie shook herself and flew back to stand on my shoulder. She stretched up onto her tippy toes to speak directly in my ear.

"Heard terrible word. Heard *witch*," she whispered. "Bad, bad word to have on the wind."

She flew up to look behind me.

"Pretty boy coming."

I shook my head, wishing—not for the first time—that I could hold her still until we finished our conversation.

"I hear him. Brenna, what else was on the wind?"

ALEXANDER

TRESSA'S bright coppery hair glinted like metal in the sunlight as I approached her spot by the lake. If I hadn't seen it up close earlier, I never would have taken it for hair from this distance.

"There you are," I called out as I drew near.

After sliding onto the glider next to her, I studied how the sunlight affected her appearance. She looked like herself, but different: everything about her shone.

Her irises danced like bold, green-blue faceted gemstones. Her lips were a rosy red. I ran a finger down the length of her forearm, admiring the soft smoothness of her skin, which had the added benefit of making her smile. Her skin, always alabaster, now had an iridescence to it.

I couldn't explain why I didn't have a stronger reaction to finding out the truth about her. Maybe it had something to do with the Second Sight she had talked about yesterday, but I couldn't be happier to be with her.

I leaned forward to kiss her when a translucent, toddler-like creature with dragonfly wings flew between us. The creature hovered, wings flapping, just in front of my face.

I choked back a surprised yelp as I jumped off the glider, nearly tripping over a tree root.

"Holy crap, Tressa! Ah... is this a friend of yours?"

"Aye," Tressa said, laughing. "Xander, this is my Precious Brenna."

The tiny girl put her hands over her mouth to cover her giggles.

"So this is who you were speaking to the first time I met you here." I thought fast, trying to process all the things I had learned over the last twenty-four hours. "So Brenna is a Sidhe?"

This was obviously wrong. Brenna spun around in front of me, hooting with laughter.

"Silly pretty boy. Do I look like Sidhe? Need to check eyes." She continued laughing as she flew to the ground and landed with a somersault at the roots of the big tree.

Who is she calling a pretty boy? I was already tired of this creature laughing at me.

Two more like Brenna wandered out from a hole at the base of the tree, stretching and rubbing their eyes.

"Brenna and her sisters are Pixies," Tressa explained.

"And Pixies are another type of faery?" I asked.

"Aye, but we prefer fae to faery."

"Okay, duly noted."

I still hadn't gotten a kiss, and I went back to Tressa deter-mined to get one. Then I remembered the Pixies and settled for a chaste, the-kids-are-around peck. To my surprise, Tressa snuggled into me and kissed me a second time.

"Don't let them fool you. They're fully-grown women. There's nothing childish about their mental capacity, just their behavior," she said.

The Pixies were sprawled on the ground as though they had run a marathon. I tried to ignore them and talk to Tressa.

"Speaking of children, I've been thinking. Before I bring Sophia back, I wanted to find out who's in charge of security on the estate."

"Security?" Tressa asked. "Whatever do you mean?"

"You keep telling me about this great danger around you. There must be some type of security in place to protect you from Unsee— "

Before I could finish my thought, Tressa frantically grabbed my arm. "No," she cried.

The three Pixies were in my face trying to cover my mouth with their hands. Their wings tickled as they brushed my cheeks and I struggled not to swat them away.

"What did I do?" I asked once the Pixies had backed away.

"You must be very careful what you say outside," Tressa said.

I would have thought it was a joke if she hadn't looked so serious.

"Or even inside near an open window. Words—sounds—travel on the wind. We don't say things outside that could help our enemies locate us."

I thought about this for a minute.

"So what about talking about... your kind?"

"Many humans talk about faeries, so that isn't as unusual. But even that we keep to a minimum," Tressa explained. "To answer your question, Shamus can tell you what you want to know. But give me a little time to bring him up to speed on... our situation." She grinned at me.

"Okay, but I need to know if it's safe to bring Sophia back before the end of the week."

"Sure and it's perfectly safe for the wee one. No fae—no matter who they are—would hurt a child. Children are prized above all else."

Brenna, who sat on Tressa's shoulder with her sisters, unabashedly listening in on our conversation, tugged on a strand of Tressa's hair.

"Yes dear, what is it?" Tressa asked with a patience that amazed me.

"The child's eyes are open. She sees," Brenna said, the raucous playfulness gone.

Tressa turned thoughtful as all the Pixies began to talk over one another.

"Oh aye."

"It's true."

"She spoke to me."

"Are they talking about Sophia?" I asked.

Tressa nodded.

"Aye, I forgot about that. I noticed something strange when she woke me here a few weeks back."

"Tressa, what does this mean? What are they saying?"

"They're saying Sophia can see the fae, like you do."

I didn't like the sound of that. Tressa kept talking about the danger in knowing of the fae; I didn't want that for Sophia.

"How can that be possible?"

"I'm not sure. Many years ago there were people who were Sidhe Seers from birth, but that hasn't happened for centuries," she answered me distractedly, lost in her own thoughts. She bit her lip. "Your mother..." She hesitated, but found her resolve and started again. "Xander, I believe your mother was a Sidhe."

"What? No." Even as I denied it, the details clicked in my mind. My mother had been under Órlaith's care. Órlaith said she had visions of the future. She had come here when she was in trouble.

"She was gone long before Sophia was born," I said.

Brenna tugged on Tressa's hair again.

"You forgot. More bad news."

"Oh yes, Brenna, you're right. What else have you heard?" Tressa turned and told me, "She heard Fred call me a witch yesterday."

"Shhh, don't say again," Brenna scolded.

"Sorry. Tell me, what else is worrying you?"

"Weird things. Hard to understand. Bad fae who aren't bad fae. Faery tricks not funny. Can't explain."

"Kerry? Megan? Did you get anything more?" Tressa asked.

They both shook their heads.

"Mixed up."

"Nonsense."

Tressa sighed.

"Well, thank you for trying. You girls go get your rest now."

WE WALKED QUIETLY BACK to Tressa's home, our fingers inter-twined, each of us lost in thought.

"Tressa, what do you think Órlaith is having me look for on the mountains?" I asked when we were close to her door.

"I really don't know. Honestly, I don't. However, I can tell you that the stone in your ring is River Rock. It comes from the Otherworld. It isn't found naturally here."

"But we found some."

"Yes, I know. I don't understand it." She was thoughtful for a minute before she went on. "You should know that your mother probably left the stone with you as a bit of protection."

"How so?"

"It muffles your voice, and the voices of those around you, so that your words can't be heard on the wind. I've been wondering whether she had a special reason to think you needed protec-tion, or if it was just motherly instinct to protect you in any way possible."

"I guess we'll never know," I said bitterly. She had touched an old wound that still festered.

CHAPTER FOURTEEN

TRESSA

hen I arrived to open the shop, I was surprised and pleased to find Holly was already there. I had worried that Fred wouldn't let her return to work.

She absentmindedly passed a dust rag over the jewelry case. She was dressed in her typical high-fashion style, every hair in place, but her eyes were still lifeless.

Matt was there, leaning across the case, speaking to her in a low, fervent tone. I caught the phrases 'listen to reason' and 'it isn't safe' before my entrance stopped the conversation.

I went to her and pulled her into my embrace.

"Oh, Holly. Finally, I get to give you a hug. You had so many supporters I couldn't get near you yesterday."

"I'm trying to tell her she can't move back in with that animal," Matt reported tersely.

I agreed with Matt that living with Fred would inevitably lead Holly to heartache, though I doubted she was ready to hear it.

"The baby deserves a whole family. It wouldn't be right to not give him another chance," Holly said.

"That's your parents speaking, not you. He hasn't changed. Don't let him hurt you again."

"It's done. I've already moved back, so stop harping on it, will you?" she snapped. She brushed past him, storming into the back room.

Matt looked defeated. He glanced at me and shook his head.

"Give her time," I encouraged him. "She's been through a lot these past couple of days."

"So help me—if he hurts her again..." Matt looked as though he could barely control his fury.

"We'll just do the best we can between us to keep her safe until she's strong enough to go against her parents and break away from him again." It was an empty sentiment and I knew it. I prayed that she would let us help her before catastrophe hit.

Matt nodded, resigned.

WHILE SOPHIA WAS STILL at her grandfather's, Alexander and I spent our evenings at my house, enjoying getting to know each other.

We fell into a quaint domestic routine, Alexander making our dinner and me cleaning up afterward. I had wasted weeks avoiding him, and we used this time without Sophia to make up for lost opportunities.

We spent the nights in my bed, getting to know each other in another way. There was an intensity to our relationship that both scared and thrilled me.

Each morning I would reluctantly leave him to go to work. While at the shop, I did little else but worry about Holly. My apprehension over her situation contrasted sharply with the happiness I felt at home.

Holly came into work sullen most days. Between Matt—still a steady morning visitor—the customers, and me, we could usually get her into a better place over the course of the day. However, she still refused to listen to anything negative about Fred.

A week after Eileen's death, Tom Lynch came into the shop. I sat at my workstation putting together a simple string of rose quartz. He held up his hand toward me by way of a greeting before heading over to Holly.

"Is there somewhere we can talk privately?" he asked.

Holly sighed and then nodded.

"Tressa, I'm taking a break, okay?"

She led the police officer into the storage room in the back, out of earshot for most people. I, of course, could hear the entire conversation.

"Holly, did Eileen ever mention someone named Chuck Sullivan?" Tom asked in a clipped, to-the-point tone.

"Yeah, he was her supervisor at work. Why?" Holly's voice sounded tired, as if she had already answered too many questions.

"Did she ever mention having a problem with him?"

"Well she didn't like him, that's for sure. Are you saying he's the one who—" her voice broke, she had trouble saying the words. "That he's the one?"

"I don't know yet, but I heard he made her life miserable. He has something against women driving trucks. Her coworkers say she always stood up to him, usually with a smart remark." Tom's voice held a tinge of pride and amusement.

"You said it was Alexander," Holly said blandly.

I sucked in a breath, shocked to hear the accusation stated so bluntly. I nearly jumped up to defend him before I remembered that I wasn't supposed to be listening.

"No. The detective on the case told me his story checks out about how his wife died, and several witnesses say he never left the bar that night."

I huffed again, indignant. They had investigated Alexander as a murder suspect.

"I'm glad it wasn't him," Holly said, "for Tressa's sake."

"Holly," Tom said hesitantly. "We have to face the possibility that it could have been—"

"No," Holly interrupted him. "Don't say it. It can't have been him. He's my husband, and he knows how much Eileen meant to me. It wasn't him."

"I don't want to believe it either."

Thinking back to the time Fred almost ran me down with his pickup, I had no problem believing he could have tampered with Eileen's brakes.

The bells chimed as new customers came in; I set down the quartz necklace and went to wait on them. If there had been more to the conversation, I missed it.

ALEXANDER PLANNED to pick Sophia up at his father's house after work, so I didn't expect to see him until the next morning. A pounding noise woke me from a deep sleep. It took a confused moment to understand that someone was knocking on my door.

Uncertain what to expect, I tossed off my nightgown, pulled on a pair of yoga pants and grabbed a t-shirt, pulling it over my head as I made my way downstairs.

At the door, Alexander held up a beaten and bloody Matt. He dragged Matt over the threshold and towards the living room.

"No, not there. Put him on the dining room table."

Alexander changed direction and set him gingerly on the table. I helped lift his legs as Alexander slowly lowered his head. Though we did our best, Matt groaned in pain.

"What happened?" I asked.

"I'm not sure. He called and asked me to get him from the alley behind Saint Francis Church. I didn't get much more from him, except that he refused to go to the hospital. I thought maybe you could help him."

Bruising and swelling disfigured Matt's face. I removed his glasses, their frame bent and a lens cracked, to get a better look at him.

His nose was clearly broken, and perhaps his jaw as well. He bled from several cuts and scrapes. Every inch of his face looked painful, and I winced in sympathy.

I continued my assessment, going down his body. He had at least one, but more likely three, broken ribs. Thankfully, his steady breathing made me think he hadn't punctured a lung. His hands, swollen and bloody, probably had some broken bones as well.

I looked up and saw that Alexander watched me intently, evidently waiting for me to say something.

"He's badly hurt. Whoever did this was serious. He should go to the hospital."

"Can you help him?" he asked, worried.

"Aye, but you know the consequences if I do. His eyes will be opened to every fae he meets. Many fae won't be happy with that. It doesn't seem like much to you now, but he may regret it later."

The words were a waste; in my heart I knew I couldn't say no. My friend needed my help.

I asked Alexander to boil a pot of water while I went to the pantry, which also served as an apothecary, and grabbed supplies.

"How can I help?" Alexander asked.

"Why don't you clean the cuts on his face while I deal with his hands?"

We worked silently, concentrating on our tasks. Through touch and temperature, I located two small fractures in his right hand. The superficial cuts clotted nearly as soon as they were clean. I dabbed them with aloe, infusing it with a bit of my essence as I worked. The skin knit together into thin pink lines.

I didn't know how much energy the rest of his ministrations would take, so I left the cuts to heal the rest of the way on their own. Then I splinted his hand.

Matt remained stoic as we worked, although an occasional gasp or groan slipped out. I pried open his grotesque, swollen eyes as gently as possible to see if there was any damage or signs of a concussion.

"Mattie, did you lose consciousness at all?"

His answer was barely recognizable, but I got that he said no.

I had to pace myself. My talent for healing had a price: each discharge of my essence or energy made me weaker. I didn't have an endless supply though it would replenish as long as I didn't drain too much of it. Since none of his injuries seemed life threatening, I prioritized easing his pain.

"You're doing great, Mattie. Can you tell me where it hurts the most?"

I listened closely, but I couldn't understand his answer. I looked over at Alexander, who shook his head.

"One more time, Matt," he said. He leaned over so his ear was above the younger man's mouth. Matt mumbled again.

"Face," Alexander said, straightening.

"Good lad. Don't try to talk anymore."

I had tea bags filled with honeysuckle root and dried pinkberry leaves I had brought with me from Faery. I dipped two of them into a cup of the hot water and then squeezed out the excess with my fingertips, infusing them with the oil from my skin. Then I laid one on each of his eyes.

I sang an invocation as I soaked two more, repeated the process. This time I broke them open and spread the contents over the length of his jaw.

I put his nose back in place with a quick snap. My heart jumped to my throat when he yelped in pain. I continued my invocation but sang it softly, like a lullaby, trying to make it sound comforting while I held my fingers on either side of the break. I willed it to heal, again using my essence to begin the process and then pulling back to let his body do the rest.

"You have a beautiful voice," Matt said, his own voice groggy and heavy.

"He speaks," I teased, happy to see my ministrations were having the desired effect. I looked over at Alexander. "I'll need your help to wrap his ribs."

Alexander nodded. I took a deep breath as I moved down the side of the table to work on Matt's chest, but my legs buckled beneath me. Alexander caught me before I could fall, helping me slide into one of the dining room chairs.

He knelt before me, looking up at my face. "Are you okay?" His brow was creased with concern.

"I'm almost done," I said, evading the question.

"You look terrible." Alarm rang in his voice. "If I had known—"

"I will recuperate," I assured him. "I just need to take care of his ribs and then I'm done."

Alexander hesitated, reluctant to let me continue, but then nodded.

He cut off Matt's shirt to save him the pain of removing it. I waited until he dropped the shirt onto the floor before I stood. It took all my effort to get up from the chair.

I reached for a bottle of pinkberry tonic, but Alexander covered my hand with his to stop me from picking it up.

"You've done enough. I'll wrap the ribs, I've done it before."

"We don't know how severely broken they are. If I get them partially healed, we won't need to worry about a rib puncturing a lung."

He looked at me, hesitating.

"Tressa, I'm scared for you. I really don't want you to do this."

With my free hand I reached up to pat his cheek, meaning it as a teasing gesture. However, when my hand shook, I nodded to concede his point.

"I won't do but a tiny bit more."

I smiled when he sighed but agreed; he was just beginning to learn how stubborn I could be.

I rubbed in the tonic, using only the smallest amount of healing energy. When I finished, Alexander refused to wrap Matt's ribs until he had carried me up the stairs and tucked me into my bed—showing me just how stubborn *he* could be.

THE NEXT MORNING, I awoke to find Alexander curled up behind me with his arm wrapped around my waist, holding me close against him. I kept still, not wanting to wake him while I enjoyed the way our bodies fit together: the feel of his chest moving against my back with each breath and how he clung to me as if afraid to lose me while he slept.

He stirred too quickly. He always seemed to know when I awoke, no matter how still I tried to be. I rolled over to stare at him.

His eyes remained closed. I took advantage of the moment to memorize his face. His dark wavy hair fell across his forehead. A trace of dark stubble covered his cheeks. I ran a finger down the line of his profile and across the scar on his jaw.

"Woman, what are you doing?" he grumbled as he stretched, his voice still groggy with sleep.

"Admiring you," I said, stating the obvious. He hooted with laughter. "How was the patient when you left him?" I asked.

My question seemed to remind him of his concern for me. He sat up, fully awake now, and began his own examination.

"What about you? Are you okay?"

I rolled onto my back and stretched my hands overhead. "Aye, fine, but hungry. I must eat something to finish regaining my strength."

"Why didn't you warn me what would happen to you?" he asked, sounding angry.

"I've never tried to heal a human like that before, so I didn't know. It took two, almost three days to make your bracelet, so that had a more subtle effect on me. Plus, your fae blood may have helped the healing power work."

He lay back down and pulled me onto his shoulder.

"As long as you're okay," he said.

"Xander, honey, the patient?"

"He's in your guestroom. I checked in on him about an hour ago. He was asleep."

"And Sophia?"

"She spent the night with Kendra. She's still there."

I settled back to enjoy cuddling for a while longer. "Did you talk to Matt about what happened?"

"Yeah, a little. It seems he's worried about Holly being back with her husband. He has it bad for that girl."

I nodded, in agreement.

"He's been watching her, trying to make sure Fred doesn't hit her again. He's even been hanging around her house. It seems the husband took offense to Matt's interest; he and two of his friends jumped him last night. Trying to teach him a lesson, I guess."

"Damn. I hope Tommy wasn't one of them."

"The cop? Matt said he wasn't."

"So why not go to the hospital?"

"From what I gather, Fred works there, for one. For another, he didn't want to bring in the law or any other undue attention to the situation. He's afraid it would come back on Holly. He's probably right to be worried."

"Why?"

"Matt said he overheard an argument before Fred and his buddies came down on him. Fred accused Holly of sleeping around. Fred thinks she's been sleeping with Matt."

I sprung up, horrified by his words. "Oh my god, we need to check on Holly. If Fred really thinks she's sleeping with Matt, there's no telling what he'll do."

"Hold up," he said, wrapping his hand around my wrist to stop me from leaving. "We will, but it was the middle of the night and my gut tells me she's okay. For right now, anyway. I would have called the police right away if I'd have thought otherwise."

The conviction in his eyes made me relax back down onto the bed.

"I was thinking," he continued. "Now that Eileen's gone, Holly doesn't have a safe place to live away from her husband. From what you told me, her parents are on his side."

I nodded. "Aye, it seems that way."

"Why don't you tell her she can stay with you? If she has somewhere to go, maybe she'll do it."

"Of course! Why didn't I think of that?"

Matt and I had been encouraging Holly to leave without giving her a place to go. The idea was so simple, so obvious; I couldn't believe I hadn't thought of it earlier.

I reached for my phone on the nightstand and called her number. It went straight to voicemail, so I left a message asking her to call me. In case Fred screened her messages, I didn't leave any details.

"If she doesn't call back by this afternoon, I'm going to ask Tommy to check on her," I said.

We lay quietly for a bit. Finally, my conscience wouldn't let me ignore my patient any longer.

"I need to check on Matt, but with all the laying of hands I did on him yesterday, nothing will camouflage my appearance anymore."

"Yeah, I noticed he reacted to it last night."

"Perhaps you should warn him before I go into the room. Come on, let's go."

"Not until I get some breakfast in you. Wait here; I'll bring you something. I'll talk to him while you eat."

CHAPTER FIFTEEN

ALEXANDER

When I entered the room, Matt was trying—with difficulty—to rearrange himself in the bed. I quickly went to help him. He sucked in air through his teeth when he leaned forward to let me prop his head with some pillows.

"Damn, that hurts," he said as he slowly leaned back.

I waited until he looked as comfortable as he was going to get before starting.

"Matt, we need to talk about Tressa. Do you remember anything from after I brought you here last night?"

"Not much—at some point I started hallucinating or something." He touched his jaw, testing it in various spots. "I thought they broke it. Thank god it's just sore."

"That's what we need to talk about. It *was* broken, along with your hand and a couple of ribs. I brought you here last night because Tressa isn't who you think she is," I said. I thought for a second and sighed; this would not be easy to explain.

"I know this is going to sound nuts, so bear with me... Tressa is a faery." I crossed my arms over my chest and waited for his reaction. He had always been good with accepting my hunches; maybe this wouldn't be so bad.

"You're telling me your girlfriend is a faery?" Matt laughed. He grabbed around his waist and grimaced as his body shook. "Stop it man, it hurts to laugh."

I nodded.

"Yeah, I know it sounds crazy. But your jaw was broken last night, and now it isn't." I held up my right arm. "It may not look it, but she fixed my hand, too."

"Come on, Xander, you're making me think you're the one who got hit in the head. You think Tressa is some kind of magical creature?"

"I take offence to the 'creature' part," Tressa said as she entered the room carrying a steaming mug.

Matt's mirth died. His eyes bulged and his sore jaw fell open. After a silent few seconds, he turned to gape at me.

I completely understood Matt's reverential expression. Tressa was breathtaking. She glimmered like a fine jewel and moved so gracefully she nearly floated. I still couldn't take my eyes off her, even after all this time.

"How's the patient today?" she asked, setting the mug on the nightstand next to Matt.

"Ugh," Matt tried to talk but merely grunted. He could only gawk at Tressa while she assessed his wounds. She spoke to him during her examination in a soothing tone, using her voice to help him relax.

She inspected his hand last, rolling her finger over the fractures. Satisfied with what she felt, she removed the splint and replaced it with a sling she tied around Matt's neck.

"All things considered, you're healing pretty well. I'm sorry I couldn't finish the process," she said.

I stiffened as I started to protest; I wouldn't let her hurt herself again, especially with Matt looking so much better. She waved me off to indicate that she wasn't intending to do any more for him, and I relaxed.

Matt turned to me, finally finding his voice. "My god," he said. "I wasn't hallucinating!"

I refrained from saying I told him so, settling instead for a smirk.

"How long have you known?" Matt asked, still wide-eyed.

"Not long."

Tressa continued with her doctoring. "I brought a tonic for you. It will help your bones heal. You should eat soft foods for a day or two. How is the pain?"

"Umm, not bad I guess," Matt conceded.

"There's ibuprofen at my house," I said.

"That's a good idea. He'll need to take something; we're going up to the Manor House. We'll have lunch there."

"No, Tressa. I don't want to impose on your grandmother. I'll just have Xander take me home," Matt protested.

"Have lunch first. I want to keep an eye on you for a few more hours, and I'll need you around when I explain to my grandmother why I opened your eyes. It would be best if she could see you to help her understand the extent of the problem."

She handed Matt the mug and encouraged him to drink. He took a tentative sip.

"This tastes good," he said with surprise. He took another swallow. "Opened my eyes, is that what you call it?" Matt asked.

"Why don't you get that medicine, Xander? Matt and I can chat while you're gone." She raised her eyebrows and tilted her head toward the bedroom door, signaling to give her some time alone with Matt.

"So did you break a rule or something?" Matt asked as I was leaving the room.

"Many," Tressa said.

. . .

Two hours later, the three of us sat with Órlaith in the living room of the Manor House. The women had insisted that Matt lay on the sofa because of his injuries. Though Matt had protested it wasn't necessary, the tension in his face relaxed when he lay down.

While Tressa explained what had happened the evening before, I amused myself by watching Matt. The younger man attempted to scrutinize Órlaith furtively. I understood from experience the shock of seeing the regal Sidhe Queen Mother sitting in place of the nice elderly woman he thought he knew.

I turned my attention to Tressa, looking for any residual effect from her ordeal the previous night. True to her word, she looked fully recovered.

If I had known how much she gave of herself when healing others, I would've taken Matt to the hospital no matter how much he fought the idea.

Órlaith listened to Tressa's story without interruption. She seemed to have no reaction, positive or negative, to the news of what Tressa had done.

Tressa worried a lot. It was hard to gauge how concerned I should be about the odd things she told me. She talked about the danger surrounding her, but I saw nothing yet that made that danger seem real.

"It is best not to let the fae know you can see through their glamour," Órlaith counselled Matt as she had with me. "Never underestimate a fae or judge them by their appearance. Some are beautiful, some are tiny, and some are funny looking—however, almost all of them are deadly if they want to be."

There it was again: another warning against a vague danger. I took Órlaith's words as another reminder to keep alert, though I would prefer to have a better idea of what form the threat would take.

"I must tell all of you, I don't know if you are helping Holly by keeping this away from the authorities. You may well be making the situation worse," Órlaith said.

Her words had Tressa calling Holly's cell phone for the fourth time that morning. It went straight to voicemail again.

"I would be pleased if you young people would join me for lunch later. I need to speak with Jenny about a dinner party I'm having later this week, so I'll make sure she prepares enough food for us all."

When her grandmother had left the room, Tressa turned to me, eyes wide with fear.

"Are you sure Holly's okay?"

Matt stared at me as well, equally anxious for my answer. I still felt convinced that she was fine, but I couldn't predict when that might change.

"She's not hurt right now, but Órlaith has a point. Let's go with your plan that if she doesn't call you by noon, we'll call Tom...."

The front doorbell rang. Shamus must have answered it, because a commotion broke out in that direction. Tressa, who always heard things before everyone else, concentrated on the voices. Her expression changed from confusion to surprise.

She jumped from her seat and beckoned me to follow as she left the room. When I caught up to her outside the living room door, I slipped my arm around her waist.

"What's going on?" I asked.

"We have guests," she responded joyfully.

I followed her gaze through the large foyer. Two identical Sidhe woman stood in the doorway. They both had metallic blue hair that hung straight to their waist. Each had a diamond shaped sapphire that hovered around their head on a silver band; they must have anchored their glamour with the jewels. I had a hard time imagining how they must look to everyone else.

When they were a few steps closer, I identified a single distinguishing feature. From a distance, they both appeared to have matching sets of electric blue eyes the exact color of their hair. On closer inspection, one twin had one blue eye and one gray eye.

"Rosheen! Keelin!" Tressa ran to them, throwing an arm around each of them. The three women huddled in a group embrace, all vibrating with excitement.

I leaned against the doorjamb and crossed my arms over my chest as I watched, astonished to see my serious Tressa become so childlike.

Two male Sidhe came up behind the women.

Gilleagán!" Tressa exclaimed, throwing her arms around the neck of a tall blonde man.

Gilleagán's hair was the same color as Órlaith's, but without the silver streaks. His brilliant blue eyes, also matching Órlaith's, had a razor sharp glint. Judging by his resemblance to their grandmother, I guessed that he had to be Tressa's brother.

Behind Gilleagán came another man of similar age and stature. Everyone in the group of Sidhe was tall, wispy, and exceedingly good-looking. They carried themselves with the same ethereal quality as Tressa.

"Hey Jewels, good to see you," Gilleagán said.

Tressa stiffened. She dropped her hug and stepped away from him. Her smile faded from her eyes, then disappeared altogether when she noticed the second man.

"Connor. What a surprise," she said flatly.

"I hope you don't mind that I decided to tag along with this guy." Connor dropped his chin and looked at her through the thick lashes of his half-lidded eyes. He took a step closer to her.

"When he told me he was coming, I couldn't resist the chance to see you, Jewels."

"Don't call me that," she said. "You both know I hate it."

Then, in a delayed reaction, something in what he said rattled her. Her eyes narrowed as she looked over the group.

"None of you seem surprised that I'm here."

"Of course not, Tressie, why do you think we came?" one of the twins asked.

"To visit Mamó, of course. No one is supposed to know I'm here." She looked warily around the group. "Who told you?"

The twins looked at each other. "I thought you told me," they said to each other and laughed. They turned to the men. "One of you must have told us."

Connor shrugged.

"I've known you were here for a couple of weeks now. I may have told the girls. Gil, didn't you tell me she was here?"

"What does it matter? We came to visit you, aren't you glad to see us?" Gilleagán asked, sounding hurt.

Tressa's neck flushed.

"Yes, of course. I'm thrilled to see all of you."

She looked discombobulated by the turn in the conversation so I walked into the foyer and stood behind her.

"Everything okay?" I asked.

She stepped back so that her shoulder touched my chest.

"Xander, these are my cousins Rosheen and Keelin." Tressa indicated with a wave that Keelin was the blue-eyed twin and Rosheen was the one with the gray eye. "And my brother Gil and his friend Connor."

"Xander? What kind of name is that?" Rosheen asked, moving in closer.

"Xander is all you need to know," Tressa told her.

"Oh, this one is yours?" Rosheen asked, grinning. "He is; I see it in your face."

"You're seeing someone?" Keelin asked. "That's great! It's about time."

All four visitors stared at us, seemingly in disbelief. I didn't understand why our relationship was such a surprise. Tressa lifted her head in a good imitation of her grandmother's regal bearing.

"We're Handfast," she said, reaching back and linking her hand with mine.

I didn't know why she said it. Tressa and I hadn't discussed anything like this, but I wasn't about to contradict her.

"You're kidding. With him?" Gilleagán hooted. "Connor, saints alive, a human has edged you out. And a scarred one, at that."

"The Jewel with a human?" Connor said, obviously displeased.

I didn't care if these men wanted to needle me, but their insults affected Tressa. Her posture wilted a little more each time they called her that name. I tried to step forward, but she held onto my forearm, keeping me next to her.

"You got it, she's with me. Is there a problem?" I scowled at them.

Órlaith's arrival in the foyer dispersed the tension in the air. She entered from the direction of the back porch, walking stiffly with her cane.

"Shamus says more of my grandchildren have arrived. Who is it that I'm hearing?"

The twins squealed and ran to her. I lost sight of the older woman for a minute as their hugs enveloped her.

"Gil, is that you?" she asked over the girls' heads.

"Aye, Mamó, it is I. Connor Dwyer is with me."

"I hope it's not an imposition, Your Grace," said Connor as he greeted her with a bow.

"Of course not, dear boy. The more the merrier."

She let her grandson hug her before she held him at arm's length.

"What's different about you? Have you changed something since the last time I saw you?"

"I haven't. Is this going to end with a punch line about me not visiting often enough?" he teased.

"Now that you mention it..." she laughed, and then she patted his cheek. "It is good to see you, dear boy."

"You too, Mamó." He kissed her palm.

"Let's not stand here in the entryway," Órlaith addressed the group at large. "Go on in to the living room. Isn't that injured boy in there?"

"Aye, Mamó. Mattie's still there," Tressa said.

MATT ATTEMPTED to rise from the sofa, but gave up when Tressa admonished him. She introduced him to the new arrivals.

"Seriously, Tressa, the people around you are always getting battered," said Gilleagán. "You're a walking disaster zone."

Gilleagán exchanged an amused look with Connor. I balled my fist, wishing I could take a swing at him.

"Geez, Tressa, can't you do anything for this guy?" Connor asked.

Matt stayed quiet, although his wary eyes told me the younger man was on alert as he assessed the scene. Matt glanced at me to signal that he had noticed the tension in the room before continuing to watch the group dynamic.

The twins cuddled up to Matt on the sofa, one on either side.

"Oh, I like his face!" Rosheen cooed.

"Poor baby, I'll kiss it better." Keelin pecked his cheek.

"Where did you pass the threshold? Did you come through Niagara Falls?" Órlaith asked, ignoring their antics.

"We came through in Switzerland about six months ago. Roe

and I have been skiing all this time, until Gil said he was coming here," Keelin said.

"I came through Niagara Falls," Connor said.

"Did you notice anything out of order at the crossing?"

"Not that I remember. Why?"

"It's probably nothing." Órlaith waved her hand, dismissing the topic.

Tressa's cell phone rang. She looked at the caller ID and rushed to answer it.

"Holly, thank goodness you called. Are you okay?" She paused to listen. "No, wait. Holly, I want you to come stay with me." Her brow furrowed. "Please, Holly? I really don't think it's safe.... But he can't make you... I'm so sorry to hear that. Are you absolutely sure that's what *you* want? We'll come get you..." Tressa blinked rapidly, holding back tears. "Okay, if you're sure. Holly, remember what I told you about the shop—that it's a safe place. Promise to remember that."

When she ended the call, everyone was staring at her.

"That was my assistant at the store. She won't be coming back to work." Tressa spoke directly to Matt and I. "Fred doesn't want her to come back. She said it was her decision, but I don't believe her."

THE CONVERSATION CONTINUED AROUND us as the newcomers prattled on about what they wanted to do while they visited. Matt, Tressa and myself seemed to be in our own world, communicating our concern for Holly through meaningful looks. After a few minutes of this, Órlaith's voice interrupted my musings.

"Why don't you young people continue to make plans over lunch?" Órlaith asked. Just then, Shamus entered the room to announce that lunch was ready.

As the rest of the Sidhe chattered on their way to the dining room, Tressa and I each took a side and helped Matt up off the sofa.

"Listen carefully," Tressa whispered. "Never give a fae of any kind your entire true name."

"Hmmm, I noticed the Xander bit," I said.

"If a fae knows your full name they can hold *Dominion* over you. They can control what you do," she explained. "The weaker-willed a person is, the less of his name you need to gain *Dominion*. You should be fine as long as you don't lock eyes with them for too long or drop your guard."

"But this is your family, Tressa. Shouldn't we be able to trust them?" Matt asked.

"I trust them not to do you any lasting harm, but fun and games may not be the same for them as they are for you."

CHAPTER SIXTEEN

TRESSA

 insisted Matt spend at least one more day with us so that I could monitor his progress. Alexander helped him into a clean t-shirt and sweatpants while I fluffed and arranged the pillows on the large, king size bed in the free bedroom of the guesthouse. It took some extra effort for Matt to ease himself onto the bed, but the pain he had experienced earlier in the day had gone.

He was mending nicely, but sleep was an important part of the healing process. I insisted he rest for a while. Not that he argued overly much; the effort of being social had worn him out. His eyes were closing before I left the room.

"Those cousins of yours are something else," he said sleepily.

"You could say that," I agreed. I smiled as I thought about my adorable cousins. As much as I loved them, I knew the devastation they could bring to tenderhearted young men.

"They're good fun, Mattie, but don't get too involved with them."

"No, of course not. I wouldn't do that to Holly."

I didn't know if he realized he had spoken aloud; he was asleep with his next breath. His words made me sad. I knew they reflected his true feelings, and Holly wasn't his to think of in that way. I loved Holly, but I didn't think Matt should pine away for her.

I found Alexander in the dining room. I was starting to tell him my thoughts when the door burst open and Sophia ran in, letting the door bang shut behind her.

"Daddy, Tressa, guess what!" She ran to where her father sat at the dining room table he used as his desk and bounded into his lap.

"I give up," he said. "What?"

"There are three more Pixies down at the lake, and two of them are *boys*!" She spoke the last word as if nothing could be more astonishing.

"Oh sure, and that would be the twins' Pixies."

I picked an apple out of a bowl on the table and took a bite before I realized that they were both staring at me. "Surely I've told you before that most Sidhe have a Pixie bound to them? And vice versa."

By their vacant expressions, it was obvious that I hadn't.

"Brenna is your Pixie," Alexander remarked—more of a statement than a question.

"I want a Pixie!" Sophia exclaimed.

"I'm sorry, honey, it doesn't work that way. It's not like a Pixie is a doll or a toy," I did my best to explain in terms she would understand. "Brenna is mine and I am hers. Family, experience, and time bind us together. It's kind of like having a best friend who moves around with you wherever you go, and who always looks out for you and you always look out for them."

Sophia nodded her head solemnly. "Sort of like Uncle Matt."

Taken off guard, Alexander let a coughing laugh escape before he managed to suppress his amusement.

"Aye, very much like that," I agreed.

"So who do Kerry and Megan belong too?"

"They belong to Miss Órlaith."

"She gets two?" the child's eyes grew wide.

"Sure, and sometimes it happens that way when you live a very long time like Miss Órlaith has."

"But what about Shamus? Doesn't he have a Pixie?"

"Shamus is a Brounie, not a Sidhe. Haven't you noticed that he looks different than Miss Órlaith and me?"

"Yeah, but that's not fair." Her expression grew indignant for Shamus, of whom she was obviously quite fond. Then her eyes went wild with excitement. She jumped down from her father's lap. "I know! I can be his Pixie."

"Well, you *are* small and you *do* follow him around," I mused.

"Let's go tell him! Daddy, can I go tell him?" She evidently sensed that he was about to say no, because she put both of her little hands over her heart and pleaded. "Please, Daddy? Pleeeease?"

Alexander shook his head. "There will be plenty of time for that tomorrow. How about you help me get dinner started?"

AFTER DINNER, Alexander helped me with the dishes. I washed while he dried. It was the first time we had been alone together all day.

I could hear Sophia upstairs, pretending to read a book to Matt. I had read the same book to her so often she had it memorized.

I rinsed a plate and handed it to Alexander. He leaned against the countertop as he dried it.

"It sounds like it's been a while since you've seen your brother," he commented.

"I haven't seen him since before my parents' death."

"Didn't he come to the funeral?"

"He was with them when they had their accident. He sent word about what happened and said that he couldn't bear to come home for their Sendoff."

Alexander put the plate in the cupboard and took the next one I held out to him. His expression showed disapproval. I had been angry myself at the time, but I still felt compelled to defend him.

"He was just too grief-stricken, you see."

"So he left you to handle things alone?"

"Oh, I wasn't alone. Not really. My grandparents and all my aunts and uncles were there."

Alexander thought quietly while we finished the last two dinner plates.

"What's the deal with that nickname he and Connor were calling you?"

I sighed heavily; I had known it would come up.

"Jewels," I said flatly. "It's just a childhood thing."

"Why does he still call you that when you so obviously dislike it? You can barely stand to repeat it to me."

He examined me with those dark chocolate eyes, as if he knew that the story ran deeper. I didn't know what to say, so I said nothing. I put a handful of freshly rinsed flatware into the drying rack.

"I just think he should treat you better, that's all," he said.

He dried the utensils, putting each one in the drawer as he finished it while I began scrubbing the pan.

"I don't care about that. I'm just sorry they were so rude to you. To be honest, Gil will always do the thing that annoys me most, but it's not like Connor to be so rude," I said.

His laugh startled me.

"What's so funny?" I asked as I placed a pot on the drying rack. I drained the water in the sink and reached for a towel to dry my hands.

"That's a no-brainer. Jealousy will make anyone into a jerk." He dried the pot and put it away. "That reminds me: we're Handfast, are we?"

I had forgotten about that too. I blushed. "I had to make them take our relationship seriously. Otherwise, you would be potential fodder for all their shenanigans. It's like saying we're betrothed."

"I know what it means."

"Do you mind terribly?" I looked away, anxious to avoid his gaze.

He gently peeled the towel out of my hands and tossed it onto the counter. He drew me to him.

"Tressa, don't you know by now that I have no intention of ever leaving your side? You can call me whatever you like, as long as I get to stay here with you." He kissed me: a long thorough kiss.

I woke up in the middle of the night, guilt making sleep impossible. I couldn't rationalize keeping secrets any longer. Alexander deserved to know the entire truth about me. I promised myself that I would tell him everything first thing in the morning.

"What's wrong? Why aren't you sleeping?" A pillow muffled Alexander's throaty voice. He always knew when I awoke.

"Xander, there are some things I need to tell you."

I sat up and hugged my legs to my chest. He yawned and rubbed his eyes, rearranging his pillow so he could lean back against the headboard. Once settled, he looked at me expectantly.

"First, I'll need to give you some Sidhe history."

"You woke me to give me a lesson on the fae?" he asked, incredulous.

"No," I said ardently. "This is about me. About us."

Here it was: the point where I had to confess to this man that I was a complete disappointment to my people, and to make matters worse, the Unseelie hunted me anyway. I fought to contain my emotions, but I failed. I choked down a gasp of pain as they burst through my chest.

"No, sweetheart. Please don't cry." He wiped tears aside that I hadn't realized were there. He sat further up and pulled me to his chest, wrapping his arms around me in a tight embrace. "It can't be that bad. Just tell me and get it over with."

"Okay." I took a deep, fortifying breath. "Before our angel ancestors parted from us, they gave their children four gifts: the Lia Fail, the Cauldron of Rebirth, the Spear of Lugh, and the Sword of Nuada. Over time, we came to take the gifts for granted and they eventually were lost.

"The Archangel Michael became incensed when he discovered our ingratitude. He vowed that none of the fae would be admitted into heaven until all four of the gifts were found, and each was safely restored to their rightful steward and used with proper esteem.

"Before our expulsion from heaven, one or another of the gifts would surface now and again. However, never had two been located at the same time. Since then, the Sidhe have searched for centuries without finding any of the gifts. There is a prophecy about how these gifts will be found."

"And this involves us, somehow?" Alexander interrupted.

"Aye, I'll explain, but let me finish the story."

He nodded.

"The Dominion Zadkiel, the patron angel of forgiveness, took pity on the Sidhe and sent a prophecy to give us hope. It spoke of how our exile would eventually end. The prophecy goes like this:

Look to The King's Jewel,
The fifth treasure of her people,
A youngest child of the youngest child-
Mother of the rebirth of the Sidhe,
Nuada's strength and fidelity will be her ally.

A new beginning shall come
When the four treasures come home.
Oh lost child, oh blessed child,
Open the gates of Annwn
And bring your people back into the light."

I STOPPED THERE, wishing I didn't need to continue. He stroked my hair; pulling the curls flat and then letting them spring back as he always did.

"So this King's Jewel is supposed to be the savior for the Sidhe?" he asked.

"We are told by our Wise Men that the King's Jewel will be the mother of the one destined to bring together and hold the four gifts, or treasures as we call them."

"This is all very interesting, but what does it have to do with us?"

"Xander, I am a King's Jewel."

His hand froze while holding a lock of my hair outstretched. After a couple of heartbeats, he released the strand.

"What does that mean?" he asked.

"The King's Jewel is the nickname given to the youngest

child of the king's youngest child. My father was my grandparents' youngest, and I am the youngest of my parent's children. I am also the first female King's Jewel in three generations.

"My people have watched me all my life. First with anticipation; they were sure that I would fulfill the prophecy. My grandfather and my uncle tried to pair me off with every eligible man they thought would be an appropriate match."

"And Connor was one of them?"

"Aye, one of the first, since his family is close to mine."

"I can see how he would be a good match for you. He's one of you. Good looking. Not damaged in any way."

I snorted.

"That good looking man was only interested in the position he'd gain by marrying me. A Sidhe woman can only bear children with her *Anam Cara*—you would say her soul mate. If not for this, I might have been forced to marry him.

"What's this about being damaged, by the way?" I asked indignantly.

"Well, he certainly appears to be unscarred."

"Beautiful doesn't mean perfect," I admonished him.

"So what happened? How is it now between you and your people?" he said, getting me back on track.

"I admit that I took my privileged life for granted. But, as I got older and still hadn't mated, people's attitudes began to change. You see, the Sidhe are not a very fertile race. I am old by fae standards for having a child, akin to a forty-year-old human woman. I began to see disappointment whenever they looked at me. I had let them down, and they began to show it more and more.

"I'm pleased to live my life outside the public eye now. Unfortunately, even though most of my own people no longer believe that I am the King's Jewel of the prophecy, the Unseelie are still looking for me. I still can't live my life in peace. And now, judging from what they said earlier, I can be easily found."

He pulled me tighter against him.

"But why would they still be looking for you?"

"While the Seelie Court lives their lives with the hope of one day entering Heaven in a state of grace, the Unseelie Court seeks to possess the gifts. They would exploit their power to conquer and rule.

"The last two female King's Jewels were kidnapped by the Unseelie Court and burned alive. Deaglan Mór, their current leader, swore on the day of my birth that he would do the same to me."

Understanding filled Alexander's expression.

"So this is where your pyrophobia comes from," he said.

"When we were children, Gil grew tired of me getting all the attention. He teased me with stories of how my predecessors died and how the same would happen to me."

A snarl reverberated in Alexander's chest.

"How can I get information on the Unseelie? I need to learn what weapons they use, their tactics, anything I can use against them."

I moved away from his side so I could get a better view of his face.

"You want to learn how to fight them?" I asked.

"What did you expect me to do, run away?"

I DIDN'T OPEN the store the next day; I had promised to spend the day with my cousins. However, I soon realized I needn't have rearranged my schedule. None of the guests at the Manor House got up from their beds until almost dinnertime. How had I forgotten what creatures of nightlife they were?

Instead, I spent the entire day fretting over my two big problems: how to help Holly and how to protect my anonymity at Pine Ridge. When I made my way to the Manor House for dinner, I hadn't resolved either one.

I could hear Rosheen and Keelin shouting at each other from halfway up the path. They were arguing over who owned a particular dress they both wanted to wear. Keelin won, if only by virtue of getting the garment on her body first.

When Shamus opened the door, Keelin descended the staircase in triumph, wearing a short, pale blue silk Cheongsam with yellow embroidery. Rosheen, still arguing, followed behind her.

"Shamus," I said, with an eye on my cousins. "I think Sophia should eat with you and JJ tonight."

Sophia skipped off toward the kitchen, delighted to escape the formal meal.

We took our seats at the table and exchanged greetings with everyone.

"Where's Gil?" I asked.

"He went out earlier," Keelin said. "He said to text him so he can meet us wherever we end up tonight."

Keelin's bubbly demeanor was in stark contrast to the identical yet sulking figure next to her.

"Keelin, how lovely you look in that dress," Connor said, fanning the girls' argument. "Don't you agree, Xander?"

Rosheen and I both glared at Connor. He knew that Alexander wouldn't have heard the twins arguing from outside. I didn't appreciate his attempt to walk Alexander into a trap.

"All the women look wonderful," Alexander said.

"Rosheen, I love your outfit. Is it your design?" I asked, trying to defuse Connor's teasing.

She brightened.

"No, but I have a new one upstairs I could wear."

"I would love to see it," I said.

Her temper now dispersed, Rosheen turned her attention to

Matt. He was back to his old self—none of the bruising, swelling or the sling from the day before. He had even replaced his broken glasses. She beamed at him.

"Well you turned out to be a cutie. Why don't you come out with us tonight?"

"Oh aye," Keelin joined in, argument forgotten. "It'll be fun."

Between the two of them, the twins cajoled Matt into joining us on our outing. They tried to do the same with Alexander but with less success. Alexander bowed out of the evening, citing Sophia and unfinished work as his reasons for staying home.

He kissed me before he gathered Sophia from the kitchen and headed home. Then Mamó retired to her room, saying goodnight just after Alexander left.

Rosheen ran upstairs to change, keeping the rest of us waiting for an hour before she came back down.

We rolled past *JR's* without going in; the twins pronounced it too small-town for their liking. I hadn't expected *JR's* to suit their needs, and I was happy to keep their frivolity away from my neighbors, even though leaving town would make it harder to get home at a reasonable hour. We drove on to Scranton in pursuit of a better place to party.

We arrived at a club the twins said Gilleagán had suggested. He stood at the entrance, waiting for us. He held my gaze as he lit a cigarette. I jerked when he flicked open his lighter, which was exactly what he had wanted. He smirked, pleased with himself.

Inside, the club was dark and gritty. Multicolored lasers shot through the darkness to the beat of music, which blared from all directions. Gilleagán led us around the crowded dance floor to a circular booth near the bar.

A server arrived as the six of us settled into the brown leather cushions.

"Shots all around," Gilleagán shouted into the server's ear, twirling his index finger to indicate the whole group.

I refused a second shot, and Matt switched to a cola for the third round.

"I'd better designate myself as the driver," he said.

After the others downed their third shot, we got up to dance. The music had a wonderful beat, although it drowned out the melody. I always enjoy the sensation of moving my body in rhythm with the music. The Sidhe are generally ardent dancers, and this time I wasn't the exception to the rule.

The crowd eventually jostled us apart, and I soon lost track of everyone. Looking around, I saw Matt dancing with the twins and enjoying their attention. Off in a corner, Gilleagán was huddled with a blonde woman—probably propositioning her.

The separation from my friends took some joy out of the dancing. The front of my head ached from the flashing lasers and the too-loud music. It seemed like a good time to go back to the booth.

I tried to step in that direction, but a wall of dancers made the way impassable. I turned, thinking to take a more circuitous route. Suddenly I had the odd sensation that people were closing in on me. The crowd condensed, blocking every direction.

My headache increased as my blood pressure rose. The pain interfered with my vision. I became more aggressive, not concerned with being polite anymore as I tried to push my way clear. I was trapped, and couldn't get free. I scanned the faces around me looking without success for someone I knew.

The lasers pulsated: red, orange and yellow lights illuminating the room with a blazing glow. The music screamed. My breathing became short and rapid; I thought I would hyperventilate. I pushed again, harder, but I still couldn't get out.

A hand reached in through the crowd and grabbed my wrist, pulling me forward. The crowd melted away.

I forced myself to take slow, deep breaths as relief surged through me. When my breathing returned to normal and my headache had subsided a bit, I was embarrassed to see that Connor held me in a close embrace. I stumbled as I stepped away from him.

"Are you okay?" The amusement in his expression seemed to mock my discomfort. It felt like a slap in the face, although I couldn't say he knew how distressed I had felt. The episode had been so strange... I had to wonder—had he hexed me?

"Dance with me, Jewels," he said.

The old nickname aggravated me even further. Over his shoulder I saw Matt heading toward us, so I bit back my retort.

"Matt, would you mind taking me home? I have a headache," I said.

"Sure thing." Matt looked over the crowd. "Should we say goodbye first?"

I followed his gaze. Keelin was spinning, the crowd spurring her on by counting her pirouettes.

"I find it's best to just slip out," I advised.

"How will they get home?"

I hesitated, wondering if I should explain flitting to him when an easy solution popped into my head.

"Gil will take them."

We passed Gilleagán on the way out of the club. He waved us over.

"You're leaving already?" he asked.

"Aye, it's late," I said. I had forgotten how much I hated evenings like this.

He snickered. "You haven't changed much, have you, Jewels?"

"Nor have you, big brother," I responded.

As I followed Matt to the car, I felt guilty for imposing on him when he had been having a good time.

"Mattie, I'm sorry to drag you away."

"Don't worry about it. It's late. My mother always said nothing good happens after midnight."

I barked out a surprised laugh.

"Your mother, clearly, is not a Sidhe."

CHAPTER SEVENTEEN

I began closing the store earlier than usual. Without Holly to wait on customers, I had little time for my jewelry making. The shop wasn't as enjoyable if I couldn't practice my craft.

I would leave early enough to freshen up before walking to the Manor House for dinner. Alexander went with me or not, depending on how late he returned from his excursions.

Sophia spent her days at the Manor House. The Sidhe in general couldn't resist children. Sophia, an exceptionally charming child, had us all enchanted. The twins played with her nearly every day when they first awoke. I had even seen Connor giving her lessons on playing the flute.

Sophia enjoyed her time with them; however, they tired her out quicker than the Pixies. After about a week with too much activity and attention, Sophia was overwrought.

Alexander and I decided a quiet evening at home was due. Alexander cooked while I helped Sophia bathe and get into her pajamas. He kept the meal simple: a hamburger and a salad. Sophia ate the burger with gusto and dawdled over the salad.

Later, she sat in my lap as I sang to her. I went through three of her favorite songs before she let sleep take her.

Alexander carried her to bed, quietly closing the door as he came out of the room. He returned to the living room grinning.

"Alone at last. It feels like we haven't had a minute alone since the first night the *will o' the wisps* arrived," he said. Alexander had taken up my grandmother's expression for her guests.

I patted the spot next to me on the sofa. When he sat, I snuggled into him.

"Tell me about your search," I invited.

"I keep finding pieces of River Rock, like bread crumbs, but I'm not convinced they're leading me anywhere. I've started going further north; the last spot we covered was near the New York State border. I think I'm too far out now, so I'm going to circle back."

"The journals aren't helping?"

"Brion described landmarks. He even sketched out small maps. If I could just find the right place and recognize one landmark, it should all be a breeze from there."

My cell phone rang.

"Who is it?" Alexander asked as I picked it up to look. Usually it was his phone interrupting us; mine rarely ever rang.

"It's the store phone." I showed him the caller ID on the face of my phone. I answered to the sound of weeping. It could only have been one person.

"Pix, are you okay?"

She took a while to find her voice.

"I came to the store, like you said I should."

"Stay right there. I'm coming." I met Alexander's eyes and he nodded.

"Do you want me to come?" he asked when I disconnected the call.

I shook my head and stood. "It will be faster if I flit."

"Will it be safe? What if he followed her?"

I waved off the threat.

"I'll flit to the back of the store and enter through the back door. No one will see me. He can't come into the store. Worst case, if I have to hold *Dominion* over him again, I will."

He got up to kiss me. "You'll be careful? Don't drain yourself too much."

"I won't. I promise."

He seemed satisfied with this. He walked me to the door.

"Call me if you need me. I'll get Shamus to stay with Sophia."

Once outside, I walked half a dozen steps as I willed the wind to gather me up. I flitted to the alley behind the store, arriving a second after the wind lifted me.

The alley was dark except for a security light that shone from the third floor of the building. After the breeze swept through, the air became unusually still.

I slipped my key into the deadbolt and unlocked the door that led into the storage room. I opened it slowly so I wouldn't frighten Holly if she were nearby.

The room was darker than the alley. I stepped inside.

"Pix?" I called as I moved further into the store. A strip of light shone from under the door of the break room. I opened the door, calling her name again.

Holly sat huddled in the corner on the floor. She covered her face with her hands. Her bent knees supported her elbows, limbs cradling her slightly rounded belly.

I rushed to kneel in front of her, heart pounding in my chest.

"Pix, are you okay?"

She didn't respond. She didn't move. I held my breath as I reached out to touch her shoulder. At last, with her hands still hiding her face, she spoke.

"I really thought he had changed this time." Her voice came out raspy and tear-soaked.

"I know you did, Pix. Look at me, honey."

She lifted her head. Her face was painful to see. Her left eye was black and swollen. The skin on her cheek from her nose to her ear was raw and red. A gash across that same cheekbone trickled blood. Finger shaped bruises covered her neck.

"He said the baby wasn't his." Tears spilled out of her good eye. "I think he would have killed me this time."

I privately agreed, but I knew better than to say so out loud.

"How did you get away from him?"

"I stabbed him with a steak knife. I don't think I hurt him too badly." Her breath caught in her throat. She swallowed painfully before continuing. "I never tried to fight back before. It startled him enough for me to get out of the house."

I didn't know what to do for the girl. She clearly needed medical attention, but was this something I could or should attempt on my own? I'd never laid hands on a pregnant fae, let alone a pregnant human.

And of course, there were the problems that would come with opening her eyes. Did I want to bring a pregnant woman into that mess?

A banging on the front door interrupted my thoughts. I tensed, thinking it might be Fred.

"That should be Matt," Holly told me. "I called him too."

I went to let him in.

A measure of relief showed in his eyes when he saw me. "Thank god you're here," he said.

"I don't know how helpful I can be," I whispered. He nodded, but I didn't think he was listening. He rushed toward the lit room and knelt, as I had, in front of Holly's balled up figure.

She reached for him and he gathered her tenderly into his arms. He rocked her, whispering calming noises as she cried. I was loath to interrupt them, but I felt an urgency to get her medical treatment.

"Pix, you need to get to the hospital."

"No, I can't. I can't go there."

"You need a doctor," Matt agreed, "and the emergency room is the only place you'll get one this time of night."

Holly buried herself deeper into his chest. "I can't go there. Fred will be there. Or if he isn't, one of his buddies will be."

Matt could hardly argue the point. He had made the same decision just a week ago. He looked up at me, clearly expecting me to have an answer.

"Let Mattie take you to the hospital in Carbondale. It's outside Fred's influence and it's not that far."

She nodded but didn't move, so Matt lifted her. I went out first to be sure that no one was outside before he carried Holly out to his car. I opened the passenger door so he could place her on the seat.

"Thanks for your help—again," Matt said. He kissed my cheek before running around to the other side of the car.

"Call me with an update."

"I will," he said before driving off at an alarming speed.

As I watched them go, I questioned my decision to send her away without doing anything to help. I resolved to learn the proper treatments for pregnant women so I wouldn't feel this helpless again.

When Matt's car was out of sight, I pulled my phone out of my pocket. This time I didn't care if Holly approved. I did a quick search, finding the number for the local police department and dialed. A woman picked up.

"May I please speak with Officer Tom Lynch?" I asked.

• • •

ALEXANDER HAD a cup of tea waiting for me when I came home. I sat with him on the sofa, sipping the tea and recounting what had happened at the store. As I described Matt racing off to the hospital, there was a knock at the front door.

"It's a little late for a house call, isn't it, Officer Lynch?" Alexander asked when he answered the door.

"Xander, I called him," I said. I hadn't yet gotten to that part of the story.

Alexander led Tom into the living room. I set the teacup on the side table, suddenly exhausted.

"Fred is in the emergency room." Tom sounded tired. "He's saying Holly stabbed him."

"Tommy," I said. "Won't you have a seat?"

Both men remained standing. Tom's face looked drawn, and he had bags under his eyes, but he still stood in what I thought of as his cop stance.

"I'm looking for Holly. She's not at their house or her parents'. I thought she might be with you."

"She's not here," I said, shaking my head. "She's at the hospital in Carbondale. The doctors want to watch her overnight. The stress of the beating may have harmed the baby."

Tom's face went ashen.

"I didn't know it was that bad. I need to speak to her as soon as possible."

My weariness had shortened my temper, and I lashed out at him.

"Fred tried to strangle her, to kill her and her baby. I don't understand, Tommy. After all he's put her through, what do you intend to do? Arrest her?"

He closed his eyes for a minute, his posture drooping.

"It was self-defense, I get that, but Fred is over in the emergency room screaming bloody murder. She needs to give her side of the story or she'll be charged with assault—possibly even attempted murder."

I nodded, seeing the sense in what he said.

"Tressa, I've made mistakes. I see now that I have to take off my blinders. Fred isn't the guy I grew up with anymore. He hasn't been for a long time; I just refused to recognize it. I promise I will do everything I can to make sure Holly's safe from him."

He wasn't the only one who had waited too long to help Holly. I had the taste of guilt in my mouth as well.

WE GOT a call from Matt just before we went to bed; Tom had come and taken Holly's statement. Matt would stay with her overnight.

I WOKE up early the next morning and went to my grandfather's library, determined to learn more about healing pregnant women.

I paged through three books, finding many references to conditions that accompany pregnancy but nothing related to treating a battered pregnant woman. There were also passages regarding chronic conditions in pregnancy, but none of it was relevant to Holly's situation.

The fourth book, an ancient text written in Old Gaelic, showed promise. I rarely read in the old language but I stumbled along following, with my index finger as I read.

Footsteps in the hallway distracted me. Gilleagán stumbled by the library door, still in his pajamas and a robe. When he saw me, he switched tracks and came into the room.

"What are you doing up so early?" I asked.

"What time is it?"

I shrugged. "It's well before noon."

He looked over my shoulder at the open book.

"What are you doing, a little light reading?" he said sarcastically.

"I'm doing research on healing a pregnant woman."

He yawned.

"Did something happen to your store clerk?"

"Aye," I said, surprised he remembered I had a clerk, let alone that she was pregnant.

He had lost interest before I even answered his question.

"Later, Jewels."

"Gil, why did you come to Pine Ridge?" I asked, my usual annoyance falling away, replaced by curiosity.

His eyes narrowed.

"What do you mean?"

"You said you came to visit me, but why? I haven't seen you in years. You didn't come to our parents' Sendoff; you've never even sent me a kind word."

He pulled a pack of cigarettes from his pocket. I could have sworn he leaned toward me when he flicked the lighter open to bring up a flame.

"Did you just come here to annoy me? To call me by an old nickname you know I hate and spark flames around me?"

He inhaled and blew out a stream of smoke.

"You've always been too sensitive and too serious. Lighten up, Tressa. Not everything is about you."

I sighed. He would never understand.

"Mamó's complaining she has seen little of you since you've arrived. Why not make her happy and join us for dinner once in a while?" I asked.

"You see, that's just the thing, Tressie," he said in a teasing voice. "I came because I wanted to spend time with both of you, but I'd forgotten the weird schedule you keep. What is it you like about the daytime so much?"

I laughed as he turned again to go.

"Baby's breath is what you need," he said. He waved and left, walking toward the kitchen.

I went back to the thick tome in front of me, surprised to see he was right. The ointment in the book called for baby's breath.

ABOUT AN HOUR LATER, Alexander found me in the greenhouse.

"You're home early," I said.

"Tressa, we need to get you to Holly." He grabbed my hand and I thought for a second that he would drag me away.

"Xander, wait— tell me what's going on. Did Matt call?"

"No, I just know that she needs you."

I quickly gathered up the sprigs of baby's breath I had been clipping and followed him out. I made him wait while I ran to my pantry and grabbed a small bottle of lavender essential oil.

As we drove out of the gates to the estate, my phone rang.

"Tressa, you've got to get over here as fast as you can." Matt's voice cracked with emotion.

"We're already on our way. Tell me what's happening."

"She's bleeding, and she's really out of it. They think she may lose the baby. We might lose her, too. She begged me not to let her baby die. Begged me."

Tears sprang to my eyes as I heard the agony in his voice.

"How am I supposed to do that? There's no one I can call but you. I'm sorry, Tressa; I know you wanted no part in this."

"Nonsense. I was afraid because I didn't know what to do. I'm better prepared now. We'll be there soon."

Twenty minutes later, thanks to Alexander's willingness to break every speed limit, we stepped out of the elevator and onto the hospital's maternity ward.

A locked door blocked the entrance to the unit. Alexander pushed the button on the wall to summon someone to open the door. Through the window I could see a burly woman wearing light blue scrubs sitting at the nurses' station. She glanced up at us but continued typing.

Alexander pressed and held the button down until the woman looked up again. Annoyance clouded her face. She looked again at the computer screen before sliding her chair over to her intercom.

"Yes?" she asked

"We're here to see Holly Moyer," I said, holding a visitor's badge up to the window. She looked unimpressed, but she buzzed the door open.

We hurried inside and down the hall, following the arrow pointing toward her room number. A uniformed police officer sat on a chair in the hallway outside the room.

"Sorry, no visitors allowed for Mrs. Moyer without proper authorization." He reached down and retrieved a clipboard from the floor under his seat. "I need to see some ID to see if you're on this list."

I could feel Alexander's anger and frustration growing, fueled by his urgency to stop a tragedy. The officer eyed Alexander's jumpy body language suspiciously. I brushed Alexander's arm to calm him.

I smiled sweetly at the policeman. "Officer, may I ask, what your name is?" I said innocently.

"Rob Turner, ma'am." He focused on me, forgetting Alexander.

"Robert, is it then?"

"No ma'am, it's Robin."

I leaned over until we were about eye to eye, the officer's expression a mixture of surprise and exhilaration.

I locked his gaze to mine.

"Robin Turner, you will let us into this room and allow us to stay as long as we like."

He remained frozen until I broke my gaze from his.

"Well, you guys go right on in and stay as long as you like," he said without so much as glancing at us again.

Alexander rapped once before opening the door. Holly lay on a hospital bed in the middle of the room, her skin nearly as white as the sheet that covered her. The starkness of the room and the equipment surrounding her bed seem to dwarf her.

Matt sat in a chair at her bedside, holding her hand. He leaned forward, his forehead resting on the bed. He looked up as we entered and put a finger to his mouth to shush us.

"She's sleeping," he whispered.

He moved away and stood with Alexander as I took his place beside her. Holly's breathing was shallow. The bruising on her face contrasted dramatically against her sallow skin. She looked decidedly worse than the last time I'd seen her.

Her eyes fluttered. She smiled awkwardly. "Tressa, you're here." Her words were barely audible.

"Aye, Pix, I'm here."

"I was thinking how silly I was, worrying about that strange flu when the real danger was right in my own home."

"Sure, and you're a mom now," I told her. "Moms worry about everything—it's what they do. It's not silly at all."

One big tear rolled down her face.

"I don't know if I'll get to be a mom, Tressa. They say I'm losing the baby."

"Well, Pix, we're not going to let that happen. You see, I have a bit of skill with healing. If you say it's okay, I'm going to try to help."

She nodded before dozing off again. I searched the room and found a small plastic basin. I washed it and my hands in the little bathroom inside the room and set the basin on her overbed table.

I set about mixing an ointment, pouring several tablespoons

of the lavender oil into the bottom of the basin. Taking the sprigs of baby's breath, I crumbled them into the oil. As per the book's instructions, I mixed them together and infused my essence into the ointment before placing it on the patient.

I sang the accompanying intonation softly as I worked the oil and bits of my spirit into the baby's breath. When the ointment was complete, I didn't rub the salve directly on her abdomen, not wanting to disturb the fetus any more than it already was. Instead, I slathered it into the pulse points on her wrists, temples, neck, and behind her knees to allow it to travel through her blood stream.

When I had finished applying all the ointment, I prayed. I prayed to the Virgin Mary, the patron saint of mothers, to intercede on our behalf. I prayed to God Himself that I had done enough to heal the damage and save the child.

Alexander and I kept vigil with Matt as she continued to worsen. She seemed to slip into a coma, which puzzled the doctors. At first I thought it was just a deep sleep brought on by rapid healing. However, as she remained motionless—except for the gentle rise and fall of her chest—for hours on end, I became convinced that my attempt at rapid healing had overtaxed her system. We were losing them both.

I took my turn staring out the room's small window four hours into our vigil. The window overlooked a main thoroughfare of the small town. The bells in the church steeple a block away struck the hour—one, two, three, four, five. I counted to myself as they rang out. As the last bell fell silent a light, soft voice whispered behind me.

"Matt?"

The three of us rushed to Holly's side. She was awake.

She reached up and touched her eye. The swelling had receded, but the greenish-yellow of a nearly healed bruise remained.

"Welcome back," I said, relief washing over me. "I think the worst is over now," I told the men.

"Tressa, is that you? Your hair, your eyes...." Still weak, Holly's voice died off before she finished her thought.

In all the worry about saving her, I had forgotten about this part. It was sad, knowing I must look like a stranger to her now.

The emotional and physical strain building up inside me collided. Suddenly exhausted, I sank into the chair beside her bed.

"Aye, tis me," I said.

CHAPTER EIGHTEEN

e brought Holly to my house when the hospital released her two days later. The doctors had placed her on complete bedrest for at least the next two weeks.

She had rejected the hospital staff's suggestion to go to her parents' home even before I'd invited her to stay with me.

"I'd rather take care of myself," she told them.

Alexander had offered to stop off on the way home from the hospital so she could pick up her clothes, but she refused to return to her home with Fred. I made a note to myself to send the twins out shopping for maternity clothes. They would enjoy that.

Alexander put her things, such as they were, in one of the guest bedrooms upstairs while I got Holly settled on the sofa in the living room. She wore one of Alexander's T-shirts that hung down to her mid-thigh and a pair of my yoga pants with the legs rolled up several inches. She looked younger without her designer clothes, styled hair and make-up. She picked up the TV remote and turned on the local news.

"Do you think they know about Fred's arrest?" she asked in a small voice. Her expression said louder than words how much she didn't want that to be true.

"It will be fine one way or the other," I assured her.

The show was in the middle of a special broadcast about the flu outbreak, which had previously been contained to the area around Niagara Falls but now seemed to be spreading south. The story disclosed nothing new. Officials still didn't know the source of the flu, nor did they have an effective treatment.

They reported on a missing hiker presumed to be lost in the woods. A recent photo of the hiker displayed in the upper right corner of the screen while the anchor read the story. The weatherman came on next.

A knock at the door interrupted the broadcast. I clicked off the television when Alexander ushered Tom Lynch into the room. He was in uniform, his thumbs hooked on his gun belt. This time when I offered, he took a seat, pulling the chair closer to Holly.

"How are you feeling?" he asked, smiling sadly.

"I'm okay, Tommy." She rubbed her belly. "The baby's going to be fine."

He exhaled deeply.

"I'm so glad, Holly. Truly." He looked around the room, his eyes brushing over Alexander and me before returning his attention to Holly. "I have bad news," he said.

Holly nodded and looked down. She played with the fringe along the edge of a pillow beneath her.

"Fred was due in court this morning. He didn't show."

"He skipped bail?" Alexander asked at the same time I said, "He's out on the loose?"

Tom nodded in response to our questions, but continued to focus on Holly. "He passed the Canadian border late last night. We flagged his passport, so if he tries to return we'll have him. I wanted to make sure you heard it from me."

Holly continued to fiddle with the fringe.

"Holly, I never thought he would take things so far. I thought he meant it when he said your leaving him had straightened him out."

Finally, she looked up at him.

"I know, Tommy. I did too."

"Another thing," Tom said. He cleared his throat and swallowed twice before continuing. Grief spread across his face. "They're going to charge him with Eileen's murder. He killed her, Holly. He cut her brakes."

Holly's eyes glistened. She fought to keep the tears from spilling out. Unable to speak, she gave him several quick nods.

"We're going to get him, Holly. The Canadians are looking for him too. If it's the last thing I do, I will get him."

There was no doubting his earnestness. Rage radiated from him in waves. Holly took his hand and squeezed it.

Tom stood to take his leave, leaning over and kissing Holly on the cheek. He turned to say goodbye when we heard the back door slam.

Keelin's melodic voice called out, abruptly evaporating the tension in the air.

"Mamó sent me down with food for your convalescing friend. Seriously, Tressa, why do all your friends end up battered?"

She came into the room holding a tray of food with a covered dish, a carafe of milk, another of water, and utensils. She carried the heavy tray with a dancer's grace: straight back and out-turned feet. She stood framed by the doorway.

Holly and Tom both gaped at her. Keelin was only the second fae Holly had encountered since my laying of hands had opened her eyes. Her coloring was much farther removed from human than my own, with her metallic blue hair and her electric blue, glittering eyes.

Tom stared at a shockingly beautiful girl, albeit with flat blue eyes and blue-black hair.

I jumped up and cleared off the table next to the sofa so she could set the tray down.

Unburdened of her load, Keelin gravitated toward the new man in the room. She danced over to Tom, holding out her hand, which he took. I doubted that Keelin had ever offered her hand to a man who didn't take it.

"Keelin, this is Tommy. He's a friend of Pix's," I said, careful not to give her too much information. I wasn't one to offer any of my brethren more of a name than they needed. "This is my cousin, Keelin. Tommy was just leaving."

Alexander, now accustomed to the effect the twins had on other men, clapped his hand down on Tom's shoulder to shake him out of his daze. He looked at Alexander as if he had forgotten what he was doing.

"Thanks for coming by," Alexander said. "Be sure to let us know if you learn anything more."

"Oh. Yeah. Right."

Alexander walked him to the door.

Keelin settled into a chair opposite Holly. The two women assessed one another. Holly played with her hair, attempting to better arrange it, which made me believe she felt lacking compared to the Sidhe.

"Keelin, this is my good friend Pix, whom I told you about. Did I mention she's expecting?" I said, knowing no Sidhe can resist fawning over an expectant mother.

Keelin now observed Holly with enthusiasm. She slid forward on her seat. "Well, you're just much too thin," she said.

Keelin uncovered the dish, releasing a waft of fresh-baked bread. Inside was a thick turkey sandwich with deep red toma-toes and dark leafy lettuce, sliced into four sections. She picked up the carafe of milk and poured a serving into a glass on the tray.

"I'm not hungry," Holly protested.

"Nonsense. Even if you're not hungry, the baby is," Keelin said, handing Holly the glass of milk.

"Pix just came home from the hospital today. The doctors have put her on bedrest. Since she has no maternity clothes and she's stuck here, I thought you and Rosheen could go shopping for her," I said.

A broad smile lit up Keelin's face. The suggestion even brought a bit of life back into Holly's expression.

"That would be great fun." Keelin leaned conspiratorially toward Holly, dropping her voice. "Better leave Rosheen out of this. The girl has no taste."

"I heard that!" Rosheen's voice preceded her into the room. Sophia was at her side, carrying a basket.

"Twins?" Holly gasped.

"Don't listen to her," Rosheen said. "I'm Rosheen Danann, fashion designer to the Royal Family. She's just a dancer."

Keelin huffed.

"Designer to Mommy and Daddy, you mean."

"Girls, girls," I laughed. "You can both shop for her."

I took Sophia to the Labyrinth Garden that afternoon. She loved to play tag inside its elaborate pattern of twisting and turning paths and multiple dead ends.

At the entrance of the garden, Sophia let go of my hand and ran in ahead of me, giggling.

"You can't get me!" she called back to me in a singsong voice.

The labyrinth was quite old; the hedges that created the walls reached well over my head. Once Sophia turned the first corner, she disappeared from view. However, I kept close behind her by following the sound of her footsteps and giggles, staying out of sight so she would think she was outsmarting me.

"I'm going to get you," I called, teasing her. Occasionally I would get closer and fake a grab at her.

We kept at it until she reached the heart of the labyrinth, where a bench surrounded by rosebushes awaited us. A bloom off the bush was the reward for any adventurer who made it this far. Sophia picked which flower she wanted: a pale yellow rose in full bloom. She waited for her prize, shifting her weight from one foot to the other with her hands clasped behind her back as I clipped it and snapped off the thorns on its stem.

We sat on the bench. She pulled her knees up and put her feet flat on the seat of the bench. She leaned against me and I put my arm over the seat back.

"Tressa, how did these flowers get here?" She twirled the stem between her fingers. The sweet fragrance from the flower spun around us.

"Miss Órlaith planted them many years ago. She planted the whole garden."

"Why?"

"She loves to grow things, especially plants. She planted all the gardens on the estate."

"Why?"

"Why do you think she did that?"

Sophia thought for a minute, holding the flower under her nose.

"She must really love plants."

"Aye, I believe she does."

She scooted around until she lay with her head in my lap, knees still bent, gazing up at the sky.

"When you look up, you don't even know you're in a puzzle," she said.

I followed her gaze and noticed storm clouds accumulating. The temperature had dropped several degrees. I would need to get the child indoors soon.

"Can I stay at Pine Ridge forever?"

The seriousness of her voice startled me. I phrased my answer carefully.

"There will always be a home for you at Pine Ridge, whenever you want and for as long as you want. You must ask your father how long this visit will be."

The child scrambled to her feet, standing on the bench. The yellow flower left discarded by her shoe. She hugged me around my neck, putting her tiny cheek against mine.

"I love you, Tressa."

"Aye, and I love you too, little one."

"I wish you were my mommy."

My heart broke at the same time as it swelled with joy.

"Me too, baby. Me too." I hugged her fiercely and then stood. "We better get going, it looks like rain."

"I'll race you!" She ran off, giggling and zigzagging her way through the second half of the labyrinth. I concentrated on listening to her direction changes to keep close behind her.

She turned into a short dead-end and then, seeing her mistake, she abruptly turned back and ran into me. We were both laughing as we busted out of the end of the labyrinth on the far side of the garden.

The sun shone through a break in the clouds and a flicker caught the corner of my eye. I jerked my head in that direction and caught a glimmer of gold in the trees. At first, I was sure the sun had glinted off Gilleagán's golden hair as he walked in the woods. When I looked again, I saw nothing.

Sophia came and grabbed my hand.

"Can we go visit the Pixies?"

"Aye, a short visit," I agreed.

We had walked halfway around the outside of the Labyrinth Garden toward the lake when I heard a noise from the woods next to us. It sounded like the crackling of the underbrush beneath a footstep. The hair on the back of my neck stood.

Someone had to be in the woods.

The labyrinth blocked us from the view of everyone else on the estate. Nobody would be within shouting distance. The Pixies might pick up my shout on the wind, but they wouldn't be able to summon help in time.

A man stepped out of the woods. Fred Moyer stood twenty feet in front of me. His arms and face were scraped and dirty. Sections of his t-shirt were torn. He looked like he had fought his way through the thicket. In his hands he carried a coarse rope, which he twisted maniacally back and forth around his fists.

My instincts screamed at me to hold *Dominion* over him. I could make him freeze where he stood while I went for help. However, he was too far away for me to lock his gaze.

Although I doubted he was after Sophia, I didn't want to take any chances. I had to get her away from him. I kept my eyes on Fred as I spoke to her.

"Lass, I need you to run to the Manor House. *Now!*"

Instead of following my instructions, she clung to my leg.

"That's the bad man from the store," she said in a trembling voice.

Fred stepped toward us. Unconsciously, I backed away from him, Sophia still glued to my side. Belatedly I remembered that I needed to be closer if I were to control him. This was difficult when it meant allowing him within reach of Sophia.

I pushed her behind me and gripped her upper arm to hold her there as I moved closer. I made eye contact with him, but something was wrong. His eyes were flat and lifeless.

"Fredrick Moyer, husband of Holly Moyer—"

"God damn right, she's my wife. Where is she?" he shouted.

Fear rose in my chest.

I tried again. "Fredrick Moyer, stop right there."

I trembled. I couldn't hold *Dominion* over him; someone else was already controlling him. He kept coming toward us.

I had to get Sophia to safety. If I ran with her, he could catch us. I couldn't be sure he would grab me and leave the child unharmed. I had no choice but to hold him off while she got to safety. Then, perhaps, I could flit away.

I whipped around and stooped to her level in one smooth motion. I grabbed both her arms, too tightly in my panic, and she yelped. I locked eyes with her.

"Sophia Alexa Mannus, you will run as fast as you can to the Manor House. Don't stop until you get to Shamus."

Nothing. She didn't move; but this was different. My magic just wasn't working on her.

"Sophia, do as I ask—quickly."

This time, she obediently turned and ran, little arms pumping.

Suddenly the sky opened up, pouring down on us. Lightning flashed. I watched her through the rain, heart thumping, until I felt confident she was on her way.

I turned back and immediately felt a blow across my face. Fred's backhand knocked me off balance. I slid on the wet grass as I tried to catch myself and fell down hard.

I tried to scurry away from him and get to my feet, but he grabbed my leg and pulled it out from under me, sending me sprawling again. I flipped onto my back. When he came at me again, I swept my leg across his knees, knocking him down. He shouted curses at me.

I struggled to my feet, looking in the direction Sophia had just gone. I couldn't see her any more. Was she safe? I asked myself, wondering if she had gotten far enough away for me to flit to help.

In that moment of hesitation, he caught me, latching on to my wrist. I couldn't move on the wind as long as he held onto me.

"You're coming with me, witch," he hissed.

"Let me go," I shouted.

He punched me, pounding down on my jaw once, twice. Pain exploded across my face and down my neck.

Desperately, using my free hand, I tried to pry away his fingers and loosen his grip. He yanked on my arm, throwing me face down on the ground. The rain matted my hair around my head. He pushed his knee into my back, crushing my lungs with his weight. I struggled to breathe through a mouth full of my own wet hair.

He pulled my arms behind me. My heart pounded in my ears as I thrashed from side to side trying to get him off me. He tied my wrists together with the rope.

He leaned over to put his mouth next to my ear. His knee dug into me as he moved. I let out a muffled groan and again tried in vain to rock back and forth.

"Witch, I told you. You will burn."

His words filled me with terror. Though I had little strength left, I fought against him with renewed vigor and managed to turn my head. I gasped in air and began to scream.

Suddenly, Alexander was there. He dove at Fred, ramming his shoulder into his torso and tackling him away from me. Fred tried to regain his footing, but Alexander punched him and knocked him right back down.

My chest heaved as I sucked in air. It felt like I would never draw in enough. I rolled to a sitting position and then struggled to work my hands free of the rope.

Alexander straddled the other man and pummeled his face repeatedly with his fist.

I wrangled myself free of my restraints, ripping open the skin on my wrists and hands.

On the next gust of wind, Shamus and Gilleagán flitted in

simultaneously, but from opposite directions. Gilleagán hauled Alexander away from Fred.

"Damn it, Xander. That's enough," Gilleagán said.

While Alexander struggled to push past Gilleagán, Fred rolled to his hands and knees. My brother held his ground between the two men.

"What's the matter, tough guy?" Alexander shouted at Fred. "Can you only hit women? Come on, I'm ready for you. I'll whip your ass."

Shamus hurried over to me and gave me his hand to help me to my feet. Pain seared through me, and I thought my knees might buckle. I held onto Shamus to steady myself.

"Xander, I'm okay," I said. I thought my words would calm him.

He turned to look at me when I spoke. I can't say what I looked like, but it must have been bad. Shoving Gilleagán to the side, he delivered a sharp kick straight to Fred's ribs. Fred collapsed back down to the ground, groaning.

Alexander would have continued beating him if Matt hadn't come sprinting around the end of the labyrinth at just that moment. He stepped between them, chest heaving, and held his hands up to stop Alexander's next blow.

"Xander," he shouted to get his attention. "I got this. You take care of Tressa."

Fred lay immobile on the ground in a puddle of mud. Though he gave no indication he would run, Matt hogtied him with the rope just in case. Then he pulled out his cell phone and dialed 911.

Shamus discretely stepped away from me once Alexander had me within his grasp. Alexander held me under my elbow as he gently examined my swollen jaw and the bleeding scrapes on my hands and wrists. His anger blazed from his eyes.

"Will you be able to take care of this?" he asked. "Should we take you to the hospital?"

I shook my head.

"I just need to get home."

Shamus cleared his throat to bring us out of our tète-à-tète.

"It would be best if she flitted. It's the fastest way to get her there," he said.

Alexander looked reluctant to let go of me.

"She doesn't seem to be very steady on her feet," he said.

"I will move with her. I'll make sure she gets there safely."

Shamus, showing Alexander a new level of respect, waited for him to acquiesce before acting.

Alexander kissed me. He nodded to Shamus, who took my hand. We walked a few steps together and then flitted on the wind to the door of my home.

ALEXANDER

I CURSED at myself as I ran to Tressa's farmhouse. How could I have been so reckless? Why didn't I add my own security measures to the fae magic Shamus had in place? The remote, cocoon-like feeling of the estate had tricked me into a false sense of security.

When I ran into the farmhouse, Shamus was in the living room filling Holly and the twins in on what had happened. Tressa sat in the chair, rubbing herself dry with a towel.

Holly had lost all her color. She hugged herself as she listened to Shamus's story. I didn't know if she could bear to hear of another brutality perpetrated by her husband.

Tressa reached out with a trembling hand and patted Holly's arm to calm her. I took a deep breath to squelch my anger; Tressa was again at the brink of exhaustion, yet still she was helping someone else. Exploding at Holly would be a serious misdirection of that anger.

Everyone stopped talking as I strode over to Tressa, gathered her in my arms, and carried her up the stairs. She relaxed her exhausted body as I carried her, turning her face into my chest and wrapping her hands around my neck. I took her to her room and eased her onto the bed.

Shamus came in behind me, carrying an armful of supplies from Tressa's pantry. He placed the various bottles, herbs and powders on the bedside table.

"I have everything taken care of downstairs," said Shamus. "The princesses will tend to Holly. Sophia is with Jenny. I'll go check on her now."

"Thank you, Shamus," Tressa called after him as he headed out.

"What else do you need?" I asked.

"Just you," Tressa said, attempting to smile. I flinched; the bruising on her face made the smile look more like a grimace.

Tressa struggled to sit up. I gave her my hand to help her as she gingerly pulled herself forward. I layered pillows behind her with my free hand and she eased herself back against them. Then she patted a spot next to her for me to sit.

She spread a white liquid from one of her jars over the wounds on her wrists. She chanted softly as she applied it, and her skin healed nearly the moment she touched it. It was the fastest healing I had ever seen her do.

She placed a couple of tablespoons of a fragrant oil in a bowl, adding a pinch of dried plant leaves and mixing them together. She rubbed this mixture over her jaw and her neck. The skin under her fingers went back to its usual pearly alabaster as she touched it, but the swelling took longer to go down.

"Will you help me take off my shirt?" she asked.

She moved cautiously forward, and I carefully pulled her shirt over her head. I clenched my teeth when I saw the purple skin underneath the fabric.

She made more of the tonic, singing softly as she applied it to her midriff. The skin changed swiftly, going from purple to yellowish-green to pearly white.

"Rub some on my back, please," she said.

"Will it work if I do it?"

"Aye, it will be fine."

This time she sat forward easily. I took the remaining oil from the bowl and rubbed it into the bruises on her back as she continued her chant. These bruises healed slower than the others, but they had disappeared completely by the time she sat back against the pillows.

Within five minutes of starting the process, she looked exhausted but completely healed.

I climbed into bed next to her and put my arm around her shoulders. She leaned against me and kissed the hand that hung over her shoulder.

"How could I let him get to you?" I chided myself. "I should've taken better care of you."

"This wasn't your fault. You found me, as you always do, and stopped him from taking me. You're a hero."

I felt like the furthest thing from a hero when I remembered the marks the beating had made on her. She looked so frail.

"I knew you needed me, but I was at the History Center Library doing research. It nearly killed me, thinking I wouldn't get here in time."

My mind went to the old photos I had found; they might help me pinpoint a landmark on Brion's map. It would be a big step towards finally finding the source of the River Rock. I saved that news for a better time. Her half-asleep voice drew me back to the present.

"I couldn't hold *Dominion* over him."

"Why? You did it before."

"Another Sidhe already had control of his mind."

It took me a minute to fully comprehend the implications of her words.

"You mean an Unseelie may have been using him to get you out past the wards?"

"Aye, could have."

A new fear gnawed at my gut. I believed that the strange stories she told me of war and blood oaths were real. Nevertheless, until now she had seemed to worry about a great many things that didn't happen. This knowledge made the danger real on an entirely new level. A crushing pain in my chest reminded me how close I had been to losing her.

After my discharge from the Marines, I thought I had left war behind me. Nevertheless, I would pick up arms if need be to protect her from this strange threat.

CHAPTER NINETEEN

TRESSA

Although I felt fully recuperated after sleeping through until the next morning, Alexander insisted I take the day off and spend it relaxing with Holly at the Manor House. I didn't think he understood how difficult it was to relax in a chaotic Sidhe household. I agreed with his plan without enlightening him.

When we arrived, Shamus roused the twins from their beds. They bustled around in their pajamas, upending everyone's routine as they enthusiastically took charge of Holly and me. They insisted that Holly lounge on the living room sofa, agreeing for once that it was the most comfortable spot in the house for her. They pointed out that the room had a second sofa, in case I should like to lounge as well, which I did not. I chose a comfortable chair next to Holly instead.

While relaxing didn't interest me, I welcomed the opportunity to discuss the previous day's incident with my cousins. Once their fussing calmed, I asked, "Keelin, Rosheen, have you noticed any other Sidhe around since you've been here?"

Rosheen shook her head. "I'm sure you're wondering who's responsible for your attack yesterday. I've been thinking about it too."

Holly, pale and drawn, spoke up timidly. "Tressa, are you sure it wasn't just Fred acting on his own? I mean, at this point I have to believe he's capable of anything."

"I can't say he wouldn't come after me on his own, but a Sidhe definitely held *Dominion* over him in that moment," I said. "Roe, on that first day when I asked everyone how they knew I was here, did you sense that anyone was lying?"

Rosheen's brow crinkled. "No, not that I recall. At first there was your comment about being Handfast..." I blushed, embarrassed she knew I had lied. "...but when Xander agreed, that made it truth," she continued.

"One of the guys told us," Keelin said. "I can't remember who we spoke to first about visiting. But with all the noise on the wind recently, it wouldn't be difficult for anyone to track you, Tressa. If they were seriously looking, that is."

"So any Unseelie who managed to cross a threshold from the Otherworld could find me." My stomach turned over. I was open game. Suddenly I remembered something. "Wait, I may have seen someone. In the woods, just before Fred appeared... but it was just a blond head, really."

"I spoke to the trees yesterday after the attack," Keelin said. "They said no Unseelie were in the woods yesterday, but there was Unseelie magic. It was confusing."

"Speak to the trees?" Holly asked, incredulous.

"Keelin has an affinity for plant life. She can speak with them and they obey her command," I explained before returning to the conversation. "Brenna told me something similar after her last trip to Faery. She couldn't make sense of it either."

"Well, the forest is on the lookout now. No one, fae or human, will get past them onto the estate," Keelin said with conviction.

"How close would they have to be to hold *Dominion* over him?" Holly asked. "Tommy said Fred was in Canada."

"Of course!" I said, understanding washing over me. "He was probably in Niagara Falls, where the flu started. An Unseelie would need to lock eyes with him to start the *Dominion*. Then the Sidhe could continue to control him until he completed the command or something broke his connection. So the Unseelie magic would be here, but not the fae himself."

The aroma of brown sugar and blueberries put an end to our conversation as Jenny arrived with a luxurious tray of food for the expectant mother. Sophia, who had come in with her, brought me a plate of her favorite pastries. I made space so that she could sit with me on the chair and share them with me.

"What about us?" Rosheen pouted. "Don't we get breakfast?"

Jenny nodded.

"It's waiting for you in the kitchen."

"Sophia, when I come back I'll take you to visit the Pixies and I'll give you another ballet lesson," Keelin said. She smiled at Sophia, who pumped her head enthusiastically, as she and Rosheen followed Jenny out of the room.

I PASSED the rest of the morning alone with Holly. She spent most of that time curled up in a brooding silence. When she spoke, her words were stilted. After the extraordinary amount of grief she had been through in the last couple of weeks, I feared she was slipping into a depression.

She wore a new outfit from the twins' shopping spree. She had styled her hair in her usual way and had applied her makeup perfectly. However, that day more than usual, it all seemed like window-dressing.

She only perked up when Rosheen came back that afternoon, wearing a watercolor print dress with beading around the neckline that complimented her complexion.

"Rosheen, that dress is simply wonderful!" Holly gushed. Rosheen twirled to give her the full effect.

"Thank you; it's one of my own designs." Something clicked in Holly's mind. Her eyes widened.

"Rosheen, you're not... but you must be... you're *the* Rosheen?" Rosheen curtsied theatrically.

"The one and only."

Holly turned to scold me. "I can't believe you didn't tell me your cousin is a famous fashion designer!"

I laughed.

"She's just my little cousin to me. I forget she's famous." This prompted an idea for how to cheer her up. "Roe, honey, Pix loves fashion design. Why don't you teach her a few tricks of the trade?"

Both faces lit up.

"Would you like that?" Rosheen asked.

"Oh, yes!" Holly said, eyes dancing.

Rosheen ran out of the room and returned with a drawing pad and colored pencils. I got up so she could sit next to Holly, settling myself into a chair by the window instead.

Rosheen pulled her chair closer to Holly, who sat with her legs stretched out on the sofa. Soon, absorbed in their conversation, they bent over the sketchpad—Holly's dark head with its short Pixie cut side by side with Rosheen's long, straight blue tresses.

I was on my own, gazing out the window, when Connor entered the room. I had avoided any intimate conversations with him since that strange moment in the club, still not trusting that he hadn't put a hex on me that night. I closed my eyes and sighed in resignation when he headed my way.

"I understand you had a real scare yesterday," he said, sitting uninvited on the arm of my chair.

"It was nothing," I said, not wanting to discuss it with him.

"That's not what I heard," he insisted. "But isn't that just like a human, to beat a woman. How can you stand to be around—"

"This was one man. Let's not condemn an entire race for the actions of one individual."

"Tressa, how can you be in a serious relationship with one of them?" His expression was a mixture of contempt and pain. "Especially when you know that I'm here for you."

"Connor, please. Let's not do this again. We settled this long ago." I felt physical discomfort at the idea of heading off his advances yet again. Though he was undoubtedly handsome, he was also self-centered and vain. I simply wasn't attracted to him.

He took my hand. I tried to pull it away, but he wouldn't let go.

"I was your grandfather's choice for you."

"What good is that, Connor? I am not your *Anam Cara*. We would not fulfill the prophecy together. Why can't you understand that?" My voice rose, taking on a sharper edge than I had planned.

The two girls on the other side of the room lifted their heads to look at us. I forced a smile in their direction. Reassured that I was okay, they went back to their sketching.

"The prophecy means nothing to me," Connor said.

His adamant tone might have convinced another, but I didn't need Rosheen's ability to know that this was a lie. My fame as the King's Jewel was the real attraction, not me as a person. If he didn't recognize that in himself, I couldn't help him.

"I am of your own kind: a Sidhe and a Royal, and quite simply the better choice for you."

"My choice is made, and you'd best accept it," I told him with as much finality as I could.

ALEXANDER

I RUSHED into the Manor House, knocking and entering without waiting for Shamus, as was our custom now that so many visitors were running in and out. I hurried to find Tressa, anxious to share with her the news of my discovery.

In the living room, Holly was on the sofa with one of the twins beside her—I couldn't tell which, since her head was down. They worked together over a large pad of paper.

I stiffened when I saw Connor sitting close to Tressa on the opposite side of the room. Connor reached out and took her hand. I waited, trying to understand what was happening, straining to hear their conversation.

"The prophecy means nothing to me," Connor said. "I am of your own kind: a Sidhe and a Royal, and quite simply the better choice for you."

I controlled my instinct to rush in and break the guy's neck. My second, more reasonable thought was to let Tressa handle her own business. I changed direction and went to find Órlaith.

As I walked to the back porch, I rolled Connor's words around in my head. He was like her. He was the better choice. I couldn't deny these truths. I was pensive and sad by the time I reached the back porch.

This room, although enclosed, always felt like the outdoors to me. The plants filled the room with a musky smell, seeming to multiply every time I returned.

Órlaith was there, as I had expected. She stood at a window, looking out toward the back of the house.

"Xander, I'm watching your daughter come up the path with Keelin. They make a good match. Sophia is very much like Keelin was as a child, and she could certainly do worse for a teacher. Keelin is a world class ballerina—in both realms."

"Can that be a good match? A human and a Sidhe?" I asked.

She turned to me, perhaps to gauge whether we spoke of the same thing. She didn't answer immediately. She walked to a chair, using her cane for support.

I took her place at the window, placing my forearm on the wooden window frame and resting my chin on my arm. I watched my baby dance her way up the path.

"What's this about?" Órlaith asked.

"Nothing."

She waited in expectant silence.

"I heard Connor tell Tressa he was better for her because I'm a human."

The old woman scoffed.

"Connor is a celebrity monger."

I didn't want to talk about it anymore.

"I think I've found the place you sent me to look for."

"That's wonderful! And what did you find there?"

"I don't know yet. I'll do some exploring there tomorrow."

She nodded.

"Remember, mention this to no one. Tell no one what you find there except Tressa or me."

"Yes, I remember."

"One last thing: what you will find there is meant for you, and you alone. Don't give it to anyone else."

This surprised me. I hadn't expected to come away with anything but knowledge, discovery and a few stones.

"What am I going to find there?"

"Sophia has returned. Let's go join the others so she can perform for us, as I can see she is dying to do."

It was impossible to get an answer from Órlaith once she had decided she didn't want to give it. I knew better than to try. I escorted her to the living room.

Sophia had assembled her audience. Matt, Holly, the twins,

even Jenny Jamison and Shamus had gathered in the room. Only Connor and Gilleagán were missing.

Sophia ran to hug me. "Daddy, you're here! Just in time to see my show."

"Oh good," I said. "I'm glad I didn't miss it." I winked at Tressa over her head.

Keelin gave Sophia a big, theatrical introduction then, hummed a tune to provide music. Sophia did a simple routine, combining the three or four steps she had learned thus far. When she finished, she curtsied to her audience as they gave her a strong round of applause.

"Brava! Brava!" Órlaith cheered. Sophia ran to her, throwing her arms around the elderly woman's neck.

"Well, Mamó, I see you've found a new child to favor." Gilleagán's voice startled the small crowd into silence. We all turned to look at him as he stood, arms crossed, in the doorway.

Órlaith smiled, but something in Gilleagán's voice made me wary.

"Yes, I have. Isn't she delightful?" Órlaith asked.

I could have sworn I saw him flinch when she acknowledged what had sounded to me like an accusation. No one else in the room seemed to notice.

"Where have you been, lad?" Órlaith asked. "I've hardly laid eyes on you since you got here."

There was a tension between them that I hadn't noticed previously. Órlaith scrutinized her grandson with an expression of confusion, tinged with suspicion.

"Is that so? Well, I'll make time to sit with you later," Gilleagán said, trying to lighten his tone. His words rang false. "Connor is waiting for me—we're going out. Girls, are you coming?"

The twins barely looked his way as they simultaneously shook their heads.

He attempted to keep his expression calm, but I was certain his composed surface covered a disproportionate amount of anger.

"Was there something going on there that I missed?" I asked Tressa after he left.

Tressa waved it off.

"That's just Gil. He never likes anyone to get attention but him, and he never gets enough no matter how much we give."

She seemed more than ready to dismiss her brother's behavior, and I was happy to do the same. I wanted to have her to myself. I was tired of sharing her with this gaggle of honking geese. Was it too much to ask to have a moment of alone time with her to share my good news from the day?

"How about a quiet dinner at home?" I whispered in her ear.

Her bright eyes met mine, her expression alight with enthusiasm. I took an extra second to admire her face. Her large round eyes, her bow-curved mouth: each detail perfectly suited to the others.

She was more than physical beauty. Her tenderness and her concern for the people around her, tempered with a strength that defied her slender stature, proved her spiritually beautiful as well.

How easy it would be to mistake her for an actual angel. She was an angel to me. I didn't understand how or why, but she had touched something deep within me. She had reawakened a part of me that I thought had been lost forever.

Now that I had experienced the world with her, I knew I would want her forever. I understood why Connor couldn't let her go.

We said our goodbyes and walked home, Tressa holding one of my hands, Sophia holding the other. I couldn't get my mind off of Connor's words. I hadn't realized that it had put me into a brooding silence through dinner and getting Sophia off to bed.

. . .

"WHAT'S wrong with you tonight? You're so quiet," Tressa asked as we got into bed. She curled on her side, putting her head on my shoulder as usual. I pulled the sheet up over us.

"I heard part of your conversation with Connor earlier."

"Please don't tell me he makes you jealous. He's nothing but an old family friend." I smiled grimly.

"I think he wants to be more than that."

"But—" I put a finger to her lips.

"It's okay to admit it. If I thought for one minute you wanted that too..." I shook my head, disagreeing with what I had been about to say. "No. I was going to say I would get out of the way, but that's a lie. I could never just hand you over to someone else. I'm not that selfless. I want you too much. Suffice it to say, I know you aren't interested in him."

Her brow crinkled.

"Then what is it?"

"I've been wondering if he's right. If I'm no good for you." I coughed to cover that I had choked up.

She surprised me by laughing. She pushed herself up to sit on her knees, tugging on me until I sat up too so we could lean back together against the headboard.

"Xander, nothing in this world could be as good for me as you are. I have never felt such unadulterated joy as I do with you. This can't possibly be wrong."

She laughed again when my expression lightened. I pulled her to my lap where she sat, straddling me. I reached up, wrapping my fingers into her hair pulling her to me. Her mouth was warm, soft, and yielding. She trailed gentle kisses from my mouth down my neck, to my chest, and lower.

IT WASN'T until much later, when I was drifting off to sleep, that I realized I had forgotten to tell her about my discovery.

CHAPTER TWENTY

TRESSA

I expected to drive at least partway to our destination, but instead, Alexander led me north into the tall pine trees that lined the property behind the lake.

"Where are we going?" I asked him for the third time.

"I'm not telling you," he said. "I found something, but I want you to see it for yourself."

We hiked through the woods without a path to follow. He was quite solicitous of me as we navigated the terrain, holding my elbow for extra stability whenever the underbrush became especially thick or uneven. However, I felt an urgency in him to move quickly. The obvious excitement that ricocheted through him amused me as I considered what could possibly make him react in this way.

After an hour of wrestling through thicket the woods began to thin, the terrain smoothing out and making it easier to walk. No longer worried for my safety, Alexander couldn't keep himself in pace with me. He kept walking a few yards beyond me before returning to my side, as though torn between staying with me and running ahead.

Each time he returned, he pointed out a different landmark: a boulder with a peculiar shape or a stream that flowed over moss covered rocks.

"You're making me think you want me to remember how to get back here," I said after his third lap.

"Exactly," he nodded, grinning.

"Do you really think I'd come here without you?"

"You'll want to know the way back, just in case," he said with confidence.

I tried to imagine what he had found. He was looking for River Rock, which only existed in Faery. Even if my grandfather had planted stones for him to find, it wouldn't be enough to merit such a fuss.

I noticed a patch of dandelions and out of habit, squatted to pull one out by the root.

"What are you doing?" he asked.

"Dandelions have several healing properties. It's always good to have a supply on hand."

"Really? And here I've spent years trying to kill them out of my yard." His voice held a note of amusement. "You may not have noticed, but I'm kind of in a hurry."

The understatement caught me by surprise, and I laughed. An odd gurgling noise cut my amusement short. I went still, concentrating on the sound.

Alexander caught the change in my body language.

"What is it, Love?" he whispered.

"I hear a rasping noise... as if someone's struggling to breathe."

"An animal?"

"No, it's a person."

I ran toward the sound, wondering if I could flit to the right place using the raspy breathing as a locater. Alexander, in step beside me, seemed to read my thoughts.

"Tressa, don't do it. There's a cliff on this side with at least a hundred yard drop. You could miss. Anyway, you don't know what happened to this person; it may not be safe."

"I see him."

I could see a spot of florescent orange about a mile in the distance. A few steps closer and I could identify the orange as a stripe on a shirt. With a destination in sight, I flitted, leaving Alexander to follow on foot.

I recognized the lost hiker from his picture on the news. He was in bad shape. I would have thought him dead if it weren't for the horrible noise he made as he struggled to draw in each breath.

The blue puffy skin of his face and hands indicated hypothermia. My mind raced to think of possible remedies or any means of helping him. Building a fire would help, I thought, but I blanched at the idea. Maybe Alexander could build one while I flitted to get help.

I knelt beside the hiker. I took his hand in mine to offer comfort and dropped it immediately, yelping with surprise. His hand was burning hot. I touched his forehead to confirm what I had already guessed; a fever, far above anything an ordinary illness would induce, was ravaging his body.

Terror filled my chest, impeding my own breathing. I pulled back the collar of his shirt to look at the skin of his neck and shoulder. As I had feared, a dense web of deep purple lines covered his shoulder, thinning as they reached up his neck.

What can I possibly do for him? This is my fault. This attack was because of me. I took a deep breath to calm myself.

I barely remembered what jewels I had put on that morning, but I felt the weight of a necklace. I grabbed the bottom of it and yanked it sharply. It sliced into the back of my neck, drawing blood, but eventually it snapped.

I watched the stones fall to the ground, knowing it didn't matter what gemstones they were. I desperately wished for a means to help him. But stones took time for their healing properties to work. They were no help in an emergency.

The hiker stirred and opened his eyes. He looked up at me with heavy lids.

"Are you an angel?" he asked, his dry lips cracking and bleeding as he formed the words.

The question startled me, but then I remembered that by ripping off the necklace I had dropped my glamour. He saw me as I really was, and surely he had never seen a Sidhe. I started to deny it, but Alexander, coming up behind me, spoke first.

"Yes, she's an angel." He moved around to kneel on the opposite side of the man. "Isn't she beautiful?"

"Beautiful," the hiker mouthed.

I watched as the life began to leave his eyes. He was dying because of me.

"No!" I shouted, as though I could stop his death by making the demand. Alexander put two fingers to his neck, looking for a pulse.

"He's gone, Tressa."

"John T. Sullivan," I said, recalling his name from the news story, "you will not die today," I yelled, staring into his lifeless eyes as though I could keep him here by holding *Dominion* over him. I wasn't fooling myself; I knew it wouldn't work. The tears I had been holding back spilled over and flowed down my cheeks, like the spring coursing over the rocks we had walked past minutes ago.

This was my fault. The thought seeped in through the fog in my brain. I lay my hands flat on his chest and pushed my essence down to infuse it into him. What was my essence, if not my life light? It might save him.

"Tressa, honey, he's gone. There's nothing you can do," Alexander said gently.

"This is my fault." I said it aloud this time in a sobbing, tear-stained voice. I continued to let my essence flow into the dead man.

"How is this your fault? Sweetheart, please stop."

I barely heard Alexander's voice anymore. An all-consuming weakness fell over me. I was dangerously close to exuding too much of myself. I tried to pull my hands away, but the flow of energy had created a connection I no longer had the strength to break. The realization fell over me: the hiker was dead, and I would die too. Exhausted, my eyes began to close of their own accord. I forced them opened for one last look at Alexander.

He must have seen it in my eyes; as soon as our gaze met, he launched himself at me. Pushing his shoulder into my chest, he wrapped his arms around my torso and tackled me away from the hiker's body.

Then he scrambled into a sitting position and gently cradled me in his lap.

"My god; Tressa, are you okay? Did I hurt you?" he asked as his trembling hands turned my face to his.

I buried my head in his chest, sobs shaking my entire body as though they would never end. Alexander let me cry, holding me close and occasionally kissing my hair. I finally gained a measure of control, my body stilling though the tears continued to flow.

"Please tell me why you think this was your fault," Alexander said when I had finally quieted. "Is it because you couldn't heal him? You must know you can't save everyone. He had been lost out here for days."

"Fae fever," I choked.

"What?"

"I've never seen it, but I've heard about it. He had a fever burning his brain and purple webbing on his skin. It's the Unseelie's favorite sickness to cast on humans. They must be here, and if they are, it's because of me."

ALEXANDER CALLED the state police and gave them rough coordinates on how to find us. We sat under a tree a short distance from the hiker's body while we waited for them to arrive. I sang a funeral lament for the poor man softly under my breath as Alexander sat quietly listening.

It took an hour for the authorities, a half dozen of them, to reach us. One officer attended the body while another took photographs. Several others scoured the area, starting close to the body and systematically moving further away.

Meanwhile, a detective questioned Alexander and me. He had wanted to interview us separately, but we refused. He asked us the same questions multiple times, changing the wording slightly each time: What were we doing there in the woods? Why did we come where there was no path? Had we known the hiker previously? Did he say anything before he passed? The questions droned on.

After a half hour, I swayed as I struggled to stay standing. Two minutes later, I sat down abruptly, trembling with mental and physical exhaustion.

The startled detective stopped speaking mid-question. He called out to the nearest police officer.

"Jones, we need to get an ambulance for this lady."

"Out here?" the officer asked incredulously.

"No," I said, swallowing to control the edginess in my voice. "I'm fine. I just need to rest."

"You may be going into shock," he warned. "You should go to the hospital."

"No, really—"

"Tom, over here!" Alexander yelled, interrupting me. Tom Lynch had just arrived. "This officer knows us, he can tell you where to find us if you have any more questions."

Tom scrutinized the activity around the dead hiker as he walked over to us. "You guys found him?" he asked when he reached us.

We both nodded.

"Tressa is a little overwhelmed. I need to get her home. Would you vouch for us with the detective here?" Alexander said.

Tom did as Alexander asked. He even offered to drive us home, for which I was grateful. I didn't think I could make it back the way we came. It was a much shorter hike to Tom's police cruiser.

Instead of taking us to our homes, we asked him to drop us off at the Manor House. Alexander and I sought out my grandmother and Shamus and asked to meet with them in the privacy of Mamó's bedroom suite.

When we explained what had happened, their first questions were amazingly similar to the ones the detective had asked. Our answers, however, were more forthcoming.

"Are you sure it was Fae Fever?" Mamó asked for the second time. I understood her hesitancy. I didn't want to believe it either.

"I'm sure," I said.

"And you're sure you didn't know this man? Maybe from the store?"

I nodded. "Aye, I'm sure."

"It still sounds like the Unseelie," Shamus said as he chomped on the end of his pipe. He was smoking in Mamó's room, which spoke to how disconcerted this incident had made him. "I'm sure they'd prefer to attack people who are important to you. These assaults on random people are misdeeds of opportunity. Practice, so to speak. But they're getting closer."

"Will the wards hold?" Alexander asked.

Shamus nodded as he pulled on the pipe.

"I've been refreshing them daily. Since the attack on Tressa, the perimeter has been warded against humans. No human can get onto the estate unless invited, and anyone with Unseelie blood won't be able to pass the perimeter."

"We must tell the others and get everyone to the estate until we have a better idea of what's going on," Mamó decided. "They'll be safe as long as they're here."

We nodded in agreement.

"Shamus, send some Pixies to Faery—Kerry and Megan would be best—with a message that we must arrange safe passage for Tressa to return home."

I sucked in a startled breath. I couldn't imagine returning to my old life.

"Mamó, do you really think that's necessary?" I did my best to control the panic in my voice.

"I'm sorry, *a leanbh*, but there is no other choice."

"Mamó, please. I don't want to go. You heard Shamus: I'm safe here."

She shook her head.

"The Otherworld is the only place we can be sure you'll be safe. Your uncle will see to it."

I looked at Alexander, willing him to demand that I stay.

"Xander?" I whispered. He brushed my cheek with the back of his fingers.

"I need you to be safe."

"Don't worry, lass. He can go with you," Mamó said.

My neck flushed with embarrassment. She made me feel like

a silly schoolgirl. Despite my embarrassment, knowing he could go with me lessened my misery.

"Alexander, I need you to run an errand for me," Mamó continued.

"You're sending him off the estate?" I asked, distressed.

"I want him to get cuttings from the herb garden while Shamus speaks to the Pixies. He'll be back before you know it. Besides, you need to sleep. Curl up on my bed and I'll have Jenny bring up some food for you," Mamó instructed. "You need to get your strength back."

Alexander lingered after Mamó and Shamus left the room. I clung to his hand, hesitant to let him go though I had no logical reason to object.

"Please don't go," I asked anyway.

"It'll be okay. You sleep now, and feel better," he said. "I'll be back before you know it."

ALEXANDER WOKE me with a kiss several hours later. He knelt on the floor beside the bed, his face eye-level with mine.

"Wake-up, Sleeping Beauty," he said.

I stretched my arms over my head and smiled, However, I was still tired. I wasn't ready to be awake. I patted the bed next to me and said, "Why don't you come curl up with me?"

He shook his head and laughed. "I've come to get you for dinner. Your cousins tell me they have a distraction planned for us this evening," he said. "Come, they're waiting on us. The girls want to put an end to this ugly day by entertaining us."

His obvious affection for my cousins made me smile. He seemed to think of them as little sisters, which pleased me. They were my particular favorites when it came to my family—after Mamó, of course.

. . .

As soon as we finished our meal, Keelin and Rosheen pulled everyone into the Manor's long, open foyer.

"Roe and I thought, since we have to spend the evening in, we could spend it entertaining each other. You know, do a little show," Keelin explained.

"Holly, we want you to just relax and enjoy," Rosheen said. She settled Holly into a couch they had set up earlier along the short end of the foyer by the back door.

They had drug several chairs from the living room and placed them around the sofa for the other spectators. My grandmother took one of the chairs next to Holly.

"I'll join Holly," Matt said. "I have no musical talent."

"Truth!" Rosheen called out, grinning at Matt.

Everyone laughed good-naturedly while Matt took the chair on the other side of Holly. Alexander claimed a large, heavily padded chair, and I sat on his lap.

Sophia started the evening with another ballet performance. Connor played music on his flute while she danced, Rosheen accompanying him on the harp. Keelin stood to the side, coaching Sophia through the newly learned steps of the routine.

She was taking her bows when Matt's phone rang.

"Sorry," he said sheepishly before answering. He looked over at Alexander.

"Kendra wants to know if Sophia can come for a sleep over tonight," Matt asked.

"Yes, yes, yes!" Sophia chanted.

Alexander was shaking his head when Mamó said, "Let the child go. There is no reason to be concerned for her."

Matt arranged for Kendra to pick up Sophia. Then he volunteered to get her ready for her visit.

After the two of them had gone, Keelin did a real performance for us. Her technique was masterful, her connection to the music primal.

I performed next, singing an ancient song about a king who had fallen for a simple maiden. Rosheen accompanied me as I sang. Her harp added the perfect melancholy sound to the sad story.

"Where is Gil?" Mamó asked when the song ended. "We should have you sing together as you did when you were children."

"Mamó, we haven't sung together in thirty years," I said, startled by the request. I hadn't thought about those times in many years. "Anyway, Gil isn't here."

"I believe that boy is truly avoiding me," Órlaith said to herself.

"I'm right here," Gil said, coming into the foyer with a dirty dinner plate in hand.

His voice, coming out of nowhere, made me jump. Where had he come from? How long had he been there in the shadows? I glanced over at Alexander, who raised his eyebrows, his face mirroring my questions from across the room.

"I missed dinner, as usual, so I was watching the show while I ate," Gilleagán said as he hastily set down his dirty plate and placed his flatware and napkin on top. Then he joined Rosheen and me on our pseudo stage. "Let's not disappoint our audience, Tress," he said. "What shall we sing?"

I smiled warmly at him. Singing together after all these years was an unexpected surprise. We had great fun as children performing for our family and our parents' friends. Our grandmother in particular was our biggest supporter.

We agreed on a song about a bird lost on the wind, a song I remembered with fondness from my childhood, but this performance didn't feel the same. In fact, it felt significantly different. An inexplicable tension rolled off Gilleagán as we sang. My grandmother scrutinized us, thin-lipped, eyes narrowed. Not the joyful expression I had expected.

When we finished, Mamó got up from the soft chair with great effort. "*A leanaí*, thank you all for entertaining me this evening. I enjoyed it very much. But it is time for me to say goodnight."

Everyone watched her leave with puzzlement. It was such a strange, abrupt exit.

"That was a lie," Rosheen whispered.

We were quiet until Keelin spoke up, breaking the brooding silence.

"Don't let this spoil the mood," Keelin said with forced cheerfulness. "Let's dance! That will be fun."

She blasted a local pop music radio station and we three girls danced. It was the perfect remedy. My mood lifted with each twist of my hips as I moved to the beat of the music. Alexander must have recognized the great effect the dancing was having on me; with very little persuasion, he consented to join me.

Gilleagán brooded for a while, leaning against the wall with his arms folded across his chest. Eventually the twins goaded him into joining us.

Two or three songs after Gil joined the party, Alexander began to cough. He excused himself to go to the kitchen for a glass of water. A minute later, Shamus pulled me off the dance floor.

"What is it, Shamus?" I asked, breathless from the exertion.

"You had better come with me."

He led me to the kitchen where Alexander sat on a stool, coughing into a napkin splattered with blood.

CHAPTER TWENTY-ONE

att found us in the kitchen after sending Sophia off with his sister. As soon as he walked in, Shamus and I shouted at him to stay away.

Fae Fever wasn't contagious to other humans once it had passed a certain phase. But, Alexander was in the earliest stages, which meant that others might contract it by touching his skin or through his perspiration.

I yelled to Matt to send in one of the fae. Connor must have been nearby; I heard Matt talking to him in the hallway. He came into the kitchen at Matt's insistence, looking with distaste at the blood soaked rag in Alexander's hand.

"Connor, I need to get Alexander to my house and away from everyone here." I worked to control my panic but my voice shook.

"You want my help?" he asked, blanching at the idea.

"I need you to let everyone know what's happening. Then get Holly and Matt out of here."

Connor looked much more comfortable with this request. He hurried out of the room.

Between the two of us, Shamus and I got Alexander to my

house and into my bed. While I pulled off his shoes and loos-
ened his clothes, Shamus grabbed a towel from the bathroom.
He handed it to Alexander as a new coughing fit brought up
more blood.

I ran down the stairs to the kitchen. Staring at my pantry, I
fought the numbness surrounding my brain to focus on a plan. I
rubbed my forehead with a shaky hand. I hadn't yet properly
recuperated my strength from the incident with the hiker earlier
in the day. Would I be able to help Alexander? I breathed carefully, afraid that even that simple action would overwhelm me.

There was no real treatment for Fae Fever. It wasn't even a
real illness; it was a spell cast to kill.

When could it have happened? It had to have been when he
went to the herb garden. He must have stepped off the estate;
perhaps he misjudged the edge of the garden?

I swallowed, pushing down the bile rising in my throat. Anger
broke through the numbness: Anger at Mamó for sending him
there. Anger at him for leaving, despite my request that he not
go. Anger at whoever it was who had done this to him.

I scanned the shelves of the pantry for the third time. Few
people survived this, and nothing in this closet would change
that reality. I closed my eyes and took several deep, calming
breaths.

The best I could do was to treat his symptoms as they arose.
An illness hex could only last for so long before it dissipated. If I
could keep his body going until the hex released its hold on him,
he would be able to get healthy again.

"What do you need here?" Shamus' voice shook me out of
my stupor. I opened my eyes to find him standing next to me,
peering into the pantry. "I'll take it up for you."

His words jolted me into action. I pulled everything off the
shelves that might be remotely helpful, filling a basket until it
overflowed. I grabbed clean towels and ran ahead of him.

Alexander was in the throes of another coughing spell as I ascended the stairs. The cough sounded like it originated deep in his chest. I could smell the blood.

I handed him a clean towel to replace the bloody one he held in his hand. His muscles convulsed with pain. A ball in my chest ached as I watched him.

When Shamus came into the bedroom with my supplies, I asked him to get me the hot water steamer from the bathroom closet and to boil some water.

"Tressa, what's happening?" Alexander asked when the coughing subsided.

"You have Fae Fever," I said, matter-of-factly. I was determined to keep a calm demeanor so as not to panic him.

He looked at me in horror.

"Bu... but how is that possible?" he sputtered.

"Xander, did you run into anyone out by the herb garden?" I kept my voice casual, not wanting to increase his distress.

"Like who?" His voice was raspy from the violent coughing.

"Perhaps a fae you didn't recognize."

He opened his mouth to answer, but a coughing fit overcame him. He shook his head instead.

Shamus brought in a large pot of water, steam rising off the top. He carried it with his bare hands since Brounies are impervious to hot or cold. He placed it on the nightstand next to the bed before going to get the steamer.

"The first thing we'll do is ease that cough," I said.

I steeped lavender, eucalyptus and tea tree in the water, a pleasant damp aroma wafting up in the steam. Shamus returned with the steamer, which he had already filled with water. I had him set it up on top of the dresser across from the foot of the bed.

"Thank you, Shamus. I'll take it from here."

"If you need me, I'll be going to wherever Matt and Holly went," he said. "I need to ward the house."

I felt a tinge of guilt; I hadn't even thought of that.

"Thank you, Shamus. Thank you for thinking of them."

He nodded stiffly before hurrying out.

I shut the bedroom door behind him to trap the warm, damp air in the room. Alexander's next attack would certainly be softer, less damaging with the steam there to help, I told myself.

I put a cup of my herbal mixture into the steamer's water to increase the soothing qualities of the air in the room.

"There was an odd shower."

"What's that?" I asked.

"While I was out—a few drops of rain fell, but the sky was so clear. Could that have been it?"

"Aye, maybe."

I dipped a towel into the pot, letting it soak up the mixture. When it had cooled enough for me to touch it, I squeezed out the excess fluid so it wouldn't drip. Gingerly, I sat next to him and unbuttoned his shirt. He grabbed my hand, stopping my progress.

"Tressa, I can't let you touch me unless you swear you won't hurt yourself."

"Don't be silly. I'll be fine." I tried to pull my hand away, but he wouldn't let it go.

"Tressa, I'm not joking. Don't you dare sacrifice yourself for me. If you did, I could never live with myself."

I struggled against the tears that blurred my vision.

"And how am I supposed to live with myself if you die?" I asked.

"You must live; too many people depend on you. You must take care of Sophia for me."

He coughed again, and it seemed to be gentler this time. I

wanted to get back to my ministrations, but he wouldn't release me, even through the painful coughs.

"Tressa, swear that you won't hurt yourself for me."

I nodded reluctantly.

"Okay. I swear."

He let go of my hand, and it seemed like his entire body relaxed. I finished unbuttoning his shirt and opened it wide to expose his chest. I covered it with the hot towel then dipped a second in the pot, wringing it out and laying it on top of the first. I did this once more with a third towel.

I put my hands palms down on either side of his chest, allowing an easy flow for my essence to move into him. A slow and steady pace might be enough to keep us both alive.

The flow of energy kept the towels warm without me needing to reheat them. I whispered a long, ancient invocation I had memorized ages ago. It was a laborious prayer, especially for the healing of mortal illnesses. I didn't know if it would be helpful in this situation, but at the very least it had a calming effect on me.

"Sing for me," Alexander requested in a groggy, sleepy voice.

I continued the invocation without faltering, but I switched to singing it to the tune of a soft, sweet love song from my youth.

When I finished forty-five minutes later, he was asleep. I took the towels off and covered him with extra blankets to keep him warm.

He continued to cough, but the severity had lessened considerably, and he slept through them. The steam in the room had him sweating. His sweat was a putrid, yellowish-green color that I took to be a good sign: I hoped it meant that the impurities inside him were working their way out.

Exhausted, I went down to the kitchen to eat something before I slept. I was determined to be vigilant about keeping my strength up so I could keep feeding my essence over to him.

After a quick sandwich, I crawled into bed behind him. It took mere seconds for me to fall asleep.

I JERKED awake from another nightmare filled with fire and Deaglan Mór. Alexander stirred and weakly patted my hand; as usual he woke when I did.

The yellowish-green of his sweat soaked my clothes, and my face was flushed where it had been pressed against his shoulder. His clothes clung to his body, drenched with sweat. I placed the back of my hand on his forehead. He burned with fever.

I stopped the steamer and opened the bedroom door to let the air cool. He was so weak I nearly had to drag him to the bathroom. Without bothering to remove our already wet clothing, I went with him into the shower and let the cold-water rain down on both of us.

I didn't get out of the shower until my teeth were chattering. I toweled off and dressed before getting Alexander into dry clothes. He sat on a chair while I changed the bed linens. Then I tucked him back in the dry bed. He was unsettlingly quiet throughout the entire process.

The fever called for a different preparation. This time I started by mixing a concoction for him to drink. It had several things in it, but it tasted mostly of lemon and cucumber.

He only took a few sips when I brought it to him.

"Xander, you need to drink. You're losing too much fluid."

He took a small amount more with my continued urging, but it still wasn't enough.

I tried another slow invocation, since the one I did last night had been so effective on his cough. I put many of the same ingredients from the drink into a basin of cool water. Then I took a sponge and systematically swabbed his face, hands, and feet with the cool tonic, singing the invocation and easing my essence into him as I had the previous night. Intermittently, I made him take more sips of the tonic.

This time it didn't help. His fever remained just as high. He had once again perspired through his clothes and through the bed linens with the ugly, yellow-green sweat. In my exhausted state, the thought of getting him into dry clothes and changing the linens again seemed daunting. I had just gotten up to start when Shamus and Mamó arrived.

Relief rushed through me at the sight of them. I was glad to have someone with whom to share my burden. I ran to hug my grandmother, and I would have hugged Shamus too if he hadn't held me off.

Mamó quickly assessed the situation.

"Shamus and I will get him cleaned up. You need to go sleep," she informed me.

"I can't sleep now. I'm the only one here with the gift of healing. I—"

"You must sleep. You need to keep rebuilding your strength, or we will lose him for sure."

Her blunt words shocked me. I nodded and turned to do as she ordered. I stopped at the door.

"You need to get him to take the tonic. He needs to drink as much as possible."

"Yes, *a leanbh*, I know this. Go."

I nodded, but I hesitated again as I looked at his expressionless face. I longed for him to turn to smile at me. I rushed back into the room and kissed his hot forehead.

"I will take good care of him, *a leanbh*. Now go take care of yourself."

This time I did as she told me.

. . .

WHEN I WOKE several hours later, Rosheen was taking a turn nursing Alexander. She hummed as she tried to get him to drink. Someone had added a plastic straw to the cup of tonic. She held the straw to his mouth.

Relief crossed her face when she saw me.

"Mamó asked me to come sit with him a while," she whispered. "Music seems to calm him, but he's not sipping the tonic anymore."

I touched his face. He didn't open his eyes or respond. The fever still had hold of him. The small beads of sweat that covered his forehead were clear, at least, which was an improvement.

Something was off, however. He still wore the clothes Shamus had put on him earlier, and they were still dry. With that high of a fever, he should have sweated through them again.

I pushed back his hair and he rolled his head sideways. I noticed what looked like a bruise at the base of his neck and pulled his collar away to see more clearly. A web of purple lines had crawled up his shoulders and was curling along his collarbones.

I took my hand away from him, trying to hide from Rosheen the fact that it was shaking.

"I'll make some fresh tonic for him. Will you stay until I get back?" I took a deep breath, grateful I had gotten the question out without my voice cracking.

She nodded, folding her arms across her stomach. I returned with two tonics, one for him to drink, one to swab his skin. Both were chilled with plenty of ice.

"Thank you, Rosheen. You've been so much help." I hugged her, holding on to her and taking extra comfort from the hug. The gesture must have worried her; she hesitated to leave.

"It's okay, Roe, I'll be fine. You can go."

"That doesn't sound like a lie, but it doesn't sound like the truth either," she said, biting her lip.

"It's the best you're going to get right now."

She nodded, gave me a second quick hug, and left.

I took a clean washcloth and soaked it with the drink I had made for him. Then I used it to wet his lips and squeeze fluid in to his mouth.

I wet the sponge with the second mixture and swabbed his face, neck, hands and feet. I infused each stroke of his skin with my energy, willing it to heal his body. Then I went back to squeezing tonic into his mouth.

Instead of singing the same invocation, I sang hymns as I worked. As I sang, prayed, and ministered, I found myself in an almost trance-like state. Perhaps I had managed to hypnotize myself.

His energy pulled away from mine. I don't know if I had realized before then how tightly our energies were entwined, or how conscious I was of his presence, until I felt it falling away from me.

I reached out to him with my internal self. I lay across him, putting one arm around his neck and the other arm around his body, as if pressing physically closer to him would make us spiritually closer. I lay my ear to his chest, listening to his slowed heartbeat as I reached out farther and farther, desperate to feel his presence next to mine.

I was drifting, searching, singing to the metronome of his heart and moving further and further away from myself when a hand grabbed my arm and ripped me from him—ripped me completely off the bed.

Stunned out of my stupor, I scrambled to keep my footing. My legs bowed, but Shamus caught me before I fell and guided me to the chair next to the bed.

Mamó grabbed my chin and then raised it so she could study my face, her own face ashen with fear.

"You could have killed yourself, lass," she admonished.

My separation from Alexander created a grief so deep I barely heard her. Nevertheless, her words pushed through the fog in my head and added guilt to the debilitating grief. I had sworn to him I wouldn't go too far. If not for my grandmother's and Shamus's fortuitous arrival, I would have broken that oath.

Alexander groaned and then rolled onto his side. I started to go to him, but Shamus held me in the chair by gripping my shoulder.

Mamó went to him instead. She touched his skin and then offered him the glass of tonic. He took two strong swallows and even tried to hold the glass while he drank, though Mamó never let go of it.

"It seems you have revived him a bit, *a leanbh*, but at what cost?" she chided me.

"Do you think he's coming out of it?" I asked. His movements had brought me a small measure of hope.

"His aura remains, but the color has paled. He isn't fully here. He isn't fully gone."

I pursed my lips to contain my annoyance. I felt like she was purposefully being abstruse, though a part of me knew I was being illogical.

"You should go eat something. We'll stay with him a while," she said.

I acquiesced, knowing she would allow nothing else. I went to the kitchen, wondering what I could piece together from the few groceries in the house.

As it turned out, I didn't need to worry about that. A tray of food lay on the kitchen table. Jenny must have sent it down with Shamus. The savory aroma of chicken soup with egg noodles and freshly made biscuits filled the air, making me aware for the first time that I was ravenous.

I ate everything. Jenny had obviously sent enough food for both Alexander and me. Chicken soup, as I understood it, was a medicinal meal served to ailing people. I ate it all myself. When I had finished, I felt considerably fortified with renewed energy.

There was a paper folded in half on the tray. I opened it to find a note hastily written in Matt's sprawling script: When can I see him?

I didn't at once recall how much time had passed since this nightmare began. Working forward from the morning we found the hiker, I thought back to when Alexander had fallen ill, how many tonics I had prepared, and the times I had slept. I calculated that two and a half days had passed.

Perhaps I was being too cautious, but I decided three days would be best. I picked up my phone, which I had abandoned on the kitchen counter several days earlier. Matt had called and texted several times. I responded to his most recent text: twelve more hours.

ALEXANDER'S CONDITION stayed much the same overnight. Mamó would no longer allow me to be alone with him. Rosheen and Keelin took turns staying with me when Mamó took respite from her post.

Shamus stayed the entire time. Mamó wanted him available to pull me away from Alexander if need be. However, this was an unnecessary precaution. I carefully checked myself; as much as I disliked it, I had given Alexander my word. I would not break my promise.

I monitored the progression of the purple webbing while I continued with my routine. I made him drink and swabbed him with tonic, slowly inserting bits of energy into each stroke and taking frequent breaks for food and naps.

Mamó sat vigil with me again the following morning. The fever still hadn't broken.

"How much more of this can his body take?" I asked her, my voice shaking.

"He's a strong man, lass. His aura is still holding."

"Tressa, can I come up?" Matt's warm familiar voice called from downstairs.

"Yes, Matt, please do," I called back to him.

I heard him sprint up the stairs. He came into the room carrying an IV pole and two bags of saline. I berated myself for not thinking of this human therapy myself. Perhaps I had done Alexander a disservice by relying only on my healing powers.

"I learned how to do this in the service," Matt said. He hung the bag from the pole and then got ready to insert an IV needle. "I spent some time assisting the medics in the field."

"Mattie, do you plan to stay awhile?" Mamó asked.

"Yes, if it's okay with you guys."

I thought it would be good for Alexander to have Matt around, and I told him as much while I watched how he went about starting the IV.

Once the saline began to hydrate him, Alexander's skin color improved. The purple around his neck quickly faded. I let myself be hopeful. Perhaps this was the boost needed to bring him through this. The hex couldn't last for much longer.

"If Matt's staying, Shamus, I need you to deliver a message to my son," Mamó said.

The unusualness of Mamó's remark took my attention away from my patient. "You're sending Shamus to Uncle Lomán? Why not send a Pixie?"

I couldn't remember a single instance when she had used

Shamus to do a simple message delivery. Shamus himself looked startled by the suggestion.

"This is too important. Shamus, I can't trust anyone but you." The wiry-haired man nodded. "I will take my leave from you as well," she said to me. "I need to have a conversation with Gilleagán. It cannot wait any longer."

"Of course, Mamó. Thank you for your help. Matt will take over." Matt nodded his agreement.

My grandmother went over to Alexander before she left. She leaned over and whispered into his ear, "Remember all I have told you of the treasure." She turned to go.

"You know I believe his color is coming back," she remarked, pausing before she slipped out the door.

When we were alone, Matt looked me over critically. "Tressa, you don't look good. Most of your sparkle is gone."

A laugh rose in my throat spontaneously. I knew he was being literal, but it was ironic how perfectly his words described how I felt inside.

"Yes indeed, I have lost my sparkle."

He looked at me with concern, "You should get some fresh air. You've been inside the house for too long. It's a beautiful day."

The suggestion sounded appealing. The breeze on my face and the smell of the forest would truly refresh my spirits. Maybe I could take a short swim in the lake. Mamó had said his color was returning, and I was sure she was referring to his aura, not his skin.

"I'm supposed to be eating and resting now," I said, hesitating.

"I brought sandwiches; they're down in the kitchen. Why not take one down to your spot by the lake?"

I touched Alexander's forehead. His skin was cooler. The purple webbing had receded to where I saw none on the front of his neck or shoulders. Alexander stirred when I pulled at his shirt to see the webbing on the back of his neck. He mumbled something I didn't quite catch. I leaned closer to him.

"Say that again," I said.

"Go. Go to the lake, see Brenna."

"You want me to go?" I said, hurt that he would dismiss me.

"I'll be here when you get back." His voice drifted off.

"He's concerned about you," Matt said. "I am too. You need to get out of here for a little while."

Alexander's slight nod at Matt's words decided it for me. I would do as they asked. "If I'm not back in an hour, will you come wake me up?"

"Sure."

"Don't forget."

"I won't." He crossed his heart with his finger, a gesture stolen from Sophia.

ONE STEP outside into the fresh air made me realize how stifling the air in the house had become. The pleasant weather boosted my belief that all would be fine.

I took several deep breaths as I walked, sandwich in hand, toward the lake. The Northern Catalpa trees were in bloom. The fragrance from their white flowers dominated the scents coming from the forest's edge.

The screech of an owl shattered the fragile peace surrounding me. I recognized the voice of this particular owl. The sandwich slipped out of my hand, forgotten as I ran the rest of the distance to the lake.

I thought my heart would stop when I saw her. She sat on the ground by the Pixies' tree trunk. She appeared as a young, beautiful woman today, though that wasn't always the case.

Dressed all in white, her pale yellow hair hung straight and long pulled over her shoulder. The Pixies, subdued for once, sat all in a row on a branch near her head.

She reached her arms out and I fell into the Banshee's embrace, tears streaming uncensored.

"Bridget, don't take him. Please, don't take him," I begged, though I knew it was futile. Banshees weren't reapers of souls, although it often appeared that way. They tended to only turn up just before someone passes, in order to help their family mourn their lost loved one.

She stroked my hair.

"Tressa, darling, you know I don't take them. I don't even know for whom I am here. You know this."

She must be here to mourn Alexander with me. Who else could it be? He had been at death's door for the last three days.

I jerked up, realizing I was wasting valuable time. Why had I come out here? I should be with him. What if he passed away and I wasn't there?

I ran three steps and flitted to the farmhouse door.

CHAPTER TWENTY-TWO

efore I could go in, I heard shouts from the Manor House. Keelin and Rosheen screamed my name as they ran toward me. I was momentarily torn, but I couldn't ignore the girls' cries for help. I wiped my tears away with the back of my hand.

They reached me before I had even taken a step in their direction. Something black was covering their face and clothes. I touched Rosheen, and the blackness came off onto my fingertips. In one horrified second, I realized the substance was soot. There was a sharp odor of smoke in the air.

"Tressa, come quick," Rosheen cried.

I wanted to go with her, but I couldn't make myself move toward what was obviously a fire.

"We can't find Mamó," Keelin wailed.

I looked at her, wanting to believe it was a hoax, a silly drama my cousins were playing. The truth was evident in Keelin's wild eyes.

A panic hit me more violently than my fear of the fire. I ran back with them. We didn't go far before I saw the flames shooting out of the Manor house's second story windows.

How could the fire have spread so fast?

Connor and Jenny came around the corner of the building, supporting Holly between them. At the same time, Connor used his cell phone to report the fire to the emergency services.

They helped Holly to the ground under a tree a safe distance from the burning building. I guided the twins over to them and encouraged them to sit with Holly.

"Where's Mamó?" I shouted at the newcomers. They all denied seeing her. Mentally taking a head count, I shouted to Connor, "What about Gil?"

He shook his head, and we all looked around us. Gilleagán emerged from the corner of the house, following the same path the others had just come. I ran towards him, but I stumbled and tripped. He reached for me, but I fell to the ground. I hastened to my feet and grabbed his arm.

"Mamó? Have you seen her?" I shouted.

"No," he said as he turned and watched the house burn. I shook his arm.

"She said she was going to talk to you. Didn't you see her?"

A piece of the roof crashed in, flames leaping up through the hole. The glass on the window closest to us burst out and I screamed, imagining the flames coming at me.

"Shamus told me she wanted me in her bedroom suite. On my way there I heard people yelling."

I didn't understand how he could be so calm when I was nearly hysterical. Someone said something behind me, but I wasn't listening.

"You mean she's still in there?" I screeched, staring horrified at the burning house. I took a few steps toward it, but when I felt the heat of the fire I froze. "Where's Shamus?" I looked frantically for him. The fire wouldn't hurt a Brounie.

"He flitted somewhere after he spoke to me," Gilleagán said.

Mamó had sent him to the Otherworld. He couldn't help her.

The heat from the crackling fire wafted over me. I took a jagged breath as I fought the nearly overwhelming urge to run away. However, my desire to save my grandmother gave me unknown strength. I took a step toward the burning building. Then another.

Someone behind me pulled me back. I turned to see it was Bridget. Her sympathy-filled cry told me it was too late. She had come to mourn my grandmother.

"No, no, no!" I yelled at her. I had to get Mamó out. No one else moved to help her, so I had to do it myself. Blinded by tears and rage, I ignored the suffocating fear and ran toward the house. I tripped over a root and fell again. I sat on my knees and screamed in anguish as the rest of the roof collapsed.

Then Alexander was there, kneeling next to me. He wrapped me in his arms and pulled me to him. I leaned on him and sobbed; deep, painful sobs. He made soothing noises as he rocked me like a child. I heard the women around me crying as well.

When the keening started and Bridget began her awful wail, I knew Mamó was gone. I grabbed onto Alexander's shirt and buried my face in his chest.

Suddenly, a pain shot through me like a strong electrical shock. I stiffened and let out a gasp.

"Tressa, what's wrong?" Alexander asked.

I wasn't able to answer him. My mind felt scrambled, as if electrical pulses were bouncing around inside of me. Finally, the sensation stopped, leaving me with a mammoth headache. I closed my eyes to block out the pain.

When I opened them again, nothing looked the same. The color of the flames was more intense. The fire seemed to be alive. Huge thick clouds of unfamiliar colors surrounded me. No two clouds were the same color. They too moved as if they were alive.

Gradually, I understood. My grandmother had bestowed her gift of Aura Sight on me. I was seeing the auras of the surrounding people. Aura Sight evidently affected the way everything looked, not just people.

I remembered that Mamó said she had been overwhelmed by the auras at first, but she learned to control how much they dominated her vision.

I stared at someone who stood away from the rest. The color of the aura was a mixture of earth tones: greens, browns, and creams. Whoever the person was, they stood perfectly still, which is why I tried gaining control of my sight with them. However, after a minute of staring I still couldn't break through to see the person beneath.

There was a group gathered close together under a tree. Their auras, though they touched, were quite distinct and separate from one another. I tried to remember what Mamó had said at that tea that seemed so long ago; something about auras having varying degrees of light and dark.

With that knowledge, I found it easy to separate the clouds between human and Sidhe. The Sidhe auras were markedly lighter than the human auras, although each individual had a different color and pattern indistinguishable by race.

Alexander still held me. I looked at his aura and at mine. His was much lighter than the other humans, so the contrast in shade between his and mine was less noticeable. Perhaps this was because he was part fae. I couldn't be sure.

Regardless, our auras weren't as distinct from one another as the others' were. They reacted and fed off each other: the edges swirled and wove together wherever they touched in a constant movement, as though caressing each other. The effect was that of making the two auras into one large patchwork aura.

I knew instinctively that this was the reason Mamó was adamant that Alexander was my *Anam Cara*. This was why our energies were so in tune. The sight of our interlocked auras gave me an odd sense of comfort.

I reached out blindly to touch him. My hand landed on his chest. I ran my hand up his neck, to his face. When I touched him, his physical being started to emerge until finally, every detail of him down to the smallest scar on his cheek was visible.

He looked the same, yet more intense. His dark eyes were a richer chocolate and more penetrating when he looked at me, which I never would have considered possible. More importantly, he looked wonderfully alive.

"Tressa, talk to me."

"You're okay." My voice was barely a whisper. "The hex has passed."

"Yes. I'm still weak, but better."

He helped me to my feet and then pulled me close again, allowing me to lean on him. The sounds of sirens wailing in the distance were coming ever closer.

"Mamó," I sobbed.

"She's gone, my love, I'm so sorry."

I nodded, unable to speak.

The firefighters arrived and worked to put the fire out. They looked like scurrying splotches of color and patterns. I turned away, not wanting to watch them, and looked to my right for the first time.

A mere three feet away stood a menacing, dark, soot and smoke colored aura. Instinctively, I stumbled backwards to get away from it. I tripped over Alexander in the process and nearly knocked us to the ground again, but Alexander kept both of us on our feet.

I sensed that the person with the dark aura had turned to look at me. He took a step toward me, and I stepped back.

"Xander, who is that?" I asked.

Alexander furrowed his brow, confused by my question.

"Who, Gil? There's no one there but Gil."

Horror ran through me. *This* was my brother? Now that I knew it was Gilleagán, his image came through the horrible darkness.

"Gil," I cried out to him as the truth seeped into my consciousness. "What have you done?"

He stared at me blankly for a moment before understanding filled his eyes. He hooted with an ugly laughter.

"Oh my god, she bestowed it on you! Of course she did. Give Little Miss Special something else for people to go gaga over." The maniacal voice spouting these words didn't sound at all like my brother. "How stupid I've been, to think she would pick me just because I'm the obvious better choice. She always intended to give it to you. I should have known she would favor you to the end—just like everyone else."

Alexander's body stiffened, alert against a possible threat. The others gathered behind us, sensing something was wrong.

I could hardly bring myself to voice the question his illogical tantrum brought to mind, but I had to know. When I asked, my voice came out dry, gruff, and raw with anger.

"Gil, did you do this?" I gestured toward the burning Manor House. I began to put things together. No Unseelie had crossed into the Human World. There has been no noise on the wind relating to the Unseelie, not even in connection to the Fae Fever. Another fae had been holding *Dominion* over Fred when he tried to kidnap me. The forest had told Keelin there was Unseelie magic, but no Unseelie. It was Gilleagán in the woods before the attack.

Alexander never left the estate the afternoon he got sick. No Unseelie could have gotten on the estate to cast the flu on him or to start this fire. No human, either, for that matter.

I remembered Mamó's last words to me: that she needed to talk to Gilleagán about something. The way that she had said it... Anger exploded through me and I screamed at Gilleagán.

"Did you KILL our grandmother?"

"Don't be ridiculous. How could you say such a thing?" He looked defensive and offended at the suggestion, and I began to have hope I was wrong, that I had made a huge mistake.

"He's lying! I've been trying to tell you," Rosheen said through shallow, quick breaths. She grabbed my arm, and I recognized her through her aura. "He was lying when he said he didn't see Mamó, and he's lying again now."

Gilleagán backed away from us.

"I had to do it. My aura had changed; she knew I had switched sides." Everyone gasped at his admission. He looked at me as though I would understand his logic.

"Nobody appreciated me like I deserved. Nobody recognized how special I am, because they were always so busy fawning over you. Deaglan is different. He values me."

There was a general uproar from the Sidhe behind me when Gilleagán spoke the name of the rebel prince.

"I guess none of you can understand. You've lived charmed lives," he said. He looked at us with disdain, took two steps, and flitted away.

Everyone spoke at the same time. Their voices buzzed around me, adding to my confusion. I forced myself to slow my breathing and concentrate. I singled out each person's voice to determine who was who. One by one, I put voices together with auras. With each one, it became easier to force my vision past their aura to see a new and more complete likeness of them.

Everyone quieted when a firefighter approached us. He was a stranger, and I found it was easier to see him through his aura than it had been with the people I knew.

"Are any of you the owner of this house?" he asked.

The twins and I exchanged a questioning glance. Since I lived on the estate and they looked like lost Pixies, I took the lead.

"Me," I said, waving my hand.

"I'm sorry, but the house is a total loss. It went up fast. Thank god everyone got out in time."

I nodded.

"Yes, sir. It was a blessing," I said, fighting not to choke on my words.

"We'll stay until we're sure the fire is out, but don't let anyone near it until you can get what's left demolished. It will be a real hazard till then."

"I'll make sure no one goes near it," I said, parroting his words. "Thank you for coming so quickly."

"Do you have somewhere to go?" he asked kindly, looking over the entire group. When everyone nodded, he took his leave.

The person with the earthy brown and green aura walked toward me. By the time she had reached our group, I realized it was Jenny.

"I'm so sorry. Thank goodness Órlaith was away; I thought for a minute she was still inside," she said as she hugged each of us.

We accepted her condolences. I told her I would keep her updated, and she left.

"Let's go to the guesthouse where we can talk," Alexander suggested.

Matt went to help Holly. I could hear her assuring him she was okay. Connor walked with a comforting arm around each of the twins.

Bridget declined to go to the guesthouse, as I expected. Instead, she went back to the lake and the Pixies. She would tell them what had happened and continue her keening.

Alexander and I took up the rear, shepherding the group down the stone path to the guesthouse.

"Why didn't the firemen find her?" Alexander whispered.

"When a fae dies, their body goes back to their ancestral home in Faery. She wasn't there," I whispered back.

Everyone gathered in the living room. Matt helped Holly onto the sofa and sat beside her, putting her legs over his lap. Rosheen and Keelin, who had washed the soot off their faces, sat on the floor in front of her. Alexander insisted that I sit in a comfortable chair while he sat on its arm.

Connor, looking uncomfortable, stood leaning on the door-frame. When everyone quieted, he moved forward to speak.

"Tressa, I had no idea about any of this. I need you to know that. I knew Gil hadn't been himself lately, but never did I imagine what he was doing."

"Truth," Rosheen said, continuing to gaze sadly at the floor. Even before she spoke, I knew from his aura that he hadn't fallen in with Gilleagán.

"Don't worry," I assured him. "We know you're telling the truth."

Reassured that we were on good standing on a personal level, Connor's demeanor took on a formal bearing.

"In light of today's tragic events, you and your family have much to do before the Sendoff. With your permission, Highness, I will return to the palace at *Tír na nÓg* and update the King on what has happened here. He will want an explanation when the Queen Mother's body appears. I can also help them capture Gil and bring him in for trial."

"You have my permission to do as you suggest, My Lord. May the Lord God carry you on a swift wind until you complete your purpose." I honored his plan with a formal acknowl-edgement.

He bowed, nodded to the rest of the room, and departed. I

looked at those who remained. The twins looked back at me with lost expressions.

"We need to get ready for a trip back to the Otherworld." They nodded. I thought quickly, deciding what preparations should take place. The need to take charge acted as a temporary buffer from my grief.

"Keelin and Rosheen, search the Manor House for anything important you can rescue," I began. "Store what you find at the farmhouse for now. Make sure nothing is there that shouldn't be found, and be sure the firefighters are gone before you begin."

"The Pixies will return with us for the ceremony, and we should take back some of Mamó's favorite flowers from her garden for her Sendoff."

"Oh yes," Rosheen agreed. "She would like that."

"Tressa, what can we do?" Holly asked, referring to herself and Matt.

"Holly, if the doctor releases you from bedrest, open up the store for me. In the meantime, please stay at the farmhouse so that it won't be empty."

Time in the Otherworld and the Human World didn't necessarily run concurrently. Short trips to Faery often lasted a longer time from the perspective of those here. I would find comfort in knowing that the life I had built here wouldn't fall apart while I was gone.

"Matt, would you help the twins search the Manor House? And it would be helpful if you could see to the demolition of it while we're away. You should move into the Guesthouse while we're gone."

Matt agreed and left with the twins, each appearing satisfied with their instructions. I gave Holly a sleeping elixir to help her nap after the stress of the day and asked Alexander to carry her to one of the unused bedrooms upstairs.

When he returned, I stood near a window in the dining room

looking toward the lake. I closed my eyes to isolate the sound of Bridget's grief-filled wail. The Banshee would help our family mourn, as she had for my entire life. Oddly, the horrible screeching sound brought a measure of comfort, though I had never understood why.

Alexander hugged me from behind and I shifted my weight to lean back against him. His warmth thawed the chill that had been building inside me. He lowered his forehead to rest it on the crook of my neck, and I felt that I, too, was bringing him relief.

"Did you see Gilleagán when you went out to the herb garden for Mamó?"

"Yes," he said into my hair. I nodded.

"Gilleagán cast the Fae Fever on you. He wanted to kill you." Alexander kissed my neck and lifted his head, nestling it against mine.

"I don't remember much. I heard you singing, and I tried to get to your voice. You were so far away from me."

So he had felt the separation of our energies as well.

"What happened to you earlier? It seemed like something hit you," he said.

"Mamó bestowed her gift of Aura Sight on me. It felt like a jolt of electricity had hit me. It was painful, at first. I couldn't see anything other than the auras until I grew accustomed to it."

"Really?" he sounded intrigued. "What does my aura look like?"

I laughed, surprising myself.

"The perfect match to mine. Our auras dance and play together whenever we are close, and they reach out to each other when we aren't."

He smiled.

"That's what it feels like, too."

"Your aura isn't like other humans," I said as I turned around to face him.

"What?"

"It's hard to describe. Auras have colors, but also shades of light and dark. Humans range in the middle of the spectrum. Seelie are noticeably lighter, and Unseelie are much closer to black." I shuddered, remembering how dark Gilleagán's had become. "Yours is much closer to ours than the other humans I've seen."

"Because I'm half Sidhe?"

I shrugged.

"I'm not sure, but that seems logical."

"I wonder what Sophia's will look like," he mused.

WE MADE DINNER. I had never eaten my lunch, and Alexander hadn't eaten in days. We ate sandwiches while discussing our plans for the funeral. I wanted him to come meet my uncle. We decided to get Sophia in the morning and take her with us.

"Xander! Tressa!" Matt shouted. The door slammed behind him as he ran into the house. He held his cell phone in his hand. "He's taken Sophia."

"Who's taken her?" Alexander demanded, tension coiling through him. When Matt hesitated, he shouted, "Who?"

"Gilleagán took her. He snatched her from Kendra's back yard."

Alexander turned to me. I flinched away from the anger that radiated from him.

"You said she was safe."

"I did. She is. She should be," I sputtered. It was unimaginable that any Sidhe would hurt a child. It was a sin even the blackest soul wouldn't dare commit. "Sidhe treasure children above all else. He will lose favor even with Deaglan Mór if he hurts her."

"Then why?"

I searched my mind for any plausible reason. Gilleagán's actions were already beyond anything I could have imagined.

"Centuries ago, the fae would take children. If they found a special child, or a particularly beautiful one, they would take them back to Faery, especially if they didn't have children of their own. That's where the stories of Changelings came from. But it hasn't happened in hundreds of years," I said.

"How will he cross realms?" Alexander drilled the question at me.

"I don't know. There are guards at every entrance, but they aren't likely to stop him." I was thinking aloud now. "He won't be able to flit with her, so whichever threshold he uses, it will take him a while to get there. The closest is Niagara Falls."

Alexander paced back and forth. I wasn't sure he was listening, but Matt was.

"We should send word that he has her so the guards are on the lookout. What's the fastest way to do that?" Matt said.

Alexander didn't look at me. The edges of his aura were sharp and jagged.

"The Pixies. They don't need a threshold," I said.

"I found a cave." Alexander finally spoke.

"What?"

"A cave. I found a cave. I was taking you to it the other day. It seems to go very deep. I hadn't gotten to the end of it yet, but the entire thing is veined with River Rock."

"That's why there was River Rock in places it shouldn't be!" I reasoned aloud. "It must be a threshold. That's why my grandfather was so secretive about it. That's why it was so important for you to find it. My god, there's a threshold to Faery right here!"

"There's something else," Alexander said. He hesitated, glancing at Matt. "I'll tell you on the way."

"Matt, go explain to Brenna what has happened. Ask her to find Shamus and tell him. He'll be wherever they laid out Mamó's body. Tell her I'll be there soon, so she needn't come back here until she sees me again." My mind raced, trying to remember any lost detail. "Oh, and tell Rosheen and Keelin to finish here and return as planned to the palace."

CHAPTER TWENTY-THREE

e made hasty preparations. I ran to my house and grabbed a velvet bag of cut stones that I kept with a small collection of jewelry supplies. They might be helpful, either for their monetary value or their healing properties. I also picked up a small dagger from my dresser drawer, spelling it to stay hidden in my jeans pocket.

Alexander met me in the driveway between the houses, a backpack slung over his shoulder. We headed toward the woods. He walked so quickly that I struggled to keep up; I lagged a few steps behind him.

We walked straight across the estate, cutting across the circuitous walkways and garden paths, toward the far northern corner and entering the woods at its thickest spot. We hadn't gone this way on the morning we had found the hiker.

Through the rougher terrain of the forest, Alexander slowed down and took my hand to assist me. I struggled more than I had the last time. My store of energy, my essence, was nearly vanquished. Alexander was silent as we walked, and I was afraid to break that silence.

I thought about Gilleagán and what possible reason he had

for taking Sophia. Was it to hurt me? Maybe he did see her as a pretty trinket, just as with the fae of old. I had never known a Seelie who had fallen. Could that be a factor? I decided it would be best not to consider what he might be planning.

Finally, Alexander stopped. He moved away some fallen branches and debris from the side of a boulder. He uncovered a gap between the boulder and the rocky mountainside behind it.

"I found this second entrance after exploring the cave. It's much closer to Pine Ridge. The other entrance wasn't on the estate itself."

He pulled a flashlight out of the backpack. "We'll only need this for a few hundred yards."

I nodded. Every threshold was the same in that once we were close enough to the Otherworld, tóirse stone along the interior would glow and illuminate the way.

The cave was narrow, but the ceiling was high. The ground was surprisingly even, considering it was uncultivated. Alexander stayed close to me as we made our way through the cave.

"We need to talk about something before we go much further," he said.

I nodded, thinking this was the point where he told me that after we had rescued Sophia, he never wanted to see me again.

"I know these people have hunted you for your entire life, and I'm sick at the idea of putting you in any more danger, but I'm going to need your help if I'm to have any hope of saving Sophia."

I looked at him, incredulous.

"You're not angry at me? You don't hate me?"

He looked mystified. "Why would you think that? I'm yours, you're mine, and nothing is going to change that. Ever."

"But this is all my fault."

He took my hand.

"No, it's Gilleagán's fault. He did this." He hesitated, as if something had just occurred to him. "Unless... is it possible that this Mór guy could have been controlling him?"

"You mean holding *Dominion* over him?"

Alexander nodded.

"No. Well, it's not likely. He would have to know Gilleagán's true name, and with a Sidhe, that's nearly impossible. We hardly even know our own true names. Our mothers whisper it to us as infants so that only our subconscious knows what it is; then they take it with them to their graves."

Alexander nodded as he took in this information. Then he stopped walking and pulled me by my hand, turning me to face him. He met my gaze and took my other hand. He spoke in a steely, serious tone.

"Tressa, I'm asking you to help me, but there's something you need to understand. When I find Gilleagán, I'm going to kill him."

I sucked in a shocked breath. Then I fought the numbness of guilt and grief that blanketed my brain, forcing myself to consider this journey's logical conclusion. The man I loved would kill my brother—or be killed by him.

We kept moving, even as I struggled to work my mind around this revelation. Since I didn't respond to Alexander's declaration, he continued making his argument.

"You think of Gil as your brother, the boy you grew up with and loved. But that's not him anymore. He killed your grandmother. He tried to abduct you and have you burned alive. He's taken my baby girl. You told me yourself that his soul is black."

"Have you had a premonition of this?" I asked, grasping for reassurance.

"No. I'm simply telling you: it is too dangerous to let him live, so I don't plan to."

"Can you promise me that you won't get killed in the attempt?"

He flinched and turned away. I knew he couldn't make that promise, no matter how much I begged.

Deaglan Mór would hunt me for as long as either he or I lived. If Gilleagán was helping him—with everything Gil knew about me—it would be far easier for the Unseelie prince to hurt me. It was hard to admit that I would be better off with my brother dead, but it was even harder to deny.

We had just reached the point where the flashlight was unnecessary when Alexander asked me to sit on a flat rock that lay near the wall of the cave. He knelt in front of me, so that we were level with each other.

He reached into his backpack. "Órlaith told me I should show this to no one but you or her, and that I'm meant to have it and nobody else. Does that make sense to you?"

He pulled a worn leather bundle out of his backpack. He unfolded leather straps to reveal a scabbard. A polished silver hilt, fashioned into a Celtic knot that I knew well, showed above the scabbard. The knot mirrored the one formed by the scar on Alexander's hand.

He drew out the sword, holding it carefully in front of him. Runes etched into the sides of the blade added strength to the weapon.

"My god," I gasped. "It's the *Claíomh Solais*."

"Yes, that's what Órlaith called it. Nuada's Sword of Light."

I dared not touch it, but I stared at it in awe. My entire life I had heard lectures about the treasures of my people. I realized then that I had never truly believed I would see any of them. I had never had faith that I was the King's Jewel of the prophecy.

"Do you understand what this is? I mean, the significance of it?" I asked.

"It's one of the treasures from the prophecy, isn't it?"

"Aye, that's right. Did Mamó actually see it?"

"No, I just described it to her."

His aura lapped around the sword, making it one with his hand. Mamó had not seen the communion of his aura with the sword, and yet she had faith. She believed Alexander was meant to bear the sword.

"Many will try to take this from you. It sings to the heart of every warrior. You will need to be careful around friend and foe alike," I warned him.

The straps of leather attached to the scabbard were a harness. Alexander slipped his arms through the straps. The sword hung between his shoulder blades, much like the backpack had done. He only needed to reach behind his head to grab the hilt and draw the sword.

He put the flashlight back into the backpack and hid the bag behind the rock where I sat.

We strode deeper into the cave.

"What can we expect when we get to the end of this?" Alexander asked.

"There are usually guards at thresholds monitoring who goes in or out. However, this is an unknown threshold, so I'm not sure what to expect. When we enter the Otherworld I can call on the wind for Henry, my bodyguard. He'll be able to come find us," I said.

There isn't a line where the Human World ends and the Otherworld begins; it's a gradual change. A fey sensation that I associated with Faery filled the air and got stronger the further we walked through the tunnel. The closer we got to the Otherworld, the more my essence returned to me, building my strength.

We pushed our way through a tangle of thin branches that covered the mouth of the cave and came out in a wide creek bed edged by dense woodland area. A grassland bordered the far side.

Water was common at the portals between realms, but this creek was frozen. In fact, everything around us glistened with snow and ice.

I should have known and prepared better. All of *Tír na nÓg* was in mourning over the death of our Queen Mother. The wintery scene overlaying the summer landscape was an expression of that grief.

"Henry, I'm here," I called to my bodyguard, pushing his name into the wind. "I need you."

Alexander turned, looking around him. He reached out and touched the flakes of snow on a frozen green leaf. "This might be a problem. We could get frostbite or suffer from exposure before we get to Sophia," he said.

I caught the smell of a stinkweed pipe. Looking closely, I saw a thin cloud of smoke rising from behind one of the thick tree trunks to the west of the cave opening.

"I think we'll be able to find what we need here."

"Here?" Alexander asked incredulously.

"Tradesman, show yourself," I called out. A face peer out from behind the tree and then retreat.

"Tradesman, you know who I am. I command that you show yourself."

The face peered out again grumbling under his breath. A small fae, not more than three feet tall, with gray scruffy hair and a pipe in his mouth staggered over to me. He wore a moss green suit and matching cap. He looked up at me with a surly expression. Reluctantly, he took his cap off and bowed.

"Aye, My Lady. How can I be of service?" he asked sourly.

"We are in need of suitably warm coats."

"And what is that to me?"

"Are you not a tradesman?"

"Cobbler is my trade, madam."

"Are you telling me that a Leprechaun of your great age and stature hasn't bartered his shoes for a wealth of other things?"

"Whatever I have, 'tis mine. What right do you have to it?"

"I look to buy something from you, that is all."

It took a bit more posturing, persuasion, and outright bribery before I could get a long, fur-lined trench coat for Alexander and a warm, ankle length cape for myself.

As we pulled on the outerwear, Henry landed on the frozen creek bed behind us with a thud that cracked the ice. The Leprechaun backed away, bowing, and then scurried off to his hollow trunk.

I ran to Henry, who had been not only my bodyguard, but also a friend of mine since childhood. I hugged him around his long scaly neck. His reddish brown and mustard skin looked like the scales of a lizard, though they were soft and warm to the touch.

He breathed through his nose, as he always did when I was around. Always acutely aware of my pyrophobia, he carefully avoided breathing through his mouth. Not that he would ever hurt me, but the occasional puff of smoke still made me nervous.

"Tressa?" Alexander sounded uncomfortable.

"Alexander, this is Henry."

ALEXANDER

THE OTHERWORLD SURPRISED ME, although I'm not sure what I had expected. In many ways, it could have been any unfamiliar place on earth, albeit a cold and wintery place.

The trees, though not exactly like the ones at home, were easily recognizable as trees. Most were a good thirty feet tall. Their trunks were bare of branches until two-thirds of the way up. The tops, clustered together, resembled a canopy of evergreens. A few of the trees, like the one where the snarly Leprechaun seemed to live were shorter and had twisted massive trunks.

On the opposite side of the frozen stream was a meadow with curly grass and a spattering of large yellow flowers frozen in full bloom.

Yet despite the familiarity, there was also an odd sense of otherness. The sky, pale lavender, gave the snow and ice surrounding us an unusual aspect. The air felt lighter, less dense. Breathing was easier. I moved faster.

A shadow fell over the sky as I shrugged into the coat Tressa had secured. The air whooshed around us. I looked up and saw a massive, scaly underbelly. I glanced at Tressa, but she and the Leprechaun were still bantering and she didn't seem to notice the beast.

The creature dropped down behind us with a thump. His weight broke the surrounding ice.

The Leprechaun ran away, disappearing into the dense forest. I crouched and reached for the sword. Before I drew it out, Tressa ran toward the beast. He lowered his head for her to hug it around its neck.

I released my grip on the sword hilt but remained crouched; stunned into motionlessness as I assessed the animal in front of me. He stood about seven feet tall, though from head to tail he measured about three times that. His wingspan was even longer. His huge claws and teeth proclaimed him as a formidable adversary—or ally—in a fight.

I finally stood and gawked as she caressed the beast. Apparently, the huge animal was an ally then. "Tressa?"

"Alexander, meet Henry."

The dragon is her bodyguard. I let that sink in, readjusting the image I'd had in my mind of a burly warrior.

"His name is Henry?" I asked, incredulous. The name didn't suit the creature.

"Well his real name is unpronounceable, so we just call him Henry."

"He's a dragon, right?"

"Aye, of course. What else would he be?"

"Don't dragons breathe fire?" I asked, astonished by her lack of fear with the enormous animal. She cooed and petted it as if it were a dog or a horse, yet it was big enough to swallow us whole.

"Henry has been my bodyguard since... well, since I was born. He's very careful about his fire breathing when he's around me." She rubbed the dragon's scaly neck. "Aren't you, boy?"

She looked at the dragon as if she were listening to it. "This is Xander. We're Handfast."

The dragon stretched his long neck toward me and sniffed then he turned his big head back to look at Tressa.

"Aye, Henry, that's right. He's human."

"You can talk to him?" I asked incredulously.

"Now stop that. Don't be rude," Tressa said sharply.

"I was just asking."

"Oh sorry, I wasn't talking to you. Dragons communicate telepathically. But I don't know if it works with humans." She glanced at Henry. "Okay, so no, it doesn't work with humans.

"Henry, what does the court know about the happenings at Pine Ridge these past few weeks?" Tressa asked.

Silence stretched on while she listened to Henry's answer. I shifted from foot to foot as I waited.

"Well, what's he saying?" I asked, impatience winning out.

She held up a silencing finger. After another minute, she turned to relay the conversation.

"It sounds like Shamus has done a good job of describing what happened until the point he told Gil to go see Mamó. She sent him back to court with a message that Gil had fallen and that I was in danger. She planned to bring everyone here as soon as she was able."

Tressa turned back to address the dragon.

"Henry, Gil killed Mamó." The raw grief in her voice prompted me to move closer to her. "I don't understand it either, really. She was going to expose him, and I guess he thought she had bequeathed the Aura Sight to him."

"No, she gave it to me, which seemed to make him even angrier. Henry," her voice cracked, "he's kidnapped a child. Xander's daughter."

The dragon snorted hot smoke from his nostrils. Tressa so trusted the dragon that she merely flinched.

"Well, Xander, you and Henry have something in common," she said. "You both think Gil should die."

I was growing impatient with this inactivity. My hands itched to do something. My daughter was in dangerous hands; I had to get her back before any harm could come to her.

"So what's the plan?" I asked, hoping to get things moving.

"There's been no word of Gil coming through a threshold yet. All the guards are on the lookout for him. They know that the human child with him is not his to take," she said, relaying what Henry had told her. She then turned back to the dragon.

"The Niagara Falls threshold is the closest to Pine Ridge, so it makes sense that he would go there. I think we should go that way to head him off."

The dragon evidently had a lot to say about that. He snorted and scratched at the ground with his huge claws, communicating his dissatisfaction with this plan.

"What's going on?" I demanded, having a hard time keeping my tone civil.

"He doesn't want us—well, especially me—to get involved in this. It's too dangerous," she translated reluctantly.

I addressed the dragon directly. "Henry, I'm going after my daughter. Believe me, nothing will convince me otherwise."

Henry snorted a black cloud of smoke, causing Tressa to step away from him.

"But the risk for Tressa is unacceptably high," I continued. "If you agree to help me find Sophia, we can take Tressa to a safe place to wait for us."

Henry seemed to approve of this idea.

"You're not going without me," Tressa said indignantly.

Henry and I both turned on her.

"Tressa, be reasonable," I said. "Gil knows you'll come after Sophia. This whole thing is a trap to get you to Mór. If Henry is willing to help me, there's no point in putting you at risk."

I felt certain Henry was telling her pretty much the same thing; still, she shook her head stubbornly.

"I will not sit at the castle with nothing to do but worry. I'd go insane. Besides, you need me to communicate with Henry, and if Sophia is hurt, I'll be able to help her more than either of you."

It was irrefutable that if Sophia were hurt, we would need Tressa. Although I despised putting her at risk, we had no other option.

"You might as well give in," Tressa said, "because I *will* have my way with this."

"Okay, fine, I give up. How do we get to the threshold?"

"We ride Henry, of course."

"Of course," I muttered.

The dragon lay down to allow us to climb onto his back. Tressa sat in front of me, holding onto a leather strap around Henry's neck. I put my arms around her and held onto the strap as well. The dragon leapt into the air with surprising grace. His expansive wings flapped with a strength that sped us through the air.

I looked down at the topography below and knew in an

instant that we were going the wrong way. "They aren't coming in through Niagara Falls," I shouted to Tressa. "They're coming through somewhere in Alaska."

"You're sure?" Tressa asked.

"I'm sure."

CHAPTER TWENTY-FOUR

TRESSA

I was grateful for the Leprechaun's cape once we were in the air. Flying with a dragon tended to be cold anyway because of the height and speed they flew. With the land completely frozen in grief, that day it was absolutely glacial.

We flew over villages with smoke curling out of chimney tops, over the city of Findias, carved into the mountainside, over a large frozen lake that glistened in the sunlight.

Henry started his descent after passing over an ancient stone cathedral that lay in ruins. As we drew closer to the threshold, the sounds of a battle floated up to us. Henry pulled up and circled around instead of landing.

He telegraphed his intentions, and I shouted them back to Alexander. "He's going to fly over so we can get a view of what's happening down there."

We flew over a battlefield several hundred yards from the cathedral ruins. I easily picked Gilleagán out of the squad of a dozen or so dark-clothed Unseelie Rebels; his golden hair blazed in the sun.

The rebels fought against three dragons, throwing their spears high into the air. They held shields that blocked the dragons' flames, evaporating the firestorm into the air.

They had taken down a young female, judging by her size, with a dragon net. She struggled fiercely to get free. Her fiery breath melted the snow and ice all around her, but the netting remained impervious to the flames. It held her captive and incapacitated.

Henry made a second pass over the fighting below, but there was no sign of Sophia.

"Henry, let's drop Tressa off by the ruins. She can wait there while we help your friends. We need to get to Gil so he can tell us where he's hiding Sophia."

Henry didn't give me time to argue. He swooped down, landing in the churchyard. I slid off him and he flew away, Alexander still on his back.

I went inside the cathedral to find shelter from the ice and cold. Most of the roof and half of the walls had collapsed long ago. I made my way to a section capable of providing shelter from the elements, a corner where the roof and walls had survived intact.

I caught the broad sounds of the fight in the distance, but not in enough detail to know what was happening. While straining to listen to the battle, I heard the crunching noise of something coming through the woods. I crouched inside the corner, feeling exposed in the crumbling building.

I froze when footsteps came my way, not wanting to draw attention to myself. When the sound of movement stopped directly outside where I hid, I held my breath.

There was a half-inch gap in the stones of the wall a bit above my head. Unable to keep still any longer, I stretched to peek through. A deer stood on the other side of the wall. She had stopped to eat a tuft of grass protruding from the ice. The poor thing was probably having trouble finding food with everything frozen.

I came out of the corner to stand by a window opening and watch the deer. A giant fireball rose into the air in the direction of the fighting. I took several deep breaths to calm myself when I thought I heard my name whispered.

"Tressa."

I looked around, but no one was there. I listened again, wondering if the sound had been traveling on the wind. A few seconds later, there it was again—louder this time.

"Tressa, over here."

Cautiously, taking cover behind the stone walls, I went toward the sound of the voice. When I reached the opposite corner of the cathedral, a shadow moved behind a large tree trunk. I hesitated, wondering if it was safe to investigate further, when the lightest aura I had ever seen stepped out from behind it.

The small bundle of light ran toward me. By the time it had reached me, I realized that the voiced calling my name belonged to Sophia. She ran head long into me, hugging my legs.

In one sweeping motion, I leaned down, swooped her up, and rushed with her into the relative protection of the far corner of the cathedral. I crouched down and hugged her against me.

The child wasn't crying or otherwise showing distress, but she shivered with the cold. Her arms wrapped around my neck with no hint of letting go.

"Are you okay? Did they hurt you?" I tried to pull her away from me so I could see her, but she wouldn't release my neck. I felt her shake her head.

"Mr. Gil said we were going on a fun trip and Daddy said it was okay. But he was being naughty, taking me away."

She spoke rapidly. Her voice held a mixture of fear and excitement. I hugged her closer, distressed that she should have spent even a second afraid.

"How did you know he was being naughty?"

"He kept saying my name—all my name and being bossy. Miss Órlaith told me that when someone who sparkles does that it means they are trying to boss you around."

Had my grandmother thought of everything? I remembered telling her that I hadn't been able to hold *Dominion* over Sophia. It must have meant something to her. I wondered if Sophia's aura had told my grandmother something. She was the only child I had seen since receiving the gift, so I couldn't say if her aura was unusual.

"What did you do when he bossed you?"

"I did just what Miss Órlaith told me to do." She relaxed her grip on my neck and sat on my lap. I wrapped my cloak around both of us. "I waited until I saw a big animal with scales and wings. She said the animal would be scary looking, but not to be afraid because they were my friend."

How had Mamó known that someone would try to bring her to the Otherworld? Or was she just being cautious with all the strange fae activity going on?

"When I saw the dragon I yelled, 'I'm a lost child and I belong to Princess Tressa,' just like she told me." Her voice wobbled as she continued. "Do I belong to you, Tressa?"

I gave her a squeeze. "Yes, my dear. You belong to me, and I belong to you."

She nodded, evidently content with this.

"Mr. Gil's friends started fighting the dragons, and I didn't know what to do so I ran as fast as I could to get away. And then I got really scared 'cause I didn't know where I was, and this place is so strange and cold, and I didn't know what to do..."

"Oh honey, you did great. What a good girl you were to do just what Miss Órlaith told you."

We sat quietly for a minute while I thought about our next move. Into the silence Sophia said, "I took a ride on the wind."

Her comment startled me out of my thoughts.

"You did? How did that happen?" Could this be true? Humans weren't supposed to be able to flit.

"Mr. Gil grabbed me and started running. Then there was a whooshing sound like the wind was blowing real hard, and we were floating on it. When he stopped we were at a lake."

The sound of an explosion much closer than any previous ones brought my attention back to our current predicament. The fact that Sophia could flit was actually helpful. If we moved out into the open, I could flit with her to the grounds of the palace. Once on safe ground I could shout to Henry on the wind where we were. I hated the idea of leaving Alexander behind, but I felt confident he would want me to get Sophia to safety.

"Sophia, we're going to try to get away from these bad guys by riding on the wind again, okay?" The child's eyes grew wide with apprehension, but she nodded. "Now, to do that, we'll need to go back outside. I'm going to take your hand and we're going to get a running start. Then you hang onto me. Whatever you do, don't let go of my hand. Do you understand?"

Another explosion in the near distance set us both on edge, but she managed another nod and grabbed my hand tightly.

When we went back to the outside, the sound of voices and shouts came through the woods. They were tracking Sophia's escape route, and I could just see some of them through the trees.

"Come on, Sophia, run!"

We ran down the side of the building, away from the fae I had seen about to break out of the woods.

We were too close to the building. Its weight blocked the

wind. We had no choice but to run out into the openness of the churchyard.

I ran three strides and the wind began to lift me, but my grip on Sophia's hand yanked me back. At first I thought she had been wrong about flitting. However, when I regained my footing I realized an enchanted rope had lassoed her, anchoring her to the fae holding the other end.

Unseelie Rebels surrounded us, their weapons pointed in our direction.

"Lower your weapons," I scolded them. "You might hurt the child."

"They're pointed at you, not her," said one of the rebels. "Give her over to us and there won't be any weapons pointed in her direction."

Sophia whimpered and hid under my cape. Her little hands grabbed onto the back of my jeans.

"This is my child. Surely you wouldn't expect a Sidhe to hand over her child?"

The same rebel, whose aura was so dark I could only pick out his red hair through it, lowered his spear. He circled around me. The others kept their spears aimed at my heart.

"Do you think we don't know who you are? You're the Jewel herself. The entire realm knows you are barren."

When he completed his circle, I was able to capture his features. He confronted me, nose to nose, with a smirk on his face. I lifted my head higher and pushed my shoulders back to feign confidence.

"None-the-less, she is mine. How dare you lasso her like an animal? Step aside and let us go on our way."

"We're not your subjects to order around," he spat on the ground. "The way I hear it, this is your brother's child."

He chanted a few words and the rope released Sophia's leg, coiling itself and hanging in the air in front of him.

Sophia's tiny voice came out from under my cape.

"I am too Tressa's." It was a weak declaration that held more fear than conviction, but for a second I thought her words had affected the Unseelie.

That hope was shattered when he muttered a few words under his breath and the rope sprang at me, wrapping around one wrist, then the other and binding them together in front of me.

The redhead grabbed my face and gruffly turned it side to side as he examined me.

"I have orders to bring you back to camp, but nobody said I had to make it pleasant."

Thorns sprouted from the rope and dug into my skin. He then spelled a metaphysical anchor to the rope to prevent me from escaping on the wind. He took the edge of his spearhead and cut off a piece of my hair, dangling it in front of me.

"A souvenir," he said, his tone mocking. He turned back to his men. "Angus, stay with them."

They marched us through the woods. I tried to loosen my restraints as we walked, but the thorns dug deeper into my skin with every small movement.

Sophia walked beside me, hiding under my cape. We fell to the end of the group; her little legs couldn't keep up with the men. All but Angus marched ahead of us.

I frequently looked to the sky, hoping to spot Henry. The dense trees made it impossible to know if he was there or not. I didn't think he was very close, because he didn't speak to me. Sophia's stride got slower and shorter until her body trembled beside mine.

"The child is tired," I said. "She will fall soon if we don't let her rest. Let me carry her."

Instead of untying me as I had hoped, Angus pulled away my

cape to look at Sophia. She stared back at him with large, scared eyes.

He took off his jacket and wrapped it around her like a blanket. Then he picked her up and held her against his shoulder. His touch with her was gentle, and without protest, the exhausted child fell asleep.

I kept a watch on Sophia as we continued our march. I felt uncomfortable having her in the arms of an Unseelie. Previously, I would have thought she was safe with any Sidhe, but Gil's recent actions had taught me otherwise.

I noticed something odd as we continued to move through the forest. When the Unseelie guard had picked Sophia up, the contrast between their auras couldn't have been greater. However, the longer he carried her, the lighter his aura became.

Slowly, the soot black gave way to a hint of auburn. It was an extremely subtle change, but it was there. If anything, Sophia's aura only got whiter. At times, it was so bright it was difficult to look at her.

We stopped at a makeshift encampment in a clearing deep in the forest. A dozen tents and campfires were scattered around the clearing. The Unseelie had melted the snow and ice in the areas around the tents, creating a bed of mud and slush throughout.

The red-haired leader of the small band disappeared into the largest tent, where I assumed Gilleagán waited for him. Angus led me to sit on a fallen tree trunk. He lay the groggy Sophia next to me, placing her head in my lap. He didn't say anything to me, but he looked surreptitiously over his shoulder before unwrapping one of my wrists.

A group of scraggly soldiers surrounded us, pulling at the coat around Sophia and trying to see her. I gathered that they hadn't seen a child for quite a while. I might have felt sorry for them under different circumstances.

As it was, their prodding made me uncomfortable. I pulled back the jacket myself, revealing Sophia's face. The crowd spoke over each other.

"Sure and she's a beautiful child."

"Anyone would want this one."

"She's clever too, I can see it."

While they chattered about Sophia, several of the men came closer. Two of them reached out. I felt certain they meant to grab Sophia and flit with her. I clutched her to me. They tried to pull her away from me, but I held her fast.

Sophia, awaken by this tousle, whimpered with fear.

"Hey, back away, mate." Angus knocked the two rebels away. "These are my charges."

With Angus standing guard, the other men gave us a more comfortable space. However, I didn't know how long or secure this protection would be. We had to get away from there. My mind raced. I had to let Henry and Alexander know where we were; I couldn't fight these men myself.

The rebels' admiration of Sophia reminded me of an old song that told the story of a lost child. I began to sing the song quietly, unsure how the crowd would react. If they didn't stop me, I could get my voice on the wind without being obvious.

The rebels reacted like every other audience I sang for, listening enraptured to my voice. I began to sing more boldly, entrancing them with my song.

Gilleagán stormed out of the tent. Enraged, he swept his outspread fingers in a circular motion, conjuring a ball of wind that he unleashed onto the camp. The squall felled some of the smaller tents; debris flew everywhere. The campfires, engorged from the rush of air, discharged flames into the wind. The camp was in an uproar of shouts and screams as debris, tents, and two rebels fell prey to the blaze. Only the ice and snow protected the forest from its ravages.

I gasped, overawed by the display. I had never seen the wind wielded as a weapon in that way.

"Don't you know she can enchant you?" he shouted at the crowd as they hurried away.

He grabbed my arm, pulling me to my feet just to backhand me across the face and knock me down again. Sophia cowered next to me.

"Gilleagán, why are you doing this?" I asked. I touched my cheek to sooth the sting of his blow. "Haven't you done enough damage already? What are you trying to prove?"

"I don't need to prove anything. I already out-smarted all of you. And for my final trick, I will hand the current Jewel over to the Unseelie for her execution."

I tried not to flinch. I had known this had to be his intention, but it was still a shock to hear him say it.

"And the child? Let her go. She has no part in this."

He came closer to us, and I cringed when he reached out to stroke Sophia's head.

"She was a special pet of Mamó's, and of yours, little sis. It will be my own special torture for you, knowing she is with me and will never return to her pitiful father. He will live the rest of his life not knowing what has happened to either of you."

I wanted to ask him what had happened to him. What could possibly have turned him into this monster? However, I knew it would be useless. He was beyond my reach.

He called to one of the men who took Sophia and me to a large tree on the edge of the clearing. He took the loose end of the rope that dug into my wrist and tied it to a branch, tethering me to the tree.

He allowed Sophia to snuggle up next to me, still wrapped in Angus's jacket. He didn't seem concerned about restraining her.

Perhaps he sensed that she wouldn't consider leaving my side. I almost wished he had restrained her so none of the Unseelie could grab her away from me.

We sat there for hours before someone brought us water and a bit of food. I let Sophia eat most of it. I ate only after she'd had her fill.

Nobody came back to check on us as evening fell. During this respite from immediate threats, I spent my time worrying about Alexander. How would he communicate with Henry and the other dragons? How would they treat a human? I worried that he might have been injured, or worse, in the battle by the threshold. I wondered if he would be able to find me.

A buzz of gossiping voices grew throughout the camp. Eventually, picking up words here and there, I pieced together that the Unseelie Rebels expected Deaglan Mór to arrive the following morning. He was coming to inspect Gilleagán's great prize for him.

My sense of urgency grew exponentially as the evening wore on and the night sky turned a deep purple. Eventually, the camp was quiet and still. The rebels had gone to bed. Sophia also slept, curled into a ball on her side.

I drew my knife from my pocket as unobtrusively as possible; I didn't sense any eyes on me, but I knew there had to be guards watching the camp. I slowly ran the dagger across the rope, cutting it little by little so as not to call attention to my movements. The rope, though thin, was tough. I worked my way through it without drawing anyone's notice.

I gingerly unwrapped the thorny cord from my wrist, reopening the cuts in the process. When I was finally free, I gently shook Sophia, wanting to wake her up but not wanting to startle her, lest she make noise. I had just gotten her to her feet when a shout came from the far side of the camp.

Within seconds, the camp was in chaos. Rebels ran in every

direction, grabbing their weapons and shouting orders. Seelie warriors flooded the campground.

I recognized Connor in the distance. He fought two Unseelie simultaneously clashing swords with one then the other. I almost cried out when a third Unseelie ran up behind him. Connor must have heard him coming because he whirled, slicing through the chest of the Unseelie at his back and lancing the second as he completed his turn. Another Seelie warrior finished off the third combatant.

A dragon swooped down breaking away treetops as it dove. Stretching its long neck, it grabbed two of the rebels with its teeth. It shook the Unseelie and threw them against a thick tree trunk. They dropped grotesquely to the ground.

More swords clashed around me, growing ever closer. Blood splattered and intermixed with the mud and slush as more Unseelie Rebels fell.

I tried to take advantage of the confusion by grabbing Sophia and running into the woods, but someone grabbed my hair and brutally yanked me back.

It was Gilleagán. He pressed his blade to my neck.

"Let her go, Gil."

Alexander was there, seeming to materialize out of nowhere.

"One-Handed Willie arrives just in time to see her die," Gilleagán said.

Alexander lifted his sword. He rolled it in a figure eight showing off the dexterity in his hand.

"Let's see if I can gut you, shall we?"

In that minute, while Gilleagán was distracted by Alexander's swordplay, I plunged my dagger into Gilleagán's leg. The force of the blade hitting his bone reverberated through my bloody hand and up my arm. He fell to the ground; yelling curses and holding his blood soaked leg.

Alexander stood over him, sword pointed at his chest. His eyes narrowed as he looked down at him.

I took in a shaky breath, remembering Alexander's words in the cave before we crossed the threshold. He swore he would kill my brother. At any moment I expected him to drive the sword through Gilleagán's heart. I wanted to look away, but I was transfixed. Alexander looked up from his captive and met my eyes. He held my gaze for a moment before looking back down at Gilleagán.

"Will they put him on trial?" he asked. I had to swallow to find my voice.

"Aye, and he will most likely be executed," I admitted.

He nodded curtly, releasing the pressure of the sword on Gilleagán's chest.

Connor joined us then. He ordered several of his warriors to seize Gilleagán. They restrained him and gathered him with other captured rebels.

"This is all that remain," Connor said, indicating the small group of prisoners. "The rest are either dead or have fled."

The battlefield reeked of blood and sweat but was devoid of bodies. The remains of those killed in the fight had returned to their ancestral home.

"I'll take them back to *Tír na nÓg*. The king will decide what happens next."

"Thank you, Connor. Whatever you do, don't let Gil get away," I said.

"Don't worry. That won't happen, for many reasons not the least of which is I swore an oath to King Lomán that I would bring him back. The king demands justice for the murder of his mother."

Once Connor and his men had their captives securely rounded up, the entire group flitted to the castle in *Tír na nÓg*.

I slumped against a tree, relief turning my body to rubber.

Sophia ran to her father. He picked her up midstride as he rushed over to me.

"Tressa, are you okay?" he asked. "My god, look at your arms."

He grabbed me, kissed me, and hugged Sophia and I in one big embrace. He inspected his daughter until he seemed satisfied she wasn't hurt. Then he turned his attention to me. His concern grew as he took in the bruise on my face and the blood on my arms.

"I'll be fine," I reassured him before he could ask. "I just need to find a catalyst. Then I'll be able to take care of it."

Henry dropped down in the clearing, carrying a branch of pinkberry leaves in his mouth.

CHAPTER TWENTY-FIVE

*H*enry delivered us to the king's castle, where Shamus met us at the door. He stepped back in shock at our disheveled appearance.

"You can't be seen like this," he said, horrified.

"I wasn't planning to, Shamus."

His look said he thought that was exactly what I had planned.

"Shamus, I haven't slept since I last saw you. Since then, my brother murdered my grandmother, kidnapped a child in my care and threatened my life. I think it's to be expected that I'm not at my best."

I regretted my sharp words when the color drained from his face. He lost his usual bustling manner.

"Aye, of course. I am sorry, My Lady," he said, bowing deeply. "The preparations for Órlaith's Sendoff ceremony have been made for this evening. You must be taken care of before you are presented."

Shamus shuffled the three of us to a suite on the third floor of the family wing of the castle. Word had somehow gotten to Rosheen and Keelin, who met us there. After they hugged us all and made proclamations of sympathy regarding our misfortunes, they took charge of Sophia, promising to get her washed, fed, and asleep in that order.

We were alone for the first time since entering the Otherworld. I looked up and met Alexander's eyes. He looked as exhausted as I felt.

"How did you know where to find me?" I asked. "Did Henry hear me?"

"I don't know, maybe. When Connor and the Seelie troops joined us, I led them to you. I just knew where you were."

I had anticipated this answer, but it soothed me to hear him say it.

"I will always be able to find you. I don't know how, but you never need to worry about that."

I nodded and gave him a small, tired smile. I had no doubt he spoke the truth. As soon as he said the words, my mind accepted it as a fact—like the fact that the sky is lavender, it just is.

"What happens now?" he asked.

"They will hold Mamó's Sendoff first. It's like a funeral," I said, addressing his questioning expression. "I want to see her again before the ceremony. They will surely give me that chance, as we weren't here while she laid in state."

"And the trial?"

"That is for the King to dictate. I expect it will be soon."

The prospect of going through a trial and repeating all that had happened was distasteful. The seediness of it made me feel as dirty spiritually as I was physically.

"We have enough time to bathe and rest. The ceremony won't be until dusk."

"A bath and then bed sounds good," he said.

. . .

THE BROUNIES HAD LAID out a gown for me. When I slipped into it, I recognized it as the gown Rosheen had designed for me for my parents' Sendoff. It had been her way of doing something to help and comfort me at the time.

The choice pleased me. It reminded me of my cousin's love for me, and it might lighten her sorrow a bit to see me wearing it.

The dress was beautiful: pure white with a dropped waistline and a long A-line skirt. She had trimmed the collar and waist with a white and sapphire braid. The gown would suitably honor my beloved grandmother, Órlaith Finna Dé Danann, who also happened to be the Queen Mother of the *Tuatha Dé Danann* of *Tír na nÓg*.

The Brounies found appropriate clothing for Alexander. He looked quite dashing in his tunic and laced boots. The only bit of color he wore was the bracelet I had made for him. The Brounies had even found a white scabbard for his sword.

Mamó had been laid in state in the grand ballroom. Keelin told me thousands had flocked to pay their respects. The ballroom, the largest room in the castle, still hadn't been large enough to accommodate them.

The two guards at the door readily allowed Alexander and I entrance. Our steps echoed in the large dark room as we walked to the center where Mamó lay in an intricately woven reed casket.

Candles lit the room, surrounding the platform that held the casket. There were hundreds of flowers, making the air heavy with their fragrance.

We knelt before her. Alexander bowed his head and prayed. I looked at her face, memorizing every pore, every strand of hair, not wanting to admit to myself that I would never see her again in this life.

"I wish there was something I could say or do to take your

pain away," Alexander said. My chin quivered as I tried to control my emotions. I shook my head.

"There is nothing," I said. "At times like this, I've heard people in the Human World say 'take comfort in the fact that she is in a better place.' However I can't take that comfort. She and my parents and all of my loved ones who have passed on before me are not in that better place. They are stuck in purgatory."

I picked a lily from a bouquet and placed it into Mamó's delicate hands.

"I've been thinking a lot about her faith. She had faith that I would fulfill the prophecy. For most of my life, I have acted as if I had that faith too, but it was a lie. I realize now that I never had any. I've been playing wait-and-see, expecting the prophecy to just happen or not. And now... Well, I can't say I have absolute faith, but I have faith in her. I understand that I will never fulfill the prophecy if I don't try."

Alexander touched my arm. I looked at him and was surprised to see tears glistening unshed in his dark chocolate eyes.

"You know that I will do anything I can to help you."

I wrapped my arms around his waist and leaned against him. It was remarkable how comforting it was to feel his body next to mine. We stayed like that for a few minutes, each replenishing the other's spirit.

"It's time we go," I said finally.

"Is there anything I should know? Any part of the ceremony I should be aware of?"

"No, just listen. If you behave as you would at a funeral, you will be fine."

Keelin was waiting in the corridor with Sophia. They wore matching dresses with soft, flowing skirts that swept to the floor. I thought how sweet it was of Keelin to display her bond with Sophia in that way. The dresses were obviously Rosheen's design. She must have created them as a part of her preparations for Mamó's Sendoff.

If the adorable child didn't win the people over with her charm, being favored so by the daughters of the king would raise her mightily in their esteem. Keelin's dress was white with the same braid accents as my own. Sophia's was a pale lavender that matched a soft summer morning's sky. She carried a ballerina doll I recognized as one from Keelin's childhood.

With a kiss on both cheeks, Keelin left Sophia with us and went off to take her place with the King and Queen.

Alexander, Sophia and I went to join my aunts, uncles, cousins and their children. We would all follow behind the body as it traveled to the ocean, where the ceremony would officially begin.

Six Sidhe warriors carried the open casket on their shoulders. The family followed in the birth order of Mamó's children. The king, being the first-born, went first with the queen and the twins. Uncle Lomán had the same golden hair and tanzanite eyes as his mother. His wife, Ciara, had the same coloring as her daughters. They made a handsome family.

With Gilleagán imprisoned, I was the only remaining member of my father's family. As such, I held last place in the procession of mourners. I was grateful to have Alexander and Sophia walking with me.

The adults in the procession wore white; the children were in pastels, which is our custom. Each family carried a lantern to illuminate the way. Alexander carried ours so that I wouldn't have to hold the flame.

Fae of all types lined the streets for a last glimpse of the great woman. They threw flowers down ahead of the procession, so we made our sad parade along a carpet of petals.

The onlookers chanted a lament that spoke of the greatness of the Queen Mother. Of the wonderful works she had done, and of how loved she had been. In the distance, nearly drowning out the sound of the lament, the Banshees of *Tir na nÓg* wailed.

As we brought up the rear, the chanting faltered. I realized the Sidhe were reacting to Alexander. One rarely saw a human in Faery anymore. Sophia on her own, I was sure, would raise a positive reaction. As it was, a negative atmosphere radiated from the crowd.

I moved closer to Alexander, a protective instinct, and he put his arm around me. We let the onlookers wonder as we walked the rest of the way, Alexander and I arm in arm as I held Sophia's hand.

The crowd fell in behind us and followed the family to the banks of the ocean. Everyone, even the Banshees, quieted to listen as a clergyman chanted the traditional Sidhe funeral rite. When he finished the final prayer, everyone joined voices to sing a hymn, the strength of which floated over the clouds to God.

The pallbearers placed the reed casket into the ocean. My sorrow overflowed, silent tears streaming down my face as Shamus escorted Mamó out toward the sea. When he was waist deep in water, he gave the casket a push and allowed the tide to take her the rest of the way across the water. The lanterns on the casket lit its way until a wind came up and pushed it out of sight.

If you enjoyed this book please take a moment to leave a short review on the page where you bought the book. Reviews are very important to authors because they help other readers find the book. Your help with this is sincerely appreciated.

THANK YOU!

ABOUT THE AUTHOR

 Belinda M Gordon was born and raised in Pennsylvania and currently lives in North-eastern PA in the Pocono Mountains with her wonderfully supportive husband, her thoughtful easy-going son, and two delightful dogs. She is of Irish heritage, which is how she became interested in Celtic Mythology. She used the Celtic Mythology, specifically of Ireland, as the starting point of her Romance/Fantasy series, The King's Jewel.

To learn more about Belinda visit her website at
www.belinda-gordon.com

www.ingramcontent.com/pod-product-compliance
Lightning Source LLC
Chambersburg PA
CBHW060758210726
48292CB00013B/696